# Birch & Beyond

*A testing time for Katie leaves her
uncertain about her future*

## Gill Buchanan

Gill Buchanan
Visit my website at www.gillbuchanan.co.uk

Printed in the United Kingdom

Second Edition 2019

ISBN– 9781083001542

## Praise for Unlikely Neighbours:

**Catherine says:** Gill's, style of writing is easy to read. This is a delightful book that once you pick it up, you won't put it down. One is able to relate to the characters, enjoying the activities of their daily lives as they become entwined. I would highly recommend this for anyone who is looking for a light-hearted holiday read or just simply to curl up with for the weekend. Enjoy!

**Jack says:** Enjoyable and thought-provoking
The writing skips along, mixing a real sense of fun with deeper - sometimes even darker - interludes. Great first book.

**Cherry says:** Perfect holiday read
Written with a light and confident touch and it certainly does not feel like a first book. Gill draws you into the lives of her characters so you genuinely want to know what happens to them all. I enjoyed the way the story is presented from the different perspectives of each person. An easy read for your holiday.

**Tom says:** Poignant and witty
This book has the feel of a novel that has come from the pen of a seasoned author on their 10th book or so. I find it hard to believe this is book #1!
I love the way the plot swings around from perspective to perspective of the characters, learning more and more about their machinations as we get sucked into the minutiae of the Middle England world.

## Praise for Forever Lucky

**Dollyrocker says:** I have just finished reading Forever Lucky and feel sad to be leaving these characters behind. Gill Buchanan has managed that most tricky of tasks here: she's created a world in which a reader can fully immerse.
Great book. Great story. Great fun.

**Jane says:** A great relaxing read - easy to get into, fun and poignant at the same time, with a feel-good ending. I liked the little personality quirks of each character.
Having really enjoyed her first book, Unlikely Neighbours, I was optimistic and this was just as good. Highly recommend it.

*To Mum – my biggest fan.*

# Chapter 1

'Happy New Year, darling,' Birch said with a subdued tone but Katie still had to gulp back a tear. It was her first New Year without David and it was moments like this that were a poignant reminder.

'Yes, happy New Year,' Julia echoed leaning over the dining table to squeeze Katie's hand.

'Shall we go through to the lounge?' Katie suggested and she felt three sets of eyes on her as she tried to shake away the memories that saddened her.

'Yes, we could turn on the telly and watch the fireworks,' Andrew suggested in an attempt to lighten the mood. They went through and the contrast from the warm dining room made Katie shiver and wrap her arms around herself. Birch quickly stoked the fire and added a couple of logs to raise the temperature in the room. Katie turned on a standard lamp in the corner which gave off a warm mellow light and sat on the edge of the sofa warming her hands against the fire.

'David always made a big thing about the fireworks.' She smiled at the recollection but then she thought of him lying in Highgate cemetery in his willow coffin, unable to enjoy anything anymore.

'Shall we put them on then?' Andrew asked picking up the TV remote from the glass coffee table.

'If you like; I'm not bothered. We could have some music on – maybe some jazz.' She looked up at Birch who was a big fan of Miles Davis and Thelonious Monk, while she only tolerated them.

Before they decided one way or another their conversation was interrupted by the doorbell ringing loud and shrill. Twice.

Julia turned to Katie, 'Alice, maybe – forgotten her key? Seems a bit early for her.'

'Maybe it's some drunk,' Andrew suggested laughing.

'I'll go,' Birch said, a serious frown on his face. 'You stay here.' He was nodding pointedly at Katie as he backed out of the room and closed the door behind him.

The amount of champagne he had drunk had lightened his mood, but nothing could have prepared him for the sight before his eyes.

'Is this a private party,' Celia slurred, lunging towards him, 'or can wives join in?' She put great emphasis on the word wives and was now close enough to him that he could smell alcohol on her breath. She was wearing a bright red, low cut party dress, which was completely out of character, her black mascara was smudged messily around her eyes and her vibrant lipstick was marking her front teeth.

'Well?' Her expression demanded an answer and she spoke loudly enough for half the street to hear.

'Celia, you know you're not invited.' He spoke quietly in the hope that she would too. 'You left me for Alistair, remember? Why aren't you at his party?'

She threw a dismissive hand around in the air. 'Turns out he's not the one for me.' She started fluttering her eyes at him in a feeble attempt at flirtation.

Birch suddenly felt very sober. 'Well, I'm sorry to hear that but as you know I'm with Katie now and what's more you and I are going through a divorce.'

'Ah!' Celia cried triumphantly. 'Ah yes, but no!'

'What are you talking about?' She was beginning to worry him.

'What I mean is,' she was staggering from foot to foot and looked like she might topple over at any moment. Birch grabbed her wrist to stabilise her.

'What you mean is?' He tried to hurry her. This interruption of his evening had gone on long enough.

2

'I mean that I don't want a divorce anymore!' She was standing uncomfortably close to him now, looking wide-eyed up at him with her blue grey eyes. In her inebriated state she was convinced that she was appealing to her husband, when actually she looked a mess.

'Don't be ridiculous,' Birch tried to keep his voice steady and was trying to steer her away from him. She pulled her wrist back in protest and immediately fell backwards on to the path.

'Oh my God, are you all right?' He crouched down and peered at her. She lay there motionless with her eyes closed for a few seconds before bursting into a giggle and lifted her head in an attempt to stand up.

'Whoops!' she shrieked delighted that Birch had taken her hand and was helping her up. 'Silly me!' She put her head on his chest. 'You see I need a husband to look after me, otherwise I might get into all sorts of trouble,' she squeaked in a little girl voice.

Birch sighed deeply. 'Celia, you had better go home.'

'What, before Katie finds out I'm here?' She raised her voice as loud as she could.

At that point the lounge door burst open and Katie stood there looking hurt and confused. Birch immediately told Celia she should go home and closed the front door on her but she banged with her fists repeatedly crying, 'I want my husband back! Give me my husband, you money grabbing bitch! He's mine! We're still married you know!'

'What on earth is going on?' Katie asked and Birch went straight over to comfort her.

'I'm so sorry, my love. This is outrageous. I can't believe she's stooped so low.'

'What happened?' Katie still didn't understand what was going on.

'She just turned up. She's drunk.'

'And she wants you back?' Katie blinked disbelieving.

'The woman is delusional. She's too drunk to know what she wants.'

'It doesn't sound like that to me,' Katie said shivering. The opened front door had let in an icy cold wind. Julia appeared with Andrew close behind.

'Everything okay?' she asked her voice deflating as she saw her friend upset.

Celia continued her tirade of insults and demands at the front door. Birch was red with embarrassment. 'I'm so sorry about all this. My estranged wife is giving me enough ammunition to divorce her on the grounds of unreasonable behaviour ten times over,' he explained, imploring his onlookers to have sympathy with him.

There was a squeal from outside followed by a concerning silence. Birch closed his eyes in despair, 'she's already fallen over once,' he informed the others.

Andrew put a hand on Birch's arm. 'Look mate, do you think maybe you and I should walk her home?'

Birch bit his lip and looked to Katie to approve the idea before he answered.

'That sounds like the best solution,' Katie said putting on a brave face.

'Right,' Birch braced himself, 'we'll be as quick as we can. It's only a few streets. You two go back in the lounge and, Andrew, let's get out of the front door as quickly as possible. I can't bear the thought of her barging in here.'

With the two men gone, Julia opened a bottle of brandy and poured generously into two tumblers.

'I don't like brandy,' Katie said with a smile but behind her eyes you could see pain.

'Nor do I, but it's good for a shock.' Julia sat next to her on the sofa in front of the fire and they both stared into the cinders as they tried to make sense of what had just happened. Julia got up and added more logs, stoking the embers to get some much needed warmth from it.

'Yes, shocking is the right word,' Katie said eventually. 'I'm wondering if my relationship with Birch was doomed from the

4

start. I mean Bethan hates him with a vengeance and Alice only tolerates him...'

'They lost their father last summer,' Julia interrupted, 'they were bound to react to any man coming in to your life.'

'Perhaps I should end it for their sakes.'

'Katie!' Julia sat upright and turned to her dearest friend. 'After all you've been through! Let's not forget that David had gambled away all your savings and left you with very little. I know you've forgiven him and I think that's the right thing to do.' She relaxed back into the cushions again. 'But you've had to claw your way out of financial ruin. You've set yourself up as a virtual assistant and worked jolly hard to build up a client base.'

'I have, haven't I?' Katie suddenly felt proud of what she'd achieved. 'Harry's been a great help of course.'

'And Birch has been really supportive; he's the light in your life, you've said as much.'

'He is. He makes me very happy.' Katie smiled as she thought of how her life had turned around when he came into it.

'Ending this relationship, what's that going to achieve apart from heartache?'

'But if Celia wants him back...'

'That's her problem. The sooner their house is sold and the divorce is all sorted, the better. Hopefully she'll move away. A long way away from Highgate Village.'

'That all seems like a pipe dream right now. She called me a money grabbing bitch.' Katie said sighing.

'I'd call her the devil incarnate,' Julia joked and they both laughed and felt better for it.

'Before this evening I'd have said that was a bit harsh.' Katie took a gulp from her brandy deciding she quite liked it.

'But now, it's her new name.' Julia clunked Katie's glass.

\*\*\*

Katie was woken early the next morning by the phone ringing. The answer machine kicked in after three rings and she heard a loud

5

manly muffled voice from downstairs that sounded rather animated. She persuaded her eyes to open and looked at her digital clock in disbelief. She hadn't got to bed until the small hours and just wanted to turn over and go back to sleep but the phone was ringing again. As any mother would, she thought the worst – one of her daughters was in trouble? – and willed herself to wake up.

Birch stirred slowly beside her frowning. 'Who the hell is that?' he mumbled.

'I don't know but they won't go away,' Katie said yawning. The phone was ringing for a third time. She rubbed her face awake got out of bed and found her dressing gown. Her calves were tight as she padded across the room and out to the landing. She took the stairs unsteadily and when she reached her study she sat down at her desk, leaned over, yawned again and pressed the button to pick up the messages.

*'Katie, Katie my love, I'm so sorry about this. New Year's Day and all that. But the thing is the new Hampstead flat, Golden Avenue, the downstairs residents have got water pouring through their ceiling. Literally pouring. They're going crazy Katie. Apparently, it's ruined their sofa already. So, I was just wondering if you could call the plumber who's been working on the place. I don't have his number. Call me back soon please.'*

Birch appeared at the door in a tartan dressing gown and brown suede moccasins, his fair hair dishevelled. 'Not that bloody Charlie boy. Not today surely!' He took one look at Katie's tired face and went straight to her side, cradling her head in his hands. 'I'm so sorry about what happened last night. I meant what I said when I got back. I'm more determined than ever to make this divorce happen.'

Katie looked bemused but managed a curt smile. That was all she would allow him right now.

'Coffee?' he asked more helpfully.

'Double espresso for me, I think.'

'Coming up toute suite,' he said cheerfully and then added, 'is there anything I can do to help sort out Charlie?'

'Thanks but it shouldn't take too long.' She turned on her mobile to find the plumber's number. As she did the house phone rang again and this time she answered.

'Yes Charlie, I know. I'm just looking up John's number now.' The battery of her mobile phone was dead so she couldn't access her contacts.

'Oh you're an angel. So sorry about this, silly question, do you happen to know where the stop cock is on this property?'

'Erm..' Katie was trying to put her mobile on charge whilst holding the handset between her neck and shoulder. 'No,' she answered vaguely, 'no actually, I don't.'

'The thing is, it might be inside the flat or outside.'

'Right,' Katie was struggling to think straight and Charlie wasn't helping. 'Okay, when I've found John's number, I'll give him a call.'

'Oh would you, you're a doll.'

Harry awoke disbelieving the vision in front of him. Natasha's soft chestnut hair was cascading down her naked back. How had she ended up in his bed? And then it all came flooding back to him. The party at Olly's Oyster Bar in Hampstead that Ben had insisted he went to; the amount of wine he had drunk and the surprising arrival of Natasha well after he was in an alcoholic haze of reckless abandon. This was a disaster. He had only just smoothed things over with her mother, Vicky Johnson–Sinclair, (one of his best clients given the size of her investment portfolio) a couple of months ago when he had gently let Natasha go as a damage limitation exercise. Despite his considered approach, Natasha had found his behaviour infuriating and got very angry with him whilst her mother had tutted a lot but at least she hadn't moved her money. He put that down to his excellent investment record.

He thought now about surfacing very quietly and jumping in the shower so that he could make out he had somewhere to go and then any encounter they had that morning might at least be brief. He slid one leg gently towards the edge of the bed and made it to the floor with his foot. Carefully he released the duvet in her direction so that she would not be disturbed as he sat up and swung the other leg out to the wooden floorboards. He stood up and took his lithe naked body daintily across the room to his en-suite shower. He was relieved to have reached the door.

'Harry! Not sneaking off are you?' Her voice was seductive even at that time of day. He turned around to see her surprisingly wide-awake, eyes smiling at him.

Birch handed Katie her coffee and sat down in the armchair in the corner of the study. She turned to face him, looking flustered.

'So what's all this about? What can't wait until tomorrow?' he asked rather unhelpfully.

'Oh, it's an emergency. Water flooding through the floor of one of his flats into the one below which is already let to a nice young couple who, as you can imagine, are going spare.'

'Can't they turn the stop cock off?'

'Apparently it's inside the flat above and they haven't got the keys.'

Just then the phone rang again. Katie raised her eyebrows and picked it up.

'Hello?'

'Are you Katie?' The young woman sounded agitated.

'Yes,' Katie said hesitantly and sighed at this new voice she wasn't familiar with.

'Ah, I'm Diane, we're the ones at Golden Avenue. Charlie said you would know.'

'Yes, that's right. I'm so sorry about all this.' She tried to soften her voice.

'Well, actually we've stopped it now.' Diane sounded a little awkward.

'Oh, well that's good, isn't it?'

'Well yes but we had to break the door down of the flat upstairs you see; the only way of getting to the stop cock to turn the water off.'

8

'Ah.' Katie thought that this sounded perfectly reasonable in the circumstances but decided to be careful how she responded as Charlie was her client after all. 'Have you told Charlie?' she asked hopefully.

'No, no we haven't. Would you give him a call?'

Birch was pulling a face which said "end this fiasco now" and pointed to the clock. They were due to be in central London by midday.

'I'll let him know,' she said and decided a text would do. She had already left messages for John the plumber to go round there and do what he could.

'Thanks, and do you know what will be happening about the damage to our flat?' Diane asked innocently as Katie's heart sank.

Natasha had showered and was browsing an issue of Tatler wearing last night's silver sequined party dress as she lounged on Harry's black leather sofa. 'Well aren't you going to offer me breakfast?'

'I'm afraid I'm not very good at that sort of thing,' Harry said truthfully. He wasn't even sure how to turn his oven on and lived on takeaways when he didn't dine out.

She looked dejected. 'Surely you eat breakfast?'

'Well,' Harry approached his Nespresso machine, 'I can make you a coffee.' He looked optimistic.

'I suppose that's better than nothing.'

'I quite often pick up a croissant or two from the bakery on my way to the office but they're not open today, obviously.' He was suddenly very pleased it was a bank holiday.

'Really Harry what you need is a good woman to look after you.'

Harry continued to have his back to her as he operated his coffee machine and let his face cringe in disbelief at that comment. Having Katie Green as his virtual assistant was all the looking after he welcomed. The coffee made he handed a cup to Natasha and drank his whilst leaning against the worktop. He considered this a safe distance as she was sprawled across the sofa on the other side of his open plan living area. She patted the cushion next to her.

Harry looked at the clock hanging above his desk, 'my God, is that the time!'

Natasha's eyes widened in disbelief but still he added, 'I'm going to have to hurry you I'm afraid; I'm expected at my sister's house shortly. We're all off to a New Year's Day concert.'

'That sounds nice,' Natasha pouted at him almost demanding an invitation.

'Yes, it's the Kensington Philharmonic. Very popular, in fact, sold out I believe.'

'Are you sure you want me to come with you?' Katie was feeling the effects of a traumatic evening followed by a rude awakening. Birch started to say something 'I...' but stopped abruptly. He went over to Katie and put his arms around her. She had an expectant look.

'Selfishly, yes,' he admitted at last. 'But I realise you're probably thinking it's the last thing you need right now.'

'You're right there.' She had no energy to dress up her reply and took a deep breath before adding, 'But still, I might as well have a hangover at your book signing as moping around here all day.'

'I love you.' He drew her to him and kissed her.

'And I love you, even if your wife is proving to be a complete nightmare.' Her eyes drilled into his as she moved away from him.

'Don't call her my wife!' he said as he pulled her back into his embrace.

'She is your wife!' Katie protested.

'Please, please can we call her my ex at least. Who knows how long it will take for this divorce to go through?' Birch ran his fingers through his hair sweeping it back from his forehead.

'Sorry,' Katie kissed him lightly, 'now where is it we have to go?'

'Covent Garden. Waterstones.' He looked at the kitchen clock and added. 'We're going to be late.'

She smiled knowing that Birch was rarely on time for anything but said nothing.

Bethan lay wide awake watching Matt's chest rise and fall with each breath as he slept. The whole house at Pond Square was quiet; no one else had stirred. Jake had been at the same bar to see the New Year in and had been chatting up a slim girl with long sleek black hair and sharp features. He had certainly not been ready to leave the celebrations when Matt and Bethan headed for home just after two o'clock. Rob, the other house-mate, who had affluent parents living in New York, had been down in Kensington at a private bash his brother was hosting. Bethan didn't know whether or not he'd made it home, although she knew he thought nothing of paying fifty quid and more for a cab.

She thought about getting up to make some tea but the flat was cold. No one had put the heating on yet and as she wasn't paying rent she didn't feel she could either. She pulled the duvet over her head and half wished that Matt would wake up. Her thoughts turned to her mother and what she used to call home. Her bed there was so much more comfortable; her bedroom always warm, light and airy. It provided a small sanctuary for her. If only Birch didn't live there now. It was wrong that he had moved in. It was as if he was trying to replace her father within six months of him dying. How could such a ridiculous man even be there? The sad fact was that she couldn't be happy in her own home. If she was still living there she could just date Matt and still have her own space. That would be better. She needed her own space. It was too much too soon with Matt.

The fact that they lived and worked together at Web Dreams was leaving her feeling claustrophobic and perhaps it was made worse by Matt being so much more senior than her at the agency. He had been promoted to account director a couple of months ago and Bethan was destined to be a graphic design apprentice for a full year which would take her into the autumn. She wanted to see it through, especially as one of their clients, Carol, otherwise known as Mrs Cup Cake, was very complimentary about her work and insisted that she spoke to Bethan every time she rang the agency. Paul Costelloe, the MD, had asked Matt to keep an eye on the account as, although he was impressed by Bethan, he knew that at just seventeen she lacked experience. When Carol had wanted to take Bethan out for lunch as a thank you before Christmas, Bethan had been looking forward to a fun and girly time, a little light relief, but Paul had insisted that Matt should go too. This turned it into a dull affair stifled by small talk. As if that wasn't bad enough, Matt had insisted they drank sparkling water rather than wine as they were heading back to work after.

Bethan had tried to keep their relationship quiet at work but Matt was all for telling everyone. 'Why not? I think it's best to be open about these things. Anyway I want the other guys in the agency to know you're taken!' Bethan was a very attractive girl; a tall, leggy blonde with pure white skin. So he chose the regular Friday evening after work, drink at the pub, to announce the fact that they were together. The news had met a half-hearted cheer from a couple of them and Bethan had blushed as a few of the men had remarked on how lucky Matt was to be dating such a stunner.

Matt snuffled and turned away from her taking the duvet with him and leaving her exposed. Sighing she got up, grabbed some clothes and slipped into the bathroom where she decided against showering and put on her jeans, socks, t-shirt and a big cream woolly jumper. She still felt cold and went to the kitchen to make a hot drink.

Katie was pleased to be home again. 'That was great but exhausting!'

'Thank you,' Birch said sincerely.

'Don't be silly. After all the support you've given me...'

'But still it was a big ask after what happened last night.'

Katie looked puzzled and searched his face for answers. 'Have you told me everything?'

'Of course. Everything you need to know. I don't think I mentioned that Celia vomited on the pavement a couple of times on the way back but....'

'Oh my God, she must have been in a really bad way.'

'As I said, she was drunk. She never used to drink much alcohol so she doesn't have much tolerance for it.'

Katie decided to change the subject. 'Let's curl up on the sofa and watch a film.'

'That sounds good. Is Alice about?' Birch was always wary of her daughters' presence.

'I've had a text from her; she'll be back later.'

Birch looked excited. 'So we have the place to ourselves?'

The doorbell rang and they looked at each other. Katie closed her eyes and sighed. 'That better not be Celia. I will not tolerate her coming round here causing trouble.'

Birch looked concerned. 'I'm sure it isn't,' he said praying and then added, 'You know, we should get one of those spy holes fitted.'

'Yes,' Katie said biting her lip. 'Put the chain on.'

'Good idea.'

The next thing she heard was Bethan's shouting voice. 'Well aren't you going to let me in?'

She was barging her way in, pushing past Birch. 'I might have known you'd still be here! Mum, Mum, I need to talk to you.' She ran to her mother's side. 'Mum, I need to come home. To live I mean. I need some space. He has to go! I can't stand him here!' She started sobbing and threw herself onto her mother. Katie hugged her daughter hoping it would calm her. Birch reluctantly headed for the room at the top of the house, where he did his writing.

Eventually Bethan stopped crying and looked up and straight at her mother. 'Mum, I want to come home.' Her tone was more reasonable now. 'But I can't live here with Birch in the house. Can't he go home to his wife?'

Katie took a deep breath. 'Is it over with Matt?'

'No! No, that's not it. I just want my room back, you know, my own space. We'll still see each other, I mean we work together so..'

'It would be awkward if you split up? At work, I mean?' Katie could see she had hit a nerve.

'No, no, I'm sure it will be fine.'

'Well you're welcome to move back home darling but Birch isn't going anywhere right now. Him and his wife are getting a divorce and Celia is insisting in living in their house. So you see...'

Bethan sprang to her feet. 'So he's more important to you than me? What do you think Dad would have thought of that?'

'You're being ridiculous.' Katie managed to stay outwardly calm despite feeling churned up inside.

'So you honestly choose him over me?'

'I choose both of you,' Katie said emphatically.

'You're impossible Mum!'

Katie knew she had to hold her ground. 'I'm sorry Bethan, but if you can't even be civil to Birch you'll have to stay where you are.'

'I hate you! You're so horrible to me!' she screamed as she turned to leave. 'And Dad would hate you too!' was her final shot before the front door slammed behind her.

Katie, stunned by this outburst, collapsed onto the sofa and burst into tears.

# Chapter 2

Adrenaline high, Bethan raced off down Bisham Gardens up to the High Street. Where would she go? She really didn't want to go back to Matt's place, especially as he had made quite a fuss about her leaving.

'What do you mean, you're moving out?' He was glaring at her in disbelief.

'Listen Matt, I'm really grateful that you let you me stay here rent free, but it's not really fair on the others, I mean Jake and Rob, and I think I should go back home now. My mother needs me,' she added rather unconvincingly as she started to pack a bag trying to avoid his gaze.

'But what does this mean for us, we're still alright aren't we?' he asked urgently as he grabbed her and pulled her close.

'Of course we are,' she said and managed to hold his interrogative stare.

'Sure?' He looked angry more than anything else.

'Yeah, course,' She was half-hearted and he looked in no way appeased by her attempt.

'So when will I see you?' he asked in a needy way.

'At work, tomorrow, silly.'

'Great,' he'd said sarcastically.

As Bethan reached the centre of Highgate village she slowed her pace and took her mobile out of her handbag. She found Harry's number in her contacts and thought about calling him but decided it would be better if she just turned up at his flat. After all, he had turned up at her place on Christmas day.

She smiled to herself as she thought back to that moment when she had opened the door to him. She was all alone and feeling really low. In fact, she had been fed up with Matt for going off so cheerily to his family fully expecting her to do the same; he just didn't seem to understand how she felt about Birch. Harry had been her knight in shining army. He had looked more gorgeous than ever that day and it had been such a thrill flirting with him over Christmas lunch. The fact that she was at her mother's house somehow made it more dangerous and therefore more exciting. Even more wonderful, she had overheard him telling Birch that he'd managed to end his relationship with Natasha. Natasha had to be the glamorous woman she had seen him with at the Hampstead bar. Thank goodness that was over; she was not the sort of woman Bethan would want to compete with.

He had walked her home at the end of the day and the amount of alcohol he had drunk had loosened his tongue. He was talking about his penthouse apartment and she only had to say, 'where's that then?' and the address had been forthcoming. Bethan had etched it into her brain until she could write it down in a safe place.

Thank goodness.

She reached the building called Clarendon House and now all she had to do was find the flat at the top. She chose the intercom button at the bottom of a line of four assuming it would be the ground floor flat and not Harry's place. Her luck was in. Whoever it was, they were obviously expecting someone and the main door clicked open. She was in. She climbed two flights of stairs, pausing for breath, her heart beating faster, and got to what had to be Harry's front door. After taking a few moments to sweep her long blonde hair to one side and apply some baby pink lipstick, she rang the doorbell. All was quiet but she had a strong sense that he was there. She listened carefully and heard footsteps the other side of the door. It was then she noticed the peep hole. A moment later the door opened and Harry stood there, his fair hair dishevelled, his blue eyes narrowed against the light.

'Bethan, what are you doing here?' He seemed surprised but not annoyed.

She put on her little-girl-lost-voice and said, 'Harry, I'm so sorry but I've got nowhere else to go. My Mum's thrown me out, would you believe it?'

16

'But I thought you were living with your boyfriend?'

'Oh that. Well it's over really. At least it is for me.'

'Oh dear, I'm sorry to hear that,' he said although he didn't seem bothered.

'Harry, can I come in?' She moved closer to him, her adoring eyes taking in his whole body, her perfume giving off a heavy spicy scent.

He looked alarmed and then flustered. 'Well okay, yes, but we'll have to sort something out,' he said vaguely.

'Of course,' she replied as her face lit up.

Ross turned to look at Elaine as they sat on the park bench wrapped up against the cold. She had a red wool scarf round her neck and up to her ears which were just covered by her short layered hair style which had tones of auburn running through it. Just her blue eyes and delicate nose peeped out.

'What's wrong? What are you looking at?' Elaine ruffled her hair with a gloved hand.

'Sorry, I'm just admiring you.'

She blushed.

'You're very pretty,' he said earnestly.

'Don't be silly. I'm just a thirty-five-year-old mum buying my clothes from Top Shop because I can't afford anywhere else.'

'What's wrong with Top Shop?' He'd heard of Top Shop but that was the extent of his knowledge.

'Nothing if you're eighteen or Kate Moss!'

'Well, I think you look lovely.'

'Thank you.' She finally accepted the compliment.

'Shall we walk round again? Somehow I don't want this moment to end,' Ross said looking out across a frosty Waterlow Park and beyond to the City.

'Oh I don't know; I need to get back really. Mum's had Jessica since yesterday evening and I've already had a text from her asking me what time I'll be home.'

Ross pursed his lips and then said, 'sorry, I'm being selfish.'

'Maybe just along the top here and back, I need to warm up. It's freezing sitting on this bench!'

'Yes it is, isn't it?' They laughed together and sprung to their feet to start walking again.

He tucked his arm in hers and drew her to him.

'That's nice,' she said. 'I can't remember the last time I was with such a gentleman.'

'Oh just trying to get it right.' He beamed at her and then added gently, 'I've messed up so badly in the past and it's a long time since I've been this happy.'

After last night, Elaine knew most of the awful truth about his past. They had shared a bottle of wine and he'd chosen what seemed like an opportune moment to tell her about when he was addicted to gambling and his wife had thrown him out of their home. At least now he was back on his feet with his own flat, even though it was rented, and his gainful self-employment. Even so, he didn't want to put so much as a foot wrong with this one.

She was looking out over the park towards the city and looked to be in her own world.

'Oh dear, have I said the wrong thing, is it too much too soon?' He searched her face for clues.

'No! It's lovely and actually, well, I think I feel the same way.' She was beaming at him now and he stopped to put his arms right around her and kiss her. Memories of last night's love making came flooding back to him and he felt an overwhelming sense of bliss.

The remains of a Chinese take-away were sprawled over Harry's coffee table. Bethan relaxed back into his sofa. 'Thanks, that was great.' She felt warm and cosy for the first time that day.

'No problem.' Harry leant back too. There was something very careful about his body language.

'Another beer?' he offered. 'Or is that taking hair of the dog too far?'

'Actually I didn't drink that much in the end last night.' Bethan smiled at him and looked delighted as she added, 'yes please.'

Harry went over to the fridge and took out two more bottles.

'So where is this Olly's Oyster bar?' Bethan asked.

'Oh, Hampstead way. Ben's idea actually.'

'Was it good?' She was determined to make conversation.

'Not bad.'

'Oh.' Bethan was finding making conversation quite hard. Perhaps he was just tired.

'How's the job at Web Dreams going?' he asked.

'It's really good actually. I'm so enjoying it. Well apart from...' she hesitated.

'Apart from? Not Paul, surely? He's a decent bloke isn't he?'

'Oh no, not Paul. No, I like him.' She looked thoughtfully into her glass. 'It's just that Matt works there too and it's getting a bit, well you know...'

'Oh I see, Matt's your boyfriend.'

'Well sort of. I mean he is but I don't think..' Bethan played with her hair twirling it round and round her finger, her eyes were softly smothering him.

'Always best not to mix business with pleasure,' Harry said knowingly and smiled at her.

'Absolutely,' she agreed and that was all the encouragement she needed. She placed her glass carefully down on the table and moved closer to him. Her eyes were fixed on his and he looked startled, as with one deft movement she moved right in and kissed him, a long slow kiss. And he responded. Could this really be happening?

*

Alice was finding it very difficult to concentrate on her A-level re-take study. It was ridiculous really. There was no boyfriend on the scene, although that didn't stop her wanting one; she had reduced her hours at The Lemon Tree to free up some time and Birch had even bought her a desk from a charity shop for her bedroom.

'It's only second hand but does the job I think and probably better than some cheap IKEA thing,' he'd said as he struggled with it through the front door.

Alice surveyed it. 'Looks like it's solid wood.'

'Yes, oak I believe. What do you think? Shall I give it a coat of paint?'

'Would you?'

'Of course. Then I thought I'd take it up to your bedroom so you'll have somewhere quiet to work.'

It was certainly quiet. Her mother was busy working in what they now called her study and Birch was tapping away in the top room. The deadline for this coursework was looming and there was absolutely no reason at all for her not to get on with it and write this piece in French on French cinema. She had even done some online research but she hadn't actually seen a French film. Maybe that was where she was going wrong. Just then she heard footsteps on the landing going past her door and then down the stairs. Without giving it much thought, and knowing it was probably Birch going down to the kitchen, she decided to follow.

He turned around when he saw Alice. 'Coffee?' he asked. 'Your Mum's having one too but she's too busy to leave her work.'

'Not Charlie again. Yes, to coffee, please.'

'Probably, yes, he's quite something. Still, your mum's earning good money out of him.'

'Yeah.' Alice realised she actually felt quite proud of what her mother had achieved in such a short time since their father died last summer. 'Mum's done really well with her business.' She sat down at the kitchen table and Birch handed her a mug of coffee.

'Yes, she has.' He looked uncomfortable and there was an awkward pause.

'Have you ever seen any French films?' she asked.

'Yes, yes I have, quite a few actually.' He picked up the drink he had made for Katie. 'I'll just deliver this and I'll be back,' he said.

She searched the kitchen for pen and paper and was surprised to find both. He was back and sitting opposite her.

'I've got to write a piece on French cinema for one of my course works and well, I suppose I could do with a bit of inspiration.'

'Oh right. Well funnily enough I've got a couple of DVDs you might want to watch. There's Les Petits Mouchoirs and The Untouchables; both great films.'

'That sounds good. So what are they about? Les Petits Mouchoirs, Little White Lies, is about a group of friends living in Paris who holiday together every year at a big villa one of them owns. Anyway this particular year one of them is involved in a dreadful motorbike accident and ends up in hospital just before they are due to go. I suppose it's about how they all tell little white lies to each other. It's actually very funny in parts but the ending is incredibly sad.'

Alice scribbled away. 'That sounds good. Have you got the DVD here?'

Birch looked awkward. 'Mmm, I'm pretty sure I didn't rescue it from the witch's den but I should be able to retrieve it, assuming she hasn't changed the locks.'

'Would she do that?'

'I wouldn't put it past her.'

'Tell me about the other film, The Untouchables, was it?'

'That one stars Francois Cluzet too. I'm a bit of a fan of his.'

'Oh yes, I've heard of him.'

'It's a fantastic film and even more amazing because it's based on a true story. Cluzet plays this guy who's paralysed from the neck down, I think, in a wheel chair anyway. Oh and he's really wealthy, an aristocrat in fact, and lives in this amazing palace in Paris. He ends up hiring this black guy, who's lived in poverty and been in prison, as his carer. He chooses him because he lets him live life to the full and do crazy things, unlike all the rest of the carers he's had who are over cautious about everything.'

'That sounds amazing.'

'Okay,' Birch scratched his head, 'looks like it's mission impossible to retrieve them from chez ex-wife then.'

Alice stopped scribbling and looked up at him with a cheerful smile. 'Thanks Birch, that's really helpful.'

Katie's head appeared at the door. 'Everything okay?' she asked, her eyebrows raised.

'Just discussing French films,' Birch enlightened her.

'Part of my A-level work,' Alice added eagerly. 'We just need to work out how we're going to get the DVD's out of Birch's house so I can watch them.'

Every Monday morning at nine o'clock, Paul Costelloe called all the staff of Web Dreams together for a meeting where they all had to talk briefly about their focus for the coming week. Matt was stood on the other side of the room and Bethan smiled at him briefly but made no move to join him.

'So this pitch for Pet Perfect who sell pet foods online is going to be key for us.' Paul was making eye contact with everyone in the room. 'We really need to win this one guys, so let's all go the extra mile, okay?'

'Yes, it's going to be massively important to come up with the right creative,' Matt added. 'I've met this client and creative is king in their book. We also need to have a winning SEO strategy in place, so Phil that's up to your team.'

'Absolutely,' Phil stood upright at the sound of his name. 'Don't worry, we're on it.'

'Good,' said Paul, 'and Bethan I think you should help out with the web page creation after your big success with the Cup Cake Company.'

'No problem,' Bethan said thinking that it was going to mean working closely with Matt which was the last thing she needed right now. Ever since she had turned up at Harry's flat she had been full of excuses every time Matt suggested that they get together and he was getting more and more frustrated with her. After all, she had only said she needed to move out and have her own space for a while. She was pretending that she'd moved back in with her mother when in fact she was still staying at Harry's place and so the deceit was making life more and more complicated.

But she didn't care. She was on cloud nine. She was going out with Harry Liversage, something she could only dream of before now. Not only that, she was living in his penthouse apartment! He was a beautiful man, an exciting guy who had money to take her out in his shiny Mercedes convertible to expensive restaurants. She loved his fabulous open plan home with its enormous plasma TV screen and gadgets she didn't even know existed. Harry was an early adopter of new technology, not caring that he was paying way over the odds. He had his own investment business and was obviously doing really well. He was the perfect man.

It was a truly wonderful way to live but Bethan still had a slightly uneasy feeling that the bubble would one day burst. Perhaps her mother would find out and forbid Harry to see her. She seemed to have some strange hold over him that Bethan could not work out. Perhaps he would tire of her; he had already more than hinted that he was a confirmed bachelor. The sex had been brief and unfulfilling the first time but she put that down to him being tired. Since then it had got better but some nights they would stay up until midnight watching some dreadful film or other and when they finally got to bed he just turned away from her and fell immediately to sleep.

It was when he gave her a key to his flat that she allowed herself to dream that this might actually go somewhere.

'Bethan, are you coming?' Matt was beckoning her from the door of the meeting room at the back of the office.

'What?' She must have missed something.

'Weren't you listening?' he sounded annoyed. 'You, me, Adam and Theo are getting together now to make sure we've got the brief covered.'

'Oh yeah, okay.' She flounced off to her desk to pick up a file and followed him into the meeting.


'Fancy a spot of lunch?' Ben said looking up from his lap top but Harry didn't respond. 'Hey daydreamer!'

'Oh sorry, what was that?' Harry shook himself back to fully compos mentis and sat up in his chair.

'Everything okay old boy?'

'Oh, well, you know.' Harry stared out from his desk into the distance at nothing in particular.

'No, I don't mate, but you're definitely not yourself these days.'

'I told you, I've got Katie Green's daughter, Bethan, living with me! Can you believe it? How on earth am I going to get rid of her?'

'Sounds like a spot of lunch and a data download would do you good. Would you like to try that new gastropub down the road?'

'Good idea.'

The place was nearly full but they managed to get a table. The waitress was cute but she could have had two heads for all Harry cared. Ben thanked her for the menus. Harry glanced at his and put it down again. When the waitress came over for a second time Ben ordered two steak sandwiches and a bottle of red wine. Harry didn't flinch.

'You know me too well,' he said simply discarding his menu.

'Well you look like your mind's elsewhere.'

'Yeah, I need to sort this. Would you believe I've got Natasha on the war path as well?'

Ben loosened his tie and leant over the table. 'Most men would give their right arm to be in your position!'

'No! No they wouldn't. Not if they actually knew what it was like. I don't get a moments peace.'

'What's she like this Bethan? I mean I remember meeting her briefly last year some time but not much else.'

Harry sighed deeply. 'She's gorgeous, stunning in fact, really sweet, only seventeen and far too innocent.'

'I doubt.' Ben gave him a knowing look.

'Well you know, inexperienced in life.'

'Mm.' Ben poured the wine.

Harry lifted his glass. 'Here's to getting my home and my life back!'

Ben just laughed. 'Maybe you should be straight with her? Why's she living with you anyway?'

Harry said nothing but looked guilty.

'I mean if she's only seventeen,' Ben continued, 'she should still be at home with her mum.'

'Yes, you're right. But I found out what all that's about. You see she can't stand this chap, Birch, who her mother's taken up with since her father died. It was all a bit quick. One minute he was the lodger keeping them from financial ruin, and the next Bethan catches him and Katie in a compromising position in the kitchen.'

'I see. She's got a point then.'

'She told me that her mum threw her out but I suspect that's not quite how it happened. I spoke to Katie yesterday and she has no idea that her daughter's moved in with me. She thinks she's still at her boyfriend's, this Matt guy she works with.'

'So hang on a minute, Bethan's got a boyfriend?'

'Well she says it's over.'

'Bloody hell, this is all a bit of a tangled web isn't it?'

'You're telling me. And that's before you consider that Natasha is texting me daily and getting more and more irate!'

'Now you've got to be careful there. Her mother's one of our biggest investors.'

'Don't I know it!' Harry had his head in his hands as the food arrived. The waitress looked confused.

'Women trouble,' Ben enlightened her and she suddenly looked worried and scurried away.

Ben was thoughtful. 'Didn't you have Birch staying with you for a few weeks?'

'Yes, that's right. Poor chaps got ex-wife issues.'

'Yes, I remember now. You said he made a great flat mate, really amenable guy. So why does Bethan hate him so much?'

'Purely because he's taken the place of her dad I suppose. Alice, the other daughter, gets on a bit better with him.'

'Looks like what you need to do is to somehow persuade the lovely Bethan that she should really be living at home and getting on with this Birch. Best all round.'

'Mm, well I suppose it's worth a try.' Harry did not feel optimistic about this outcome.

'You know it might help to put some distance between you and all these unruly women. How about a trip to the big apple to see that Garcia chap who's looking to do some serious investing in the UK?'

'Now there's a thought.' Harry suddenly looked brighter. 'Mm, a trip across the pond; I like that idea.'

# Chapter 3

Stephen Cardell rang at nine o'clock precisely. Katie had barely sat at her desk but grabbed a pen and paper before answering cheerily, 'Stephen, good morning.'

'Katie, morning to you.' He was brusque. 'Have you got a minute?'

'Yes, of course,' she said wondering why he was even asking that as she was his virtual assistant.

'The thing is, I've been really pleased with your work and it's no reflection on you, but..'

Katie worked out what was coming next, it was pretty obvious, and alarm bells started ringing. She was trying to remember how much she billed him each month; how much money she would be losing.

'... I've decided my requirements have changed and I've found someone who I feel can better meet them. You see I'm looking to do more with social media.' It sounded like he was reading from a prepared script.

Katie remembered now, a conversation they had had when he had asked her how much she knew about Twitter. She'd fumbled some sort of response on the lines of not a great deal but she was willing to learn. But even then her heart had sunk at the very thought of going down that route.

'I totally understand Stephen,' she responded bravely and then added, 'I have enjoyed working for you.' But as she said it, she admitted to herself that of all her clients he was the one she had never really felt totally at ease with. Whilst Charlie was a bit of a loose cannon at times, she was always more relaxed with him and they had shared many laughs.

'Well thank you for that. No hard feelings. And if you'd like to continue until the end of the month?' It was all very matter of fact from him.

'Of course, I'll do that and I'll send you my final invoice.' She put down the handset and sighed. She had just lost her first client. All the other virtual assistants, she had come across online, had said that clients would come and go; nothing to worry about. As a knee jerk reaction she reached for her mobile and called Julia's number.

'And how's my business woman of the year extraordinaire doing?'

'Stephen's just sacked me.'

'Stephen? Oh the coaching guy. Sounded like a bit of a prat to me.'

'Yes, that's the one.'

'Oh dear, sounds like you need perking up, it's a bit early for me but how about a rendezvous in Fegos later?'

'Good idea, let's make it at eleven, I've got a few urgents to do for Charlie.'

'Yes, eleven works for me, with a bit of a juggle.'

Julia was sat next to a lukewarm radiator and had already got the cappuccinos in.

'Oh, thanks darling.' Katie took her coat off. 'Not very warm in here, is it?'

'No, the heating seems to be on the blink. Anyway, Stephen's gone. Good luck to him, that's what I say.' Julia lifted her cup to her friend.

Katie laughed. 'I can rely on you to make me feel better, instantly!'

'Good!'

'But it doesn't alter the fact that next month I won't be invoicing him and I rely on every penny.' Katie took a sip of her coffee and licked the froth from her lips.

'But I thought Birch was still paying rent for the top room. I mean I know he lives with you now but he needs to contribute.'

'Absolutely but I have a feeling that the eight hundred pounds a month he gives me is under threat.'

'Oh, why's that?'

'Birch's lawyer is making noises about maintenance payments to Celia starting now while the divorce is going through.'

'But that could take years.'

'Yes, exactly. The thing is she doesn't earn much with her music lessons; they lived on his income.'

'But she's got the house, hasn't she? I mean she's living there which means he can't.'

'I know, but let's face it she's not going to be reasonable about all this, is she? I mean she's saying now that she doesn't want a divorce, so he's having to divorce her.' Katie's eyes were cast down as she added, 'after the New Year's Eve fiasco I wouldn't put anything past her.'

'I see what you mean.' Julia held a pained expression.

'She's told her solicitor she won't agree to mutual consent and he needs to wait five years!'

Birch was pacing the hallway like an expectant father when Alice got back from her shift at The Lemon Tree. She looked at him quizzically as she hung her coat up. 'Everything all right?' she asked.

'Yes, oh yes,' Birch answered as he continued pacing. Suddenly he stopped and looked straight at a bemused Alice. 'I don't suppose you're free for half an hour or so?'

'Well I was just going to chill out for a while after my shift.'

'Of course, of course.'

'Actually, if you have managed to get those DVDs, you know the French films, I thought I'd...'

'Ah! That's exactly it. You see the thing is I haven't. Got them, I mean. I know this is going to sound odd but do you think you could come with me to retrieve them as it were?'

Alice let out a confused giggle.

'Not that I'm frightened of my ex-wife or anything.' Birch scratched his head. 'I just think safety in numbers.'

Alice sighed as she put her coat back on. 'Come on then, let's go.'

Matt had sent Bethan an email saying that a few of them were meeting for an update on the pitch for Pet Perfect. He had been curt with her that morning in front of a couple of colleagues leaving them with puzzled expressions. Not wishing to provoke him Bethan made sure she arrived in time.

Matt was waiting for her. 'Close the door.'

'But what about the others?'

'They're not coming.' He looked pleased with himself.

'What?' Bethan scowled back at him.

'We need to talk.'

She sighed and sat down reluctantly on the other side of the table to Matt. 'Okay, fire away,' she said with an air of resignation.

'Me fire away? I think you're the one that's got some explaining to do.'

'What are you talking about?' Bethan was wondering if it was something to do with her work now.

'Us! Remember? Or is there no us anymore?'

Bethan kept her eyes down to the table, not daring to meet his glare. 'Listen, I'm sorry,' she began.

'What? Sorry you're seeing some other bloke?'

Bethan's face reddened. 'What makes you say that?' She knew she was trying her luck but surely Matt hadn't spotted her in the sort of places she went to with Harry. She had at least made sure they'd avoided the pubs and restaurants she knew Matt might frequent.

'Bethan, it's bad enough that you've been lying to me so far...'

'Okay, okay, I'm sorry. I am seeing someone. I'm sorry Matt, it's over between us.'

'Sorry! You're not sorry! How could you!'

'But I am.' Her eyes were pleading now. 'It was just too much for me... with us.... living and working together.'

'You seem to be forgetting that we still have to work in the same office; we're even working on the same accounts!'

She said nothing, worried about inflaming the situation further.

'And everyone knows about us!' he shouted. 'What am I supposed to say to them now? Huh?'

She looked anywhere but at him. There was nothing she could say to make a difficult situation better. Matt was clearly angry and she could see his point.

'Well, Bethan?' He was glaring at her, willing her to respond.

'I'm sorry, that's all I can say. I'll tell people, if that helps.'

'No! No it doesn't help!'

She got up to leave the room. 'I can't say anything more.'

'Well I can! I can make life very difficult for you here.' He stood up and leant in towards her. 'Paul has a lot of time and respect for me.'

Bethan was shocked that he could be so cruel. 'What are you saying? That you're going to get me into trouble with Paul because I've ended our relationship?'

'You better watch your back. That's what I'm saying.'

Tears started rolling down her cheeks, she wiped them away with the back of her hand, grabbed her notepad and made her way quickly back to her desk. She checked her mobile and was really pleased to see a text message from Harry. Until she read it.

Birch could not get his key in the lock. 'Oh blast!' He tried again.

'No, don't force it,' Alice advised. 'Are you sure that's the right key?'

'Oh yes, she's gone and bloody well changed the locks, hasn't she?' Birch took a furtive look at the windows to see if he could spot Celia. He could hear a violin playing and it sounded very much like a pupil. He whispered, 'Let's scurry off and try plan b.'

They made their way down the street so that they were out of sight, before they stopped.

'Now,' Birch said looking quite excited, 'how's this?' You go and ring the doorbell while I hide behind the hedge. Then, when she answers I'll get in before she can stop me. The element of surprise you see.'

Alice looked amused. 'But what will I say to her?'

'Mmm, good point, erm, how about asking her if she's found God yet?'

She giggled. 'I'm not sure I'll be able to keep a straight face.'

'Well you can't pretend to sell dusters as we don't have any. What else is there?' Then he had an idea. 'Got it. There's a local election coming up, why don't you pretend to be a candidate canvassing for the Tory party?'

'Aren't I a bit young for that?'

'She won't have time to work that out, I intend to be quick. Oh, and I should apologise now for any reaction you might get from her. You do look quite like your mother so I doubt she'll be generously spirited.'

'Has she met my Mum?'

'A couple of times but only briefly. The first time was when Celia was living with this Alistair chap, or at least we thought she was, and we came round here and she was in the hallway. It was so awful for Katie.'

'Right, well thanks for telling me.' Alice looked concerned now.

'Don't worry, she won't hurt you, well you know, unless looks could kill.'

Bethan read the text from Harry for the third time.

*Hi B, I've had to pop over to New York on business for a few days so won't be around. You might want to move back in with your Mum, I've spoken to her and she'd be happy to have you home. I'm going to be tied up in meetings and on a different time zone so don't worry if you don't hear from me. H x*

She immediately felt depressed. How could he do this to her? And calling her mother; that was the last thing she needed. Everything was going wrong, her job, her relationship. Suddenly she didn't know how she was going to get through the day. She saw Paul come out of his office and Matt immediately approached him. As they spoke Paul glanced over towards her and then they both disappeared inside his office. She was convinced they were talking about her. Tears were running down her cheeks and she wiped them away dismissively and turned her back on awkward momentary glances from her colleagues. She felt an enormous impulse to break free. The situation at Web Dreams was intolerable. Not caring what the consequences might be, she grabbed her handbag and coat and made for the door. Outside she let the tears flow as she walked towards the High Street not knowing where she was heading. The air was still and damp with mist. All around her was grey. She reached Fegos and the warm orange glow the other side of the window tempted her in.

Celia waited for Henry to finish his piece, Mozart's German Dance – which needed to improve dramatically before he went for his Grade one examination – and then went to the front door. When faced with Alice she looked startled and annoyed that this stranger was interrupting her lesson.

'Whoever you are, whatever you want, it's not convenient right now, I'm teaching.'

Alice was about to say her line when Celia peered at her and said, 'do I know you?'

Birch suddenly appeared from behind the hedge and barged into the house past Celia pushing her to one side carelessly.

'What the hell! What the hell's going on?'

Alice decided to come clean. 'We just need a couple of DVDs that's all. They're for my French A-level you see.'

'I don't believe this!' Celia turned and went after Birch. She found him in the living room rifling through DVDs, selecting some and creating a separate pile. 'What are you doing with those? You can't just barge in here and take what you like!'

Henry, who was just nine years old, placed his violin down carefully and looked on, fascinated by the scene before him.

Birch stood up and faced her. 'Yes, I bloody well can!' he shouted. 'This is my house as much as it is yours and you should not have changed the locks. And! These are my DVDs! You always hated the foreign ones anyway.'

Celia was shaking with indignation. 'I don't care! You can't just barge in here when you want.'

He took his attention away from the DVDs momentarily as he stared at her and said, 'you just don't bloody get it do you?'

'Stop swearing in front of Henry!'

'Stop being such an unreasonable bitch then!'

'You bastard! Get out!'

Henry looked nervous and started to sidle behind the sofa.

'Look you've upset Henry now!' Celia blamed her husband.

'Not my fault! Anyway it was not so long ago you wanted me back. Or were you so drunk on New Year's Eve that you can't remember when you made a scene at Katie's house?'

Celia was furious. 'How dare you? Get out! Get out now!'

'Not until I've found the films I want,' Birch said in a self-righteous manner that riled her even more.

'That's it! I'm calling the police!'

'Oh for goodness sake woman! You are beyond ridiculous!' He spotted the DVDs he wanted and grabbed them along with a couple more and made for the door.

'I'm still ringing the police!' Celia was shouting as Birch started to leg it down the street. Alice was waiting for him at a safe distance.

'Got them!' he said with a delighted grin on his face, adrenalin still high.

'Oh great. Was she okay with it?' Alice asked.

'Not exactly, she was threatening to call the police.'

'What? Why on earth would she do that? I thought it was your house too.'

'Too right it is! She should never have changed the locks.'

Alice looked worried. 'You don't think she will ring the police do you?'

'I wouldn't put it past her.' Birch smiled in the face of adversity. 'Come on then, we've got some films to watch.'

Bethan was staring out of the window, an empty cup in front of her. It was getting dark now and had started to rain. The waitress came over. 'All right?' she asked casually.

She shook herself from her thoughts. 'Oh yeah.. sorry... do I have to go now?'

The waitress smiled gently. 'Take your time. Only we're closing soon.'

Bethan looked around her. The cafe was almost empty. She decided it was too late to go back to work and she couldn't face it anyway. Not today. She got up and hugged her coat around her. Out on the street she meandered along with no particular plan, not caring that she was getting wet in the rain. When she saw the general store she decided to go in and buy something she might eat later. She grabbed a ready meal for one of chilli con carne with rice and a bottle of Sauvignon Blanc, the cheapest she could find, after a quick scan of the shelves. The man on the till looked at her through narrowed eyes.

'I hope you're not drinking alone this evening,' he said as he smirked at her.

Bethan frowned and said nothing as she punched in her PIN. 'Do you have a carrier?'

'Ooh, have to charge you for that love. Five pence it is.'

Bethan scratched around for change in her purse but could not find any.

'Don't worry about it; I'm feeling generous.' He flicked a plastic bag open and handed it to her.

She shoved the two items into the bag and made for the door.

'Forget your manners, did you?' he shouted after her.

Bethan gulped back more tears and started to make her way up to Fitzroy Park where Harry's apartment was. She didn't want to go there but what choice did she have. It occurred to her that Harry might still be there and that his text message was just his way of brushing her off and trying to persuade her to go back to her mother's house. Deep in thought she didn't notice the vagrant jump out in front of her.

'You got some change love? I know you have, pretty girl like you.'

She jerked back away from him startled by his sudden appearance. His face was weathered, dark with dirt and his grey beard long and wiry with bits of debris tangled into it. He wore a big black coat with a piece of rope tied round it and he smelt musty. Alcohol wafted from his breath and he was waving an empty vodka bottle around.

'No need to be afraid darlin', I'm not going to hurt you,' he said lunging towards her as she walked backwards away from him feeling scared now.

'I'm sorry I don't; I really don't. I don't have much money myself.'

'Liar! You selfish cow! You don't care, off to your cosy home!'

Bethan checked the road for traffic and crossed quickly. The man followed her. 'Give us your money, go on.'

'Go away! Leave me alone!' She looked around her, desperate now. There was no one except an elderly lady who was scurrying away.

'Just give us a quid or two. Pretty please?' He looked at her mockingly.

'No!' she shouted out loud hoping to attract attention and started to run as fast as she could in her heels.

She ran and ran without looking back. Her legs felt heavy and her stilettos were crippling but fear propelled her on. After turning a corner she slowed, her breath was heavy now and she had the taste of blood in her throat. She cursed herself for being so unfit. A couple of young women were coming towards her deep in conversation and laughing together; oblivious to Bethan's plight they simply walked around her. When she got close to the flat she dared to turn round and scan the street for the tramp. She couldn't see him but she couldn't be sure in the dark. She rushed up to the front door of Clarendon House and fumbled to find the keys in her handbag. Finally, she pulled them out but dropped them immediately on the door step in her haste. She burst into tears again as she picked them up and through the blur and with her hands trembling, she eventually managed to get the key in the door. Once inside she took her shoes off and staggered up the two flights to Harry's flat. As soon as she made it through his door she sank to the floor, inconsolable with tears. Eventually she found a tissue in her handbag, blew her nose and looked around her. All was quiet, cold and dark. Harry really had gone.

# Chapter 4

Katie gasped when she saw the balance of her bank account and something propelled her to jump up from her seat. She scanned the credits column on the screen. Apart from the amounts she invoiced her clients there was nothing. She made her way up the stairs to the attic room wondering how on earth she was going to tackle this but knowing she had to.

She knocked on the door before entering.

'Hello?' Birch turned immediately. He looked surprised but pleased to see her. 'To what do I owe this unexpected pleasure?'

She stood there before him feeling really uncomfortable and took a deep breath before she said, 'I'm sorry to have to bring this up but your rent money is...'

'Oh God I'm so sorry,' he said interrupting her painful speech. 'I know, I've been meaning to talk to you about that.'

She raised her eyebrows in anticipation.

'There's never a good time to impart bad news is there?'

'Oh no.' Katie needed to sit down and took the armchair in the corner of the room.

He went to her and knelt beside her taking her hands in his. She found this intimacy awkward given the nature of their discussion. He sensed how she felt and reluctantly let go of her hands.

'The fact is that Celia's solicitor is saying she needs a hefty monthly income from me to continue to live, and I quote, the lifestyle she's become accustomed to. Which, by the way, doesn't resemble anything I remember.'

'How can she do this?' Katie sprang to her feet in frustration and walked over to the window where she could stare out onto the park which was being deluged with a heavy rain shower.

'That's our wonderful legal system for you.' Birch rolled his eyes.

'But surely that's all decided when the divorce goes through?'

'Yes, but apparently, according to Jonathan, if I don't pay her anything now it may reflect badly on me in the long run.'

Katie sighed in disbelief.

'She also says she's unable to teach music any more as she is so stressed by the marriage breakdown, which of course is all my fault.'

'But wasn't she in the middle of giving a violin lesson when you and Alice went round there the other day?'

'Yes, she was. Anyway, what with my legal fees, and of course, her legal fees, I'm really struggling. God, I'm so sorry Katie. I feel like I'm letting you down.'

Katie felt deflated. 'It's all so unfair isn't it?'

He looked down in shame. 'It seems so.'

'Can't your lawyer do anything?'

'Yes, you're right. I should really put pressure on Jonathan. I think, like Sandgate, he's living in the past and he needs a jolt to plant him firmly in this century and the land of scheming ex-wives.'

'Why don't you go and see him? It might be better face to face,' Katie suggested willing him to take action.

'Yes, you're right. I'll call him this afternoon to fix up a time.'

Katie tried to smile.

'The other thing is,' Birch looked brighter, 'The Times pay me well. I'll see if I can squeeze some more work out of them. They are always saying how pleased they are with my reviews. Yes, I'll contact Justin, the editor and see what I can do. Maybe I should take him out to lunch?'

'Right,' she said not feeling so optimistic. And then as the full reality of the situation dawned on her she added with a big sigh, 'and I will have to get another client on board. Pronto.'

'I will get you some money,' he said as if the full enormity of the issue had now dawned on him. 'I can't live and work here without contributing more. It's not right.'

She wondered if that might mean that he may feel he had to leave. She'd got used to having him around; they got on so well. Without him she was stuffed financially anyway.

'How desperate are things?' he asked.

Katie bit her bottom lip. 'We're overdrawn. More than overdrawn. With the rent money you give me we can just about get by. But I haven't had any...'

'I hear you.' He looked thoughtful. 'Listen, I feel I owe you an apology. I didn't know how bad things were. Maybe I've taken you for granted but I certainly didn't mean to. I love you Katie and I love being here with you.'

'Oh Birch, the last thing I want is for you to leave.'

'Phew!' he said looking relieved and then with a lighter touch, 'there's always Mum.'

'No! No, you can't ask Sylvia again.'

'She wouldn't mind, honestly, she's great like that. Anyway she really likes you.'

Katie remembered her fondly. 'Perhaps we should invite her to stay again? She told me she really enjoyed Christmas.'

'Oh she did, she loves it when there's lots of people round a table.'

'Even if she doesn't know most of them!'

'That doesn't faze her!'

They were both laughing now. 'That's better,' he said, 'I hate to see you down. Hey, we can dine out this evening, on The Times! I haven't done this week's restaurant review yet.' He went over to her and took her in his arms. 'What do you think?'

'Sounds lovely,' Katie said.

'Yes, we'll make sure we sample a good portion of the wine menu, just so we can give the reader a full insight into what this unassuming Turkish restaurant has to offer.'

'Turkish! Do the Turks even drink wine?'

'They do when they're in Hampstead!'

Elaine checked yet again that all her staff were where they should be and Le Bistro was looking smart and tidy. Since the owner had refurbished the place last year it had taken on a new elegance with antique matt patterned tiles on the floor; bookshelves painted stone blue and reaching up to the high ceiling; and simple but stylish dark mahogany wooden tables and chairs. It had been transformed from having a rustic charm to being a classy eatery, exceeding the best Highgate Village had to offer. They certainly got more passing trade from visitors to the area as a result of the changes but Elaine was sure they had lost some of their loyal local customers as she had been forced to put the menu prices up.

'The menu should reflect the venue,' Adrien Moreau had said when he broke the news to Elaine. Whilst he owned the place and had impeccable taste in furnishings, he was not interested in a hands-on role and left the day to day running to her.

Elaine was fiddling with some fresh flowers at the back of the restaurant when he came up behind her.

'Bonjour Elaine,' he said to her back making her jump.

'Oh, Adrien, hello, sorry I....' She turned to see he was immaculately dressed in a dark Armani suit with silver cufflinks and his aftershave, an intoxicating mix of lemon and neroli came over her in a wave.

'Surely you were expecting me?' he asked.

Indeed she was, she had spent all morning psyching herself up for this meeting. 'Of course,' she said outwardly confident, inwardly dreading what was about to come. 'Would you like to come up to the office?'

He looked unsure and let his critical eyes smother his surroundings. 'How about we start down here? Perhaps one of your staff could serve us some drinks?'

Elaine beckoned Emma, her most competent waitress, over. Adrien selected a table at the back. 'Not many customers, are there?'

She decided not to rise to that bait. It had been really useful talking through this meeting with Ross the evening before. He had persuaded her she should stand firm and not be intimidated by Moreau.

41

'He has to understand the implications of his decisions,' Ross had said and she knew he was right but convincing the owner was a different matter.

'I've been looking at the figures you sent me,' Adrien said as he neatly removed a file from his black leather attaché case. 'Revenue is falling; this is a situation that I cannot tolerate for much longer.'

'It is since we put the menu prices up. We've lost some of our local business. You have to remember we're still in a recession and eating out is a luxury for most people.'

'I have invested significantly into this venture and we must find a way to make it pay,' he said defiantly.

'Well I have suggested running promotions, such as set menus before 6 o'clock; two courses for £12.95, that kind of thing. Many restaurants do this.'

'But it lowers the tone!' he said raising his voice so that the staff were startled. 'We must maintain standards and draw people in with our exquisite cuisine. After all, Jean Ducasse, is an exceptional chef.' He was leaning in towards Elaine now, 'I want this to be a destination restaurant with, who knows, a Michelin star one day!'

Elaine remembered the ridiculous argument she had had with Jean just the other day when he had refused to let her promote a special on the menu even though he had ordered far too much turbot and it would not last another day.

She looked around her and was grasping at straws when she said, 'look, look out of the window at the people passing by. Do they look like the type who are seeking out a gourmet meal? It's February. These are local people and if they are anywhere at the moment, they are probably in Fegos having coffee.' He seemed to be listening so she continued, 'and at lunch time they want a quick bite to eat, maybe they are working, or maybe they look at this place and think they can't afford it.'

Adrien straightened his spine and peered down at Elaine's diminutive figure. 'Your attitude is getting me nowhere! You have no comprehension of the restaurant trade! Perhaps you should be working in this Fegos fiasco of a place!'

Katie reached for her mobile and called Ross, not quite sure what she was going to say to him.

'Hello Katie, how are you?'

'I'm okay thanks.' She was unable to mirror his upbeat tone.

'I take it Birch is still renting your top room?' he asked tentatively.

'Oh well, yes, well yes and no.'

Ross was confused and said nothing. She went on to explain, 'what I mean is, he is, but his divorce is making life very difficult for him, financially I mean.'

'Ah.' There was only a moments pause before he said, 'Would you like to run your ad in the magazine again?'

'Yes, yes I would. The trouble is...'

'Don't even think about it. The space is yours, free of charge, whenever you want it.'

'Oh Ross you're very kind but...'

'Katie, it's nothing. Your late husband picked me up when I was down and I will always be grateful to you for that.'

'Thank you Ross.'

'I take it you need some new clients as soon as?'

'Yes, that's exactly what I need.'

'Okay, let me think about this. How about we get a bit more creative this time and interview some of your existing clients? Then it will be like a testimonial. They always work well.'

'That sounds great, but how much will we be able to get into half a page?'

'A full page, let's make it a full page. With a photo of you.'

'But Ross...'

'No buts. When are you free? I could come round and take a photo of you at your desk.'

Bethan had drunk all the milk from Harry's fridge and, apart from being really hungry, she had drunk more than enough coffee for one day. She was amazed that all his cupboards were empty; she had checked every one and only found condiments and a bottle of tomato ketchup. He really did eat every meal out, one way or another. She reluctantly decided she needed to go to the village shop for provisions. It was two o'clock in the afternoon and the rain had cleared leaving a bright blue sky. It was definitely daylight. There would be more people around than there was last night. But still she was reluctant to venture out.

Matt had rung three times and each time she had let the call go through to her voice-mail. She assumed he was wondering why she wasn't at work and didn't bother to listen to the messages he left. Having drunk the best part of two bottles of wine the night before to numb the shock of being threatened by a vagrant, she had woken just after ten o'clock that morning and decided it would be better not to go in to work at all than to turn up so late.

So when her phone rang again she was about to ignore it when she saw Harry's name light up.

'Harry!' she struggled to conceal her excitement. 'Hello,' she said in a more measured tone.

'Hi Bethan, how are you?'

She suddenly felt very optimistic. Perhaps all that stuff about her going back home was just a safety thing while he was away. 'I'm okay, missing you.'

'Bethan, darling, where are you?'

'What do you mean, where am I?

'Well, it's just that Paul's been on the phone asking if I know where you are.'

'Oh! Yes, well I didn't go in to work today.'

'I see. Are you not well?'

'Yes, that's right, well I'm not too bad but you see something hideous happened to me last night.'

'Oh my God.' He sounded worried. 'What was that?'

'I was attacked on my way home.'

'Attacked? Bethan, that's awful! Are you hurt?'

'Not exactly. Traumatised though.'

'That's dreadful. Did you ring the police? What actually happened?'

'It was some tramp; he was trying to get money from me. Anyway he really scared me.'

'Oh Bethan, I'm so sorry. Are you sure he didn't hurt you?'

'No, not as such.' She was biting a finger nail. 'He really frightened me. I ran all the way home. It was dark and I thought he was following me.'

'Did you get home safely?'

'Yes, eventually.'

'Thank goodness.'

'Mmm, well anyway, when will you be back?'

'Oh, a few days. I have an open ticket. Listen, do you think you should call Paul?'

She didn't answer.

'Or shall I let him know what's happened? You see he's worried about you as you haven't turned up.'

She wasn't going to turn down this offer. 'Yes please Harry, will you call him? Tell him I'm still in shock, I'm actually quite nervous about even going out.'

There was a pause before Harry said as gently as he could, 'are you at my flat?'

'Yes,' she replied uncertainly, 'is that okay?'

'Of course it is darling but you don't want to be on your own at a time like this?'

'No, not really but I'm not going back to Mum's.'

'I take it she doesn't know what's happened?'

'I don't suppose she even cares.'

'That's just silly Bethan. Of course she cares.'

She started sobbing.

'Look, I'm going to call your Mum and let her know. You shouldn't be on your own right now.'

'Oh Harry I wish you were here.'

He sighed loudly enough for her to hear.

'You don't care about me really, do you? You just want to chuck me out of your flat!'

'No, I do care; of course I care. Listen I'm sorry but I have to go into a meeting right now but I will ring your Mum and Paul for you.'

'And will you ring me again later?' she was hanging on to the last threads of hope.

'Yes, okay, I'll call you later. Now for goodness sake look after yourself.'

Elaine looked at her watch for the umpteenth time that day. Since Adrien had left her waiters were all creeping around her is if she might snap at any moment. Emma had tentatively asked her if she was all right at one point.

Elaine had sighed. 'I'm not sure I am,' she had replied finally, no energy to lie.

Emma reached across to gently touch her arm. 'You're such a good manager; I hope you don't leave.'

Elaine smiled knowingly. 'Thanks, but I'm not sure it's up to me.'

Ross turned up when she still had half an hour to go. 'I got your text,' he said looking concerned.

She didn't need to say anything. He gave her a hug before looking straight into her eyes, 'don't worry about a thing. I'm sure it will all work out. I mean, who else is he going to get to run this place?'

She sniffed back a tear, 'I don't know but I'm not sure I can put up with this for much longer.'

Emma approached cautiously, 'if you want to go now, that's fine, I'll hold the fort. After all, we're not too busy.'

'Thanks Emma, I think I will.'

'Good idea,' Ross agreed and then added, 'I'm taking you to the pub for a drink.'

The Flask had a log fire going and Ross nabbed a table for two nearby just as its previous occupants were leaving.

'Here, let's sit here near the fire,' he said as he helped Elaine with her coat. 'What would you like to drink?'

'Glass of red, I think.'

'Good choice, I'll just go to the bar.'

Elaine checked her phone. There was a text message from her mother which simply said: please phone Mum x. This was the norm. Her mother resisted even having a mobile phone but Elaine had persuaded her of the benefits especially if emergencies arose. She was worried now. Was it something to do with her daughter, Jessica? She called her mother.

'Hello dear,' her mother answered cheerily.

'Mum, everything okay?'

'Yes, of course.'

'But you sent me a text.'

'Oh yes! So I did. What it was, Jessica needs to go in fancy dress tomorrow to school. She has to dress as a character in a book she's read.'

'Oh God, that's all I need,' Elaine considered abandoning her drink with Ross just as he put a large inviting glass of Cabernet Sauvignon in front of her.

'No, don't worry, we've managed to do it. She's going as Felicity Wishes and wearing that pink fairy outfit she had for her party last year.'

'Isn't that too small for her now?'

'Yes, it is a bit but I've managed to let it out. It's very short now on her but she's wearing thick tights so she'll be fine. Oh, and we've made her a pink wand to match.'

'Oh Mum, you're so brilliant! Thank you.'

'No problem. Will you be home soon?'

'Yes, I,' Elaine had a pang of guilt, 'I will, but I'm just having a quick drink with Ross.'

'All right, I'll see you soon. I must meet this Ross chap some time. Enjoy your drink.'

'Thanks Mum.'

Ross smiled, 'everything okay?'

'Yes, except I feel bad about relying so heavily on my Mum to look after Jess.'

'Well you're here now and after the day you've had you deserve a drink.' He picked up her glass and put it in her hand then raised his own. 'Here's to Monsieur Moreau getting stuck in the tunnel on his way back to Paris.'

Elaine managed a smile, 'I hope he chokes on his own ghastly aftershave.'

Katie drove quickly round to Harry's place and parked outside. She had been in a state of heightened agitation since his call.

'It was just supposed to be for a few days.' Harry had explained. 'Katie, I've been trying to persuade her to go back home to you.'

Birch had tried to calm her down too but it was no good she had to see her daughter. Luckily another resident was leaving as she arrived and she managed to slip in through the front door. She climbed the stairs as per Harry's instructions until she reached the top and braced herself as she rang the doorbell. It was some time before Bethan answered but when she did Katie threw her arms around her.

'Oh my darling!'

'Mum!' Bethan looked really pleased to see her and sank into her embrace.

They went inside and Katie looked around. The flat was surprisingly tidy when compared with Bethan's bedroom at home. There were a couple of empty wine bottles in the kitchen and a third open on a coffee table in front of the television which was showing an old episode of the American show, Friends. An empty take-away pizza box was also on the table. Bethan sat down and turned the television off.

Katie sat beside her. 'So,' she said calmly, 'tell me.'

'I'm fine really, Harry will be home in a couple of days.'

Her mother looked doubtful. 'Darling, he told me what's happened. He said you were attacked.'

'Well, yes I was, but that was last night. It was dark by the time I left Fegos.'

'And you were on your own?'

'Yes.' Bethan's eyes were shifty. She sighed before adding, 'Something bad happened at work and I just needed to be alone for a bit so I went for a coffee, okay?'

'What happened at work?'

She said nothing now and avoided her mother's gaze. Katie gave her time.

'Matt was really horrible to me. He said he was going to make trouble because I finished with him.'

Katie looked puzzled and then she said, 'but that's not right, he can't say something like that.'

'Well he did Mum!'

'Okay, I believe you. So is that why you didn't go in today?'

Bethan looked uncomfortable. 'Well yes but it was also because I didn't want to go out after last night.'

'Have you been here all day?' Katie was beginning to realise the effect of this incident on her daughter.

'Yeah,' Bethan shrugged and looked away.

'Tell me about what happened last night.'

'This horrible dirty man, this tramp, he jumped out at me and demanded I gave him money.'

'Did he hurt you? Did anyone see? Did you call the police?'

Bethan started crying and Katie held her. 'Sorry, in your own time.'

'He frightened me!'

'Darling I really think you should come home with me. Surely you don't want to be here on your own after this.'

The doorbell rang and they both looked at each other. Katie stood up. 'I'll go.'

'Mum, there's a peep hole. See who it is.'

'I will,' she said calmly.

Peering through she saw a very attractive looking woman, probably the same age as Harry. She crept back into the living room and whispered to Bethan, 'It's some woman. Shall we ignore it? She's bound to want Harry and well, he's not here.'

Bethan looked alarmed.

'Harry I know you're in there!' Natasha shouted from behind the door. 'Don't pretend you're not. I saw the lights on from outside.' She banged loudly with her fist several times. 'For God's sake open this door!'

49

Katie's eyes widened. 'She'll go eventually,' she whispered but Bethan was looking more and more worried.

'Harry I'm not going anywhere until you open this door!' Natasha was getting irate. 'And! My mother will move her investments if you don't speak to me.'

'Perhaps I should go and talk to her?' Katie mouthed to Bethan and then steadied herself and went to the door. She opened it slowly and peered round.

'Who are you?' Natasha demanded with a look of horror.

'I'm sorry but Harry isn't here.'

'Oh don't give me that rubbish,' she said barging in to find Bethan cowering on the sofa. 'And just who the hell are you?'

Katie said, 'I'm Harry's virtual assistant actually and I can tell you that he is currently in New York on business. I'm just looking after the place until he gets back.' She was pleased she had come up with a reason to be there.

Natasha was not convinced and was already noticing the empty pizza carton and wine bottles. 'Does Harry know you've been using his place as some sort of doss house?'

Now Katie was affronted. 'Don't be ridiculous. We've just had a pizza and a glass of wine, where's the crime in that?'

'Are you sleeping with Harry?' She directed her question at Katie. Bethan looked flabbergasted.

'Excuse me! I'm Harry's girlfriend!'

Natasha laughed mockingly in her face. 'Don't be ridiculous; you can't even be legal!'

'I'm seventeen actually. Anyway who are you to come barging in here?'

Natasha looked fierce. 'Huh! I happen to be his girlfriend, actually! His real girlfriend! Not some child pretending at it.'

'Listen,' Katie decided to intervene before things got physical. 'The fact is that Harry is in New York at the moment and so he's not here.'

The wind out of her sails, she threw her handbag over her shoulder and turned to leave. Before she reached the door she turned back and scowled. 'You'd better be out of here; I shall be telling Harry that you've been taking liberties. Virtual assistant indeed!'

Katie looked surprised but didn't react. With Natasha gone she turned to her daughter. 'Now will you come home with me?'

# Chapter 5

'Charlie, just stop there a minute,' Katie said, scribbling furiously on her notepad.

'Sorry doll, am I going too fast as usual? The thing is this place down Cholmeley Crescent, well it's cryin' out for Bob the builder to have a go at it and turn it into flats.'

'So you haven't actually bought it yet?'

'Nah, I've tried to secure it, get them to take it off the market but it's no good, the owner still wants it to be sold at auction. Which is tomorrow you see.' Charlie rattled through his sentences with great speed.

'Right, so you're going to the auction tomorrow?'

'Ah well, there's the snag.'

Katie was still wondering what all this was about. 'The snag?'

'Yeah.' For a rare moment Charlie hesitated. She waited.

'I've got this important meeting with my accountant and my bank manager and, try as I might to get them to be a little bit flexible, they're just not buying it. And especially when I said I was looking to take on another development.'

'That doesn't sound good,' she said more as a reaction than anything else.

'No, no, it's all fine. It's all good. I just need to sort a few things.'

'Okay,' she said uncertainly.

'So, the thing is,' again he paused for breath, 'well I thought you could go for me.'

Her mind was whirring. 'Go to the auction for you?' She was convinced he didn't actually mean that.

'Yeah, that's it doll. You go to the auction to bid on this Cholmeley place. What d'ya say?'

'But Charlie I've never done anything like that before. I'd be out of my depth. I really don't think it's a good idea.'

'Darlin' honestly, you are one of the cleverest women I know. You're mega. I know you can do it and I promise you it's easy. All you have to do is stick to the ceiling price I give you which is three hundred thousand. Maybe three fifty. Well actually tops would be four hundred. Yeah, that has to be it. It wouldn't be worth doing for any more than that.'

Katie felt giddy. 'Charlie, I'd love to help out really..'

'I'll pay double time from the minute you leave your house to when you get back, how's that?'

She considered that the money would be very useful. 'You know you're nearly up to your maximum hours this month already, don't you?'

'Am I doll? No problem. Just bill me for all the hours you do. You're worth your weight in gold, really you are.'

Katie knew she had to seriously consider this extracurricular work for Charlie even though it frightened the life out of her. 'So what exactly would I have to do?'

Sylvia carefully removed her tan suede coat, folded it neatly and put it on the seat next to her. She decided to leave her canary yellow scarf on until she warmed up as the train was quite cool. She had boarded at Sandgate, the end of the line, so it was empty but she knew only too well that by the time they reached London it would be crowded with day trippers and she would have to have her coat on her lap which was a nuisance but she knew that if she put it on the overhead rack, she might waltz off the train without it.

Her memory was pretty good for her seventy-five years, which she attributed to her addiction to Sudoku, which she played daily on her ipad. Most of her friends were amused that she even had a tablet and Birch had laughed when he first saw it.

'Mum, you really are a silver surfer now! I thought you said you weren't going to succumb to the digital revolution?'

'Ah, well darling, when the nice man in John Lewis showed me how easy it is to use, I thought, this is brilliant! Do you realise I can watch the BBC on this little lovely?'

Sylvia was halfway through that day's Sudoku puzzle when a well-dressed gentleman approached her cautiously from the aisle.

'Madam, may I be so bold as to introduce myself?'

Sylvia blinked away from her puzzle to look up at the man who had a pleasing appearance, if lacking in height, and a lovely smile. 'Oh, yes, please do. You want to sit here? I don't mind.' The seat opposite her was still free.

'That's very kind but actually I'm in first class.'

'Very nice too,' Sylvia said, wondering now what all this was about.

'Yes, anyway, the name is Reggie and I was just wondering if you would like to join me for a drink in my carriage?'

She seemed to be having this sort of encounter quite frequently these days. There were always two options: be boring and say 'no' or throw caution to the wind and go for it. 'Why not?' She popped her tablet into her handbag and picked up her coat.

'Follow me,' Reggie said with a broad grin.

Sylvia was quite surprised that by a drink he had meant a gin and tonic and not a hot beverage, after all, it was ten o'clock in the morning. But she decided that this too was a live-a-little moment and at her time of life you really had to relax into it, rather than resist.

It turned out that Reggie was a retired army major who had served in the Falklands and he had been staying with his daughter who lived in Folkestone. He had an apartment in Kensington, preferring city life to the countryside which was far too quiet for him, and had lived alone there since his wife had died five years ago.

'Anyway cheers,' he said clinking glasses with her. 'Thank you for joining me.'

'Well this is all rather pleasant but you know I only have a ticket for back there.' Sylvia waved her hand in the direction of the next carriage.

'Oh, don't worry yourself with all that. I'll sort out the guard when he pops along.' He settled back into his chair, 'Now, tell me about yourself. What took you to Folkestone?'

Sylvia laughed. 'Darling I live there, don't I! Well Sandgate actually, little Georgian place on the sea front. Rather gusty but lovely view from the summer room.'

'Sounds fun. Do you pop up to London for a spot of shopping every now and then?'

'I have been known, but no, my son lives in Highgate Village, that's where I'm off to.'

'Ah, north of the river. What does he do?'

'Author, Birch, he writes novels, you may have heard of him. And a column in The Times.'

'Well blow me if I haven't read one of his novels recently. Good stuff. You must be proud of him.'

There was a comfortable pause as they sipped their drinks. Reggie sat up making himself as tall as he could manage. 'So, gentleman on the scene is there? Someone to take you out for a spot of fine dining every now and then?'

Sylvia admired his openness in a way. 'I get plenty of offers,' she smiled and thought of Jack, her first love, a struggling artist who would have made a totally unsuitable husband in her parents' eyes, but who was undoubtedly the love of her life. The black and white photo she had of him had faded but his beautiful smiling face still shone out at her. As in the picture, he had always had a glint in his eye and his dark moustache matched his curly hair which he wore quite long. How she had adored him; he was her kindred spirit. So he was the man that any suitor now had to live up to, otherwise what was the point?

The man she married, Arthur, the local GP, boring Arthur, was the height of respectability but duller than a wet weekend in Margate. He might have been welcomed with open arms into her family, and for a little while in the euphoria leading up to their wedding day she somehow convinced herself she would grow to love him, but in the end she could only keep up the pretence to all around her. The fact that he smoked wasn't even an issue when they met in the sixties, in fact it was considered suave, sexy even, but of course by nineteen ninety when he died of lung cancer any doctor knew the risks only too well.

'I bet you do,' Reggie said as he gazed into her eyes. 'Another G&T?'

'Why not?'

Birch watched as his mother climbed carefully out of the first-class carriage, the hand of a man he didn't recognise steadying her. In what seemed like a slightly intimate exchange they nodded to each other and the man was quickly on his way whilst she strolled less urgently along the platform, trailing her suitcase on wheels behind her, with her head held high and not a care in the world.

'Mum,' he waved as he called.

She spotted him. 'Darling, this is good of you to meet me here on the platform.'

'Mum, it's good to see you,' he held her briefly. 'How was your journey?'

'Rather splendid actually.'

'Anything to do with that chap I saw helping you alight before he scurried off?'

'Everything to do with Reggie actually!' She giggled.

'Mum, have you been drinking?'

'Yes, two G&Ts. In first class as well.'

'Really?' Birch was quite surprised even though he knew his mother had eccentric tendencies. 'Are you dating this Reggie?'

'Oh no, nothing like that. Ships that pass in the night I expect.'

'You expect?'

'Well we did exchange mobile numbers but what of it.'

'Right,' Birch was bemused but let it go. 'I'll hail a cab if you don't mind paying?'

'Lovely, I can't abide the underground,' she said and then fully grasping what he'd said she added, 'Short of funds, how come?'

'In a word: Celia.'

'Dreadful woman! Never did like her. I hope you don't mind me saying that now, darling?'

Birch looked at her and smiled, 'Well it's never held you back before!'

'And now she's being difficult, is she? She needs something large and rude sticking up the f-holes on that screechy cello of hers!'

Alice was watching the faces of the young family round the table as she cleared their plates. The mother was pale faced with dark circles under her eyes and her hair was long and lank, the roots much darker than the ends. She had complained earlier that her son's meal was too hot for him to eat. This was feedback that Alice hadn't come across before and she wasn't quite sure what to say but she picked up the plate, despite the protesting cries of the child. 'I'll see what I can do,' she said and disappeared into the kitchen. Marcus, one of the other waiters was loitering.

'How do I cool this down? Quickly.'

He looked puzzled. 'Put it in the fridge?'

'Seems crazy but..' She found the fridge and popped it in.

'Isn't that a hot meal?'

'Yeah, the mum thinks it's too hot for her precious son.'

'Oh, table nine! Yes, she does look rather tense.'

'That's the one.'

Alice checked the food. It now seemed cold to her. Was that what she wanted? 'Wish me luck,' she said as she took it back.

Now she noticed the boy had left most of the food on his plate anyway.

'Everything alright?' she asked out of habit but immediately wish she hadn't. The mother was too busy fussing over her children to notice.

Her husband looked up. 'Could we have the pudding menu, please?'

The mother scowled at him. 'No pudding if he doesn't eat his main course.'

He had an air of resignation about him as he said, 'Well, we'll have a look anyway,' and smiled at Alice.

She consoled herself with the fact that she'd got the A grade she needed for her French A-level when she sat her re-take in January.

Nottingham University had already confirmed that she would be able to start her degree in September. University was going to be an escape route away from waitressing, away from home. But actually, rather oddly, she was enjoying life at Bisham Gardens now. She couldn't quite put her finger on it but Birch's presence seemed to be a force for the good and she could see how happy he made her mother. She had a calmness and serenity about her that Alice had never noticed before. It was quite disconcerting because it made her question how happy her mum actually was with her father for all those years. But then she would consider that her and Birch were very much in the honeymoon period of their relationship when things always seem rosy. That must be it.

Birch held the door open for his mother to enter The Lemon Tree before him. 'Oh this is rather nice,' Sylvia commented.

Alice spotted them and went straight over. 'Hello, this is a surprise,' she said brightly and seemed genuinely pleased to see them.

'Just wondering if we can have a table for a bit of lunch?' Birch asked looking round; it was pretty full.

'Ooh give me a minute, we should be able to squeeze you in.'

'Are you sure this is a good idea?' Sylvia whispered to her son. 'I mean I don't want to cause trouble for Alice.'

'Well if they can't fit us in we'll go elsewhere.'

Alice was back. 'Table eight have just finished their coffee so should be leaving very soon. There are some seats over here while you wait if you like?'

'That's very kind,' Sylvia smiled at her.

Paul had sent Bethan an email asking her to come to his office for a chat at three o'clock that afternoon. She had spent the whole day so far worrying about what he was going to say to her. She knew that Carol at The Cup Cake Company was happy with her work and she had played her part on the team that won the Pet Perfect account which was considered a major success at the agency. But Matt had been so off with her since she had left him; he was being childish and she wondered what she'd ever seen in him. Even so she was upset by his behaviour and was convinced that he was telling Paul things about her that just weren't true in order to get back at her.

Matt was standing in front of her. 'Paul wants to see you now,' he said in the manner a school teacher might send an errant child to the headmaster.

Bethan hid her nerves and looked straight at him as she replied, 'I know.' She picked up a notepad and pen and made her way over to his office.

'You making notes, are you?' he said in a disparaging way that was totally uncalled for. Everyone around him looked up from their work and stared at Matt.

'Come in, Bethan, sit down.' Paul gave her a half smile but he looked disturbed.

She sat neatly crossing her legs and waited for him to speak.

'Listen, I'll get straight to the point; I'm broadly happy with your work, in fact in some areas it has been outstanding, but it's obvious you don't have a good working relationship with Matt and that does cause me concern.'

Alarm bells were going off in Bethan's head. Her worst fears were about to be realised; she was going to be sacked.

'He tells me you contributed very little to the Pet Perfect pitch but when I've spoken to others on the team they said you did most of the graphics for the presentation. What's the truth, Bethan?'

She took a deep breath. 'I did all the graphics, I was here until gone eight o'clock doing them the night before the run through. Matt wasn't here to see me but he must have known. I emailed them to him when I'd finished.'

'I see.'

'Would you like to see the email?'

'Yes please,' he was looking straight at her but then had a change of heart, 'actually no, I believe you. I don't want to turn this into a witch hunt.'

'Carol's happy with my work,' she added while she had his ear.

'I know she is.'

'In fact she wants a meeting with me tomorrow to discuss two new pages and some more functionality for her website. Matt said he'd have to come with me but when I told her she said she wanted to see me on my own.'

'I see. Why do you think that is?'

'She likes me and she likes my work. There's no need for Matt to be there. He just doesn't...' she stopped herself.

'Doesn't what?'

She sighed as she searched for the right thing to say.

He was tapping his pen repeatedly on the desk during an awkward pause. 'It doesn't take a genius to work out that since you and Matt split up your working relationship has suffered.'

He had hit her with the crux of the matter and Bethan felt she had nothing to lose now. 'But it's him! He's the one causing trouble. I've been working hard and no one else has a problem with me.'

'Mmm,' Paul sat back in his chair, 'Matt is a real asset to this agency,' he said with conviction but then he paused before he added, 'but you two need to get along.'

Bethan's heart sank as she knew that wasn't going to happen.

Paul must have sensed her dismay. 'I'll talk to Matt and...' he took a sharp intake of breath, 'it's against my better judgement but I will do what I can to keep you two on different accounts. How does that sound?'

'I'm sure that will help. And thank you,' she said in relief.

'And as for that meeting with Carol tomorrow, I'll let you go on your own.'

'Oh that's great. Thank you Paul. I won't let you down.'

'I shall get a full report from Carol after the meeting so you had better not.' He smiled now. 'Okay, that's it but will you ask Matt to come in please?'

Bethan left the room smiling and went over to Matt's desk. She approached him cautiously and said gently, 'Paul wants to see you.' She wasn't going to gloat; she was bigger than that.

'Right,' Matt replied looking confused.

The Lemon Tree had quietened down by the time Birch and Sylvia had finished their lunch. Alice delivered two coffees to their table.

'Thank you Alice,' Sylvia said with a smile. 'What time are you here until?'

'Oh, another hour to go,' she replied rolling her eyes before adding, 'Mum tells me you're staying with us for a few days.'

'Yes, that's right. I hope that's okay?'

'Of course it is.'

'Birch tells me you got the grade you wanted in French to go to Nottingham University.'

'Yes, that's right,' Alice was surprised he'd told her. 'I'm really looking forward to it.'

'I bet you are. I did French too, as a mature student you understand. When I was your age it was all about marrying someone suitable and having children. Anyway, when I graduated I worked for a translation agency for a good few years. That was after Birch's father died.'

'Oh wow, you'll have to tell me more about that!' Alice noticed that her manager, Margaret, was glaring at her from across the room. 'I'd better go.'

Sylvia looked across at Margaret, 'she's all a bit unnecessary isn't she?'

'Mum, behave, you'll be getting Alice into trouble,' her son said light heartedly.

Alice giggled and went to clear another table.

# Chapter 6

Sylvia produced two ten-pound notes and handed them to the taxi driver, 'keep the change,' she said even though the meter displayed very nearly that amount. Katie was attempting to find her purse in her handbag.

'Don't be silly!' Sylvia stopped her. 'It was my idea to get a cab after all.'

'And what a brilliant idea. I'm sure parking in Piccadilly would be a nightmare. Of course, we could have got the tube.'

'Darling, I don't do the underground. There are some things that once you're in your seventies just aren't worth the bother,' she threw a hand nonchalantly away from her in no particular direction.

Katie smiled at her; she loved her attitude to life and thought how she was the perfect companion for this morning's mission impossible. 'You know if you weren't with me now, I think I'd be a nervous wreck!'

'Well, I must admit I was a little surprised when you told me what Charlie wanted you to do. He must have a lot of faith in you.'

'Mm.. crazy man that he is!'

They both looked up at the entrance to the Meridian hotel which loomed above them, 'Well, look, we have a brief; all we have to do is stick to it.' Sylvia said but Katie wasn't reassured. Sylvia tucked her arm through Katie's and added, 'listen, you can blame me if it all goes wrong.'

'Don't be silly! And it can't go wrong!'

'Of course it won't.'

'It might.' Katie feared the worst.

'Yes, it's a possibility.'

'Oh Sylvia!'

The room had a stately feel with tall double doors at the entrance, cream panelling on the walls and glitzy chandeliers and there was a swirly cobalt blue and yellow patterned carpet. But any thoughts of this being a palatial place were brought firmly down to earth by the casually dressed misfit of potential buyers that looked like they might be anything from nervous first timers to wide boys.

They were stood at the back and Katie surveyed the room. 'I can see how Charlie would fit right in!'

'Oh what fun!' Sylvia stifled a laugh. 'And look at us! Far too respectable. Do you realise this is Max Mara?' She placed her hand on the neat tangerine shift dress she was wearing under a gold linen waisted jacket.

'You have a point. We don't exactly blend in, do we?' Katie started laughing, now. 'Charlie could have warned me!'

'Well at least we look as if we can afford a property or two!'

'Oh the irony!'

Elaine had just dropped Jessica off at school. So often it was her mother who did the school run and Jessica's year two form teacher, Miss Singh, did a double take when she spotted her at the gate. Elaine had smiled and waved meekly, almost apologetically. The teacher in turn acknowledged her. Just as she got back in her car she saw a text message appear on her mobile from Ross.

*Fancy meeting for coffee at Fegos? R x*

It was her day off from the restaurant and she had planned to do some much needed housework. Her mother was very fit for her sixty two years but, with all the time she spent looking after Jess, it was difficult for her to keep the house clean and tidy as well. Since she'd been dating Ross she had seen very little of her mother and that was yet another pull on her heart strings.

*Lovely idea but I have lots to do at home. E x*

She braced herself as she pressed send hoping it wouldn't offend him. The reply came quickly.

*The sun is shining, it's too nice for housework. Meet me at Fegos at 10am - it's important! R x*

Calm and assertive, she thought. That was Ross all over. But what could be so vital, she wondered.

*What's important mysterious man?*

His reply made her smile.

*You have to turn up to find out! :) x*

She flicked her eyes skyward and started up her engine.

When she got home she found her mother in the garden pruning her David Austin roses.

'Alright dear?' her mother looked up and discarded another handful of brown leaves from her gloved hand.

'Yes Mum.' She suddenly decided to give her a hug.

'What was that for? You're not eloping with Ross are you?'

'You got it in one! No, of course not. But he wants me to meet him in Fegos; says it's important.' She put her hands out as if to say 'search me'. Her mother looked puzzled. 'I've no idea what it's about,' Elaine added.

'Well you must go. Sounds exciting.' Connie got back to work with her secateurs.

Elaine was thoughtful. 'Mum, how about I invite Ross round for supper this evening? I mean you haven't met him properly yet, have you? I'll cook.'

Connie looked delighted. 'That's a nice idea. I'll look forward to that.'

'So which lot are we bidding on?' Sylvia whispered.

Katie had circled the relevant property in the auction catalogue. 'Lot 15, so it shouldn't be too long now; that was Lot 7.'

'Yes, they're going quite quickly aren't they?'

64

'And that,' Katie pointed to a figure pencilled on the sheet in front of her, 'is our absolute top budget.'

'I'm going to have to get my reading glasses out, I can't see it.' Sylvia started rummaging in her handbag.

'Whatever you do, don't say it out loud!' Katie warned her.

'Oh yes, of course.' She put a pair of tortoiseshell-framed glasses on the end of her nose and took a covert look. 'Got you.'

'Lot ten, three-bedroom terrace, in need of renovation,' the auctioneer announced in a cavalier fashion. He was smartly dressed and had three henchmen standing behind him, keeping a careful eye on proceedings.

'What happened to Lots 8 and 9?' Katie asked.

An Asian man in a cheap suit the other side of Sylvia gave them an irritated stare.

'Sorry,' Sylvia said and looked as if she meant it.

He smiled and said quickly, 'lots 8 and 9 were sold before the auction.'

'Oh!' Sylvia and Katie exclaimed simultaneously looking horrified. Katie shrugged her shoulders. 'Well, Charlie didn't say anything about properties selling before we even got here.'

Sylvia squeezed Katie's hand. 'Have faith. Visualise a good outcome,' she closed her eyes as if she was doing just that. Katie giggled and Sylvia joined in. The man in the suit was not impressed and moved away from them.

The two women watched as the auctioneer worked the room, checking out how people were bidding. It was often a raising of the auction catalogue rolled up in one hand. The auctioneer was careful to be sure of every bid; the idea of not being able to as much as scratch your nose was a myth it seemed. Lot 15 was announced and Katie took a deep breath to try and calm her nerves.

'Best of luck darling,' Sylvia said, 'I'm right here for you.'

'Three floors. Looks like you've got three non-self-contained flats. Start low at three hundred thousand. Not going to go below three hundred. In the air...'

He nodded to a man on the other side of the room. 'Yes, 300... 310.... Yes, 320... do I see 330? 340 standing up..'

Sylvia whispered into Katie's ear, 'when do we bid?'

'When it looks like they've all given up.'

'Right, I see. Good tactic.'

'380... right at the back of the room. 390... in the aisle 395...'

Sylvia looked pointedly at Katie, 'Now?'

'Still with you in the aisle sitting at 395..'

'400!' Katie raised her catalogue to get his attention.

'400, we have a new bidder at the back.'

'405,' the man in the aisle shouted out.

'Damn!' Katie let slip, 'we've lost it.'

'405 it is. Another bid anywhere else? If not, selling it for 405.'

The whole room was quiet for a couple of seconds. The auctioneer, raised his gavel.

'407!' Sylvia was raising her hand as she shouted the figure out.

Katie was beside herself, 'that's too much!'

'407,' the auctioneer repeated, his eyes going back to the previous bidder. The two women watched the back of his head carefully while he thought about it. It was an excruciating moment. Katie half wanted him to bid again and if he did, she would grab Sylvia and drag her out of the room before she did any more damage. But that would mean that they had failed to secure the property for Charlie. She was stuck between a rock and a hard place. The man shook his head.

'407, then. With the lady at the back at 407.' He looked round the room. Nothing. 'It's sealed at 407. Make no mistake.' The gavel came down. Bang!

'You bought it, madam,' he nodded to Sylvia, who was beaming. 'Well done.'

'Oh my God, Sylvia! We've gone seven thousand over!'

'Oh well, I'm sure Charlie will be pleased. If not, I'm happy to invest the extra 7K myself.'

'Really?'

A text from Charlie appeared on Katie's phone, which simply said:

*Well?*

How was she going to answer that? One of the henchmen was approaching Sylvia, 'this way madam, for the paperwork,' he said politely but Katie still found him menacing.

'I think I need a drink,' she said, resigned to her fate.

'Excellent idea,' Sylvia said, 'lunch is on me.'

Birch walked into Le Pain Quotidien to find Harry already sat at a table and talking into his mobile. 'Yes, that all sounds good. Thanks for the call and as I said, Katie, my assistant will set up the meeting. Good day to you, sir.' He looked up at Birch and stood to shake his hand. 'Sorry about that mate.'

'No, not at all. Thanks for meeting me; I know you're a busy man.'

'No problem.' They both sat down. 'Katie tells me your ex is causing you a financial headache.'

'To put it mildly.' Birch raised his eyebrows. 'It started off straight forward; she had an affair, left me and agreed to a divorce. She also agreed that we would put our house up for sale with the proceeds going fifty fifty. That was the end of last year. Since then she's had a change of heart, is denying her affair with Alistair, wants me back and won't even let me get an estate agent through the door to do a valuation!'

'My dear chap, this is not good. Let me get you a coffee,' Harry responded as he got up to go to the counter.

He returned with a cappuccino for Birch and said, 'Have you got yourself a decent lawyer?'

'Good question. Jonathan Taylor has been the family solicitor for many years and being in Sandgate he's not quite as expensive as London firms.' Birch was pensive. 'But I am beginning to wonder.'

'It might be worth switching to one with a bit more clout?'

'I'd love to but I just don't have the money. Celia's solicitor is insisting I pay maintenance even before the divorce settlement.'

'That way she is in no hurry to proceed with the divorce,' Harry deduced.

'Exactly. Which is the last thing I want. It's not fair on Katie, all this.'

'Mmm. She sounded pretty miffed about it when she rang me.'
Harry looked thoughtful. 'Okay, so if you don't mind me asking, what does Celia know about, in terms of what you earn?'

'Well there's the book sales and my column in The Times. That's all I've been doing. But I have been approached to do some freelance work. Some guy rang me just the other day, actually, he's putting together some guides to eating out in London.'

'That sounds good.'

'Yeah, would be easy money but no doubt I wouldn't get to keep it.'

'Mmm.. so you need a way of hiding some of this income?'

'Too right I do. But nothing dodgy or knowing my luck I'll get into trouble.'

'I was thinking about an offshore account. Perfectly legit. I've got a corporation set up on Jersey with an account I use for any money I don't want to get thrashed by the tax man. I don't see why I couldn't open up a second account for you and perhaps you could get any money from your freelance work put into the new account?'

'That sounds good. Will it cost me anything?'

'No, no, not at all, just leave it to me.'

'And it's definitely above board?'

'It's not illegal to have an offshore account,' Harry said choosing his words carefully. 'Whether you declare it to Celia...'

'Mmm, strictly speaking..'

'Put it this way, my dear chap, I doubt she's being squeaky clean about her end. I mean doesn't she earn any of her own money?'

'Ah, well that's a good point because she claims to have given up teaching but I'm pretty sure she's still got the little blighters turning up to screech the place down with their tuneless violins.'

Harry laughed. 'Well there you are. She's not playing by the rules. Let's get this account set up for you then. You up for it?'

'Yes. Yes, the more I think about it, the more I like it. I could stop doing The Times restaurant articles which she knows about and free up some time to do these London restaurant reviews which would pay handsomely.'

'I like your thinking, but won't The Times be sorry to see you go?'

'Well, if they are, I'll say I want a new contract, better pay and for the money to go into a new account.' Birch suddenly had more fight about him.

'Even better,' Harry grinned at him.

'Thanks Harry. I feel much better now.'

Elaine found Ross in Fegos reading from a file of official looking papers.

'What's all this then?'

'Hello, thanks for coming.' He got up to kiss her.

'Did I have any choice?' she said playfully.

'What would you like?'

'A cappuccino, please.'

'Right, I'll go up and order; I haven't seen a waiter all the time I've been here.'

While he was gone she looked around the cafe. There was only one other table occupied and the lack of clientele revealed the shabbiness of the decor in places, something she hadn't noticed before. Ross came back with the drinks.

'Why is it so empty in here?' she asked.

'Ah well, I wondered the very same thing the other day and well it turns out that place is up for sale.' Ross lifted the papers he had on the table and then straightened the edges so that they all sat squarely together.

'So, what's that?' Elaine nodded to the papers.

'It's the notice for sale for this place,' he said lowering his voice and leaning forwards.

'What on earth have you got that for?'

'Hang on a minute,' Ross took a deep breath and composed himself. 'Let me rewind a bit. The owner of this place, a Mr Gim.. on.. do, died a month ago and left this place to his son, Paolo Gimondo. Anyway, it turns out he's not interested in taking it on and he wants a quick sale. Nobody is sure why it has to be sold speedily, but consequently it's on the market at a very good price.'

Elaine was still puzzled. 'You're not seriously thinking of buying it, are you?'

Ross looked offended, but then smiled. 'Actually,' he reached across and cupped her hands in his, 'I thought we could buy it together.'

Her eyes widened in disbelief. 'But... how? I mean how on earth do we afford this place?'

'Well, I thought we could put a business plan together and take it to a bank. Or maybe go for a venture capitalist or crowd funding. That's all the rage these days.'

'I have to say, Ross, you are full of surprises. And here's me thinking I'm being a bit radical inviting you round for dinner with my Mum and Jess this evening.'

'Lovely idea,' Ross said without hesitation, 'but don't you see what this could mean?'

'I could leave Le Bistro before I get sacked!' she said rather flippantly.

'Exactly. Not that I think you will be sacked but I know how much you hate it there.'

'Mm,' Elaine had to agree with that much.

'Just think,' Ross was getting excited, 'this is a prime location, coffee shops are so on trend and we could make this place special. Oh and did I mention that there's a flat above included? I could move in so that I don't have to pay rent anymore and that's one less expense.'

'I suppose so.' Elaine looked around her; there was definitely room for improvement.

'We could maybe add a deli as well? It's big enough,' Ross added.

'That sounds good but hang on a minute, before we get totally carried away, how much is this place?'

He braced himself and flicked through his papers to find the exact figure. 'Four hundred and fifty thousand pounds.'

'Whoa!' Elaine swung back in her chair. 'No way!'

'The turnover's around two hundred thousand a year,' Ross continued trying to make the sale price more palatable, 'and there's the potential to increase that.'

Elaine's brain was ticking over fast. 'What about your My Mag business?'

'Well, I could continue it..'

Elaine looked doubtful, 'do you know how much work is going to be involved in running a place like this? Especially to begin with.'

'Or I could sell it to raise some capital and invest it in this place.'

She sat back in her chair and dared to dream. 'If we ran it together I'd be able to see more of Jess, pick her up from school more often.'

'Of course you would. Morning and lunch would be our busier times I suspect and we wouldn't be open in the evenings.'

'Oh Ross it's an attractive idea but we're never going to be able to raise that kind of money. I suppose I have got a bit put by but I have that earmarked for Jess if she goes to university.'

'Oh no you mustn't touch that,' Ross said frowning at the very thought.

'So what are we going to do then?'

'There's only one way of finding out. How about you leave it to me to do the research and see what's possible.'

'Okay. Sounds like a plan.' She looked around the cafe again, 'Oh Ross, just think...'

Sylvia led the way down Piccadilly towards her chosen restaurant, The Wolseley. The sun had managed to burn off the earlier cloud and it was beginning to feel like spring.

'Why's it named after a car?' Katie asked trying to keep up with Sylvia's energetic pace.

'It used to be the car showroom for Wolseley. But you wouldn't believe it, it's a magnificent art deco building with marble flooring!'

'Sounds interesting.'

They were walking past the Royal Academy of Arts when suddenly Sylvia stopped in her tracks. Katie looked at her questioningly.

'Is this it?' They were looking at a pavement sign advertising an exhibition by one Jack Harvey. It looked like he painted Mediterranean landscapes.

'No,' Sylvia murmured looking unsteady now.

'What's the matter?' Katie asked concerned. 'Are you alright?'

'Nothing.' Sylvia stood tall and shook her head. 'Nothing, it's nothing.'

'Do you know his work? This Jack Harvey?'

'No, no I don't. I don't know what I was thinking. Now, let's move on.'

They reached the restaurant and Sylvia turned to Katie. 'Why don't we call Charlie now and tell him? Get it over with. Then we can enjoy our lunch?'

'I suppose so,' Katie was biting her lip and fumbling in her handbag for her mobile.

'I'll talk to him, if you like. Honestly, I'm happy to bridge the gap if necessary. The last thing I want to do is get you into trouble.'

'Okay, well, when we get to our table.'

As they entered they immediately looked up to admire the grand art deco design and ceilings high enough to hang vast wrought iron chandeliers from. The black shiny columns were trimmed in gold and the interior was full of Italian influences as well as some exotic Eastern touches. They were led to a table by a young waiter who could not have been older than eighteen, through a crowded bustling restaurant full of media types and tourists coming to soak up the atmosphere. Katie sat down. 'This is wonderful.'

'Isn't it just. And the food's amazing.'

They were handed menus and Katie started to look.

Sylvia glared at her. 'But first the phone call to Charlie?'

Katie braced herself and retrieved her mobile phone. As she pressed the call button she crossed her fingers.

'Charlie?'

'At last doll! What's going on?'

'We bought it.'

'You did? Fantastic. Well done doll! What's the damage?'

Katie thought how appropriate it was on this occasion to call it damage. 'We had to go a little over your top budget I'm afraid.'

'How much?' he was quick to ask.

Katie was screwing her face up as she said reluctantly, 'seven thousand.'

'What, you bought it for 407?' He was struggling to hear her over the background noise of the restaurant.

'Yes,' she said loud and clearly.

There was a slight pause which was only moments but enough time for Katie to fear the worst.

'That's alright doll. Yeah, you did good. No, I'm pleased you've secured it. This one's going to be a nice little earner.'

Katie's expression gave away the relief she was feeling. Sylvia was beaming. 'All okay?' she mouthed. Katie gave her the thumbs up.

'Listen, we need to move on this one,' Charlie continued, 'so let's meet at the property asap and see what's what. Then you can get all the trades lined up.'

'Of course, Charlie.' And then everything told her not to say this but still it came out anyway. 'Are you absolutely sure about the extra seven grand?'

'Seven! Seven big ones, that's nothing!' His voice was lighter now. 'I knew you'd go over a bit. I had a sort of ceiling in my head of twenty grand over actually, so you done good girl.'

Katie's sigh of relief was audible. Sylvia summoned a waiter over. 'Two glasses of Prosecco please, we're celebrating.'

Katie put her mobile away and Sylvia looked excited. 'So, Charlie was okay about it?'

'Yes! Would you believe he'd reckoned on us going up to twenty thousand over his "top" budget! He was just really pleased that we bought it.'

Sylvia smiled knowingly.

'And I have you to thank for that,' Katie added as the waiter returned with two flutes of sparkly.

They raised their glasses amiably to each other, 'Success!' Sylvia said. 'We make a good team, don't we?'

# Chapter 7

Birch saw his solicitor's name come up on his mobile.

'Jonathan, how are you?'

'Good, good thanks. Listen, just ringing to let you know that I've agreed that figure we discussed for maintenance payments up to the divorce settlement with Brockett Fieldings.'

'Well I suppose it could have been worse,' Birch said wondering how he was going to live on the remainder of his income. 'Did you mention my advance she stripped out of the joint account right at the start of all this?'

'Yes, I've pushed that point but Judith is not admitting to the fact, other than to say that they won't expect the maintenance payments to be back dated to when you filed last year.'

'How very conciliatory of them!'

'Look I know it's tough but if you don't pay maintenance now, you'll be in a far worse position when it comes to the final settlement.'

'Worse than this? Honestly, I'll just be working to hand money over to Celia. Meanwhile, poor Katie will be virtually supporting me!'

Jonathan was tight lipped at the other end of the phone.

'And what about putting the house on the market?' Birch continued in an angry tone.

'Ah, well, she doesn't want the house to be sold.'

'But that's ridiculous! It's my only asset, apart from the car which she monopolises.'

'I know and we can force her to sell, but it's going to take time.'

'Bloody hell! This is enough to drive you mad!' Birch was running his hand through his hair. 'There must be something we can do.'

'Do we know what the situation is with the guy she was having an affair with? Alistair, isn't it?'

'Search me, Jon, I've no idea. Maybe he's moved in with her?'

'Is there any sign of that?' Jonathan continued carefully.

'How would I know? I'm not spying on the place. I went round a while back to retrieve some stuff and she was teaching like she always did to one of those spoilt brats who could singularly drive you insane.'

'Perhaps you should go round there again?' Jonathan suggested. 'In fact, your best bet is to move back in.'

'What? Are you crazy?' Birch sprung from his chair and went over to the attic window.

'No, I'm telling you it would be in your best interests to take up residency there; sleep in the spare room.'

'That's like saying that it would have been in the best interests of the Jews to move in with Hitler!'

'Well, you would at least be able to see what she's up to. It would unnerve her too probably.'

'It would unnerve me, I can tell you!'

'All right, well why don't you think about it?'

'Now let me see, how long do I need? About one millionth of a second. Yep. Thought about it. The answer is no. I value my sanity too much. You know it's funny but, even though it was her who instigated all this, I've since realised how bad my marriage actually was.'

'Is,' Jonathan said with emphasis. 'You are still married.'

'Oh stop it. Don't go all high and mighty on me.'

Jonathan took no notice. 'And that's why you need to move back in. I'm telling you, it's your quickest route to a divorce.'

Birch was beside himself. 'It's truly official; the law is an ass.'

Jonathan was laughing now. 'Let me know what you decide.'

Birch staggered downstairs in despair and lurched towards the coffee machine in the kitchen. He was in no mood to write now. His cappuccino delivered efficiently, he retrieved his cup. The doorbell rang and he wondered which one of Katie's daughters had forgotten her keys this time.

Celia stood calmly in front of him, dressed attractively in a grey ankle length skirt, with a dusky pink silk blouse under a short black jacket that was nipped in at the waist. Her make-up had been exquisitely applied and her hair smoothed into a bob. She smiled at him. He could only manage a stunned silence in response.

'Hello Birch,' she said as if she'd only been away for a while but was back now expecting a welcoming committee. 'May I come in?' she asked as if that was a perfectly reasonable request.

'What?' Birch was still reeling from his conversation with Jonathan. 'What!' His voice was getting louder. 'What do you want?'

'Can we talk inside? I really don't want to hold this conversation on the doorstep.' She was the epitome of reasonableness.

'I really don't want to hold this conversation at all!' His voice crescendoed over her.

She looked puzzled at his heightened state. 'I just want to talk to you,' she said sweetly. This pleasant demeanour was most disarming.

'After your performance on New Year's Eve!'

'I'm sorry about that.'

'You're sorry! Marvellous.'

'Birch, can we drop the sarcasm. I have something serious to tell you.'

'Five minutes,' he said and stepped back to allow her in.

They were stood in the hallway. Celia looked around her and waited to be shown into the living room. It didn't happen.

'Are we alone?' she asked.

'We will be, for the next five minutes.' He shot a sardonic smile at her.

There they were, face to face. She looked down to the floor and then cocked her head up in a coy fashion. 'Is there somewhere we can sit?'

Birch marched down the hallway into the kitchen and she followed him and sat at the table. He remained standing and took a sip of his coffee, not bothering to offer her a drink.

'Will you sit down?' she asked.

He sat reluctantly, 'let's get to the point shall we?'

'Yes, I owe you that.'

Birch's expression was one of confusion now. Why had his fractious wife of recent years turned into some kind of irritating angel?

'Birch, I've made the biggest mistake of my life. I'm so sorry.'

'What on earth have you done?' He imagined she'd blown up the house or their car or both.

'Isn't it obvious?' she asked in an appallingly sickly sweet way.

'At the moment I'm about as a bewildered as any man could get. Just spit it out woman.'

She sighed deeply. 'I know my behaviour has not been exemplary in recent years.'

'Not exemplary! You had an affair!'

'Yes, yes I know, but will you let me finish?'

'Please do.'

'Birch, I made a terrible mistake.. my affair with Alistair.. and well, as I tried to tell you before, it's over now. When it was a snatched moment here and there it was exciting, novel, but as soon as we started living together, I saw him for what he was.'

'Oh, and what was that? A man unable to keep you in Jimmy Choo's shoes?'

'I can see you are hurt.'

His eyes widened until they nearly popped, but still she continued, 'I can see I've hurt you badly, but I'm here to tell you I'm deeply sorry and I really do want you back. I want us to rekindle the love we had,' she was swaying happily as she remembered, 'when we first met. I know we can make it work.'

'You are unbelievable! After everything you have put me through, you honestly think you can waltz back into my life? Have you even considered that I might have moved on?' He saw her expression change from serene to hurt and stopped himself. His lawyer had warned against him divulging any information about his relationship with Katie or indeed anything to do with the setup at 12 Bisham Gardens. The stance relayed between his and her lawyers was that Birch was simply the lodger.

Celia shook off any notion that he wouldn't take her up on her offer to reunite. 'The thing is, Birch, we just make the same mistakes when we seek new partners. My therapist says..'

'Your therapist? Since when have you had a therapist? And how much is that costing me?'

She ignored him and continued regardless, 'my therapist says that it is better to heal the broken relationship than to go on repeating the same patterns with new people.'

Birch put his head in his hands and prayed for this hellish moment to be over. He was struggling to find the words that would put her straight whilst not blurting out something that would displease his lawyer. Celia was encouraged by this pause in his thoughts, so much so, that she was moved to say, 'Birch, I wasn't going to tell you this today,' her eyes were ignorantly playful, 'but I've had an interior designer round to look at the house.' Her face had lit up with excitement.

'Whatever for?' The blood was draining from his face.

'A complete refurbishment. Decorated throughout. New furniture. Don't you see, a new start. For us!'

'Hang on a minute! We simply don't have the money. Please tell this interior designer not to bother coming back. What with your lawyer's fees and mine we can't even consider something like this. You'll bankrupt me!'

'But don't you see there's no need for lawyers now. There's no need for you to continue lodging here. This is a fresh beginning for us.'

With a look of total disbelief he swayed his head from side to side trying to portray the negative. Then, even though he could have throttled her at that moment, he stood up slowly. He was shaking as he said very deliberately, 'no bloody interior designer. No bloody fresh start. Now get out. Just get out!'

She looked unsure for the first time and rose steadily to her feet.

'Now!' he yelled his patience lost.

'But think about it. Please, at least, think about it.'

He was chasing her down the hallway. At the door she hesitated and turned towards him. He grabbed her arm to move her out of the way, flung the door open and pushed her out. 'Just go!'

Bethan was in Carol's large kitchen which was warm from the heat of the oven as well as the sun pouring in through the lantern window of the garden room. She was sat at her dining table and watched Carol pull out a tray of chocolate cupcakes from the oven. They smelt delicious.

'I'll need to let these cool a bit before I decorate them but there's some vanilla ones ready to go if you'd like to try one?'

'I don't mind waiting,' Bethan replied as she took another sip of her tea.

'Okay, well I'll leave those there.' She placed the cakes onto a cooling rack and took off her apron, 'and come and join you.' She looked all around her. 'Now where's my tea?'

'It's just there.' Bethan pointed to a mug on the island work surface.

'So it is,' she picked up the cup and went to join Bethan at the table.

'I love your kitchen, it's so light with the French windows onto the garden and the sky lights.'

'Yes, I love it too. We actually had this built on as an extension for the business. The kitchen was tiny before, it wouldn't have worked at all. Of course Nev didn't see it at first. He said let's start small and make some money before we spend any. But I said I'll go mad trying to mass produce cakes in this poky room.'

'I don't blame you,' Bethan said as she smiled in agreement.

'What's your kitchen like?' Carol asked.

Bethan wasn't expecting that question. 'Oh, I suppose it's quite big... but you know I'm back home now with Mum?' She sighed as she continued, 'so it's a case of sharing it with whoever is around which is quite a few people at the moment.'

'Oh?' Carol seemed interested.

Bethan bit her bottom lip. 'Anyway we're here to talk about your website.'

Carol sat up straight and shook herself ready. 'Yes, of course we are. Now first things first, I'm very pleased with the website; I've certainly seen a dramatic increase in sales.'

'That's good! And there's more I could do, I mean we could optimise it for search engines and get you on some local directories. You could even start a blog,' seeing the look of dismay on Carol's face she quickly added, 'I could help you with that.'

'That all sounds great, but you know what I'm thinking, what would really make a difference and allow me to scale up would be if I could get into one of the supermarket chains, say Waitrose?'

'Waitrose? Wow, that would be amazing.'

'Yes, wouldn't it. Of course if I managed to land a contract like that, I would need to take someone on.' Carol was animated now and looking straight at Bethan.

Bethan was surprised by what she was hearing. 'So what sort of person have you got in mind?'

Carol leaned forward onto her arms and asked, 'are you any good at baking?'

Harry didn't recognise the number that came up on his mobile.

'Hello?'

'Is that Harry Liversage?'

'Yes, and you are?' he sounded irritated.

'Charles Steer, I'm a partner at Cordell Moss & Steer, based in Guildford.'

Harry racked his brain as to why this solicitor would want to call him. 'How can I help you?' his tone demanded a speedy answer.

'It's about your uncle, James Liversage, I suspect you are not aware of his demise.'

Harry's parents had died in an horrific car accident when he was twenty and he'd not been so good at keeping in touch with his extended family since. 'What, he's dead?'

'Yes, that's right. He had a fatal stroke.'

Suddenly he regretted not paying more attention; he had fond memories of Uncle Jimmy who always seemed to understand his own take on life.

'Are you still there?' the solicitor asked.

'Yes, yes I am. Thanks for letting me know. Will there be a funeral?'

'There was, yes, very quiet affair. I believe someone tried to contact you but you were in New York at the time.'

'Oh gosh, yes, I have recently been over there. I'm sorry I missed that.' Harry was trying to take it all in. 'Did you know my uncle?'

'Well, yes, I'm his solicitor. You see you've been named in his will. In fact, you're his sole beneficiary.'

Harry plummeted to his chair, taken aback by this news. 'Sole beneficiary? That's unexpected.'

'Yes, he said he thought you'd be surprised when he asked me to draw up the will. Anyway that's the way it is.'

Harry remembered the Victorian terrace where his uncle had lived, which was near enough to the restaurants and shops of Guildford, while also being close to a golf course. He'd played since he was young and Harry had often thought about taking up the sport himself. Jimmy had never married or had children but had always had a girlfriend or two on the scene and lived life to the full. Perhaps he was too hedonistic, given his relatively early death. He can only have been sixty.

'So how much are we talking about?'

'I don't suppose you could pop into the office so we can sort out the finer details?'

'Oh yes, of course,' he looked at his on-screen diary. It was pretty full for the next week. 'I tell you what, I'll try and pop down tomorrow. It will mean moving a few things around in my schedule.' He looked across the office and caught Ben's eye as he added, 'so I'll have to confirm, but shall we say twelve noon?'

# Chapter 8

Sylvia and Alice were preparing moules marinière amiably in the kitchen at Bisham Gardens and the air was filled with smells of white wine, garlic and parsley.

'Mum never cooks anything like this,' Alice said as she chopped parsley. 'In fact, I don't think she's ever done anything French even.'

'Well, I thought as you're a French student and I used to be a translator it was the perfect choice!' Sylvia said with a flourish.

Alice smiled. 'Dad would have had a go at something like this but he never had time to shop for the ingredients. He always conjured something up from whatever was in the fridge.'

'And was it good?'

'Yeah, usually.'

'I suspect your Mum's too busy these days with her work.'

'Yeah, I suppose so. I think she's doing quite well actually. I mean actually making some money. I thought she'd find it too techie at first.'

'You underestimated her,' Sylvia said gently.

Alice was thoughtful. 'She's changed.' She held a faraway look. 'She's definitely changed since Dad died.'

'I suspect she's had to.' Sylvia stroked Alice's arm briefly and then said, 'now we need to set the table before we put the mussels in. It will all happen very quickly after that. Will Bethan be joining us this evening?'

'We always lay a place for her and then just hope.' Alice raised her eyebrows to show her displeasure at her sister's behaviour.

'I see. Well it would be lovely if she did. I'd like the chance to get to know her a bit.'

'You're too nice! You know she doesn't like Birch. I mean, I don't think it's as much him, as the fact that he appeared on the scene just after Dad died.'

'It must have been a difficult time for you all.'

'Yes, it was. And it doesn't help that Bethan went off with Harry Liversage who's far too old for her, twice her age in fact. It's obvious he's not bothered with her really. She's just delusional about him.'

'Young love,' Sylvia had a dreamy look. 'I was in love with a wholly unsuitable man once...'

Katie appeared at the door. 'Everything okay in here? Smells good.'

'All under control, Mum. It'll be ready in...' She looked to Sylvia to end her sentence.

'Ten minutes.'


Bethan was mulling over what Carol had said to her at their meeting. It had come as quite a surprise. Even when Bethan had said she had no experience of baking, Carol seemed unperturbed.

'Well, I would want you mainly for developing the website and marketing; I realise that's where your main skill set lies,' she had explained.

'That sounds good, but would I need to do some baking? Would I have to do it at home?'

'Oh no, it would be here. It would have to be here - health and safety and all that. And I would teach you, of course.' Carol looked thoughtful before she added, 'I would be the main baker and it would just be a case of when I was really stretched.'

'Mm.' Bethan was really tempted but Carol's proposition raised as many questions as it answered. She took the bull by the horns. 'So, sorry to ask this but, how much would you be able to pay me?'

'No need to apologise. That's a perfectly good question. How much are you getting now? You're doing an apprenticeship aren't you?'

'That's right so it's not much more than the minimum wage.'

'Oh well, I could definitely top that. Give me some time to think about it.'

'Of course.'

'It will all depend on me getting the Waitrose contract.'

'There is another problem.' Bethan thought it best to be honest.

'Oh?'

'Yes, I think I'm tied in for a year at Web Dreams so that would be until November.'

'Oh, I see. Yes, well I wouldn't want to tread on any toes there but actually, thinking about it, that might work out quite well because it's going to take me a few months to win a major contract I suspect.'

Overall Bethan felt very warm to the idea of working for Carol. It gave her a good feeling to be with someone who appreciated her. Whilst she enjoyed her work at Web Dreams, Matt was still creating an atmosphere and she feared that it didn't bode well with regard to her securing a permanent position there. She imagined his reaction should she announce that she had a job elsewhere; how brilliant would that be!


'Are you alright, Birch?' Sylvia asked discarding another mussel shell to a large bowl in the centre of the table.

He was in deep in thought and didn't answer.

'Birch?' Katie nudged him.

'Sorry,' he shook his head and rubbed his eye lids. 'Sorry, what was that?'

'Are you alright?' Katie asked trying to be gentle but concerned that he had been in a strange mood since she got back home from the auction.

'Yes, yes. Yes, I'm fine.' He looked round the table at everyone and forced a smile.

'This is really good, Alice,' Bethan said smiling at her sister. 'And you actually made it? I mean, it wasn't from M&S?'

'It was Sylvia really,' Alice replied.

Sylvia threw her head back. 'Darlings, I was there merely for guidance of this classic French dish.'

Bethan laughed and Katie was surprised by her reaction.

'How's your job going, Bethan?' Sylvia asked.

Bethan looked pleased with herself. 'Well actually it's going well. Very well, in fact. I had a meeting with my favourite client, Carol, yesterday.'

'Is that Carol Cup Cake?' Alice asked.

'Carol from The Cup Cake Company, yes.'

'Ooh, I like cup cakes,' Sylvia chimed in and put her fork across her bowl indicating she had finished.

'So are you doing more work on her website?' Katie asked.

'Yes, she's really pleased with what I've done so far and I'm going to start a blog for her and improve her SEO.'

'That's search engine optimisation,' Alice explained.

'I'll take your word for it,' Sylvia said and kept her eyes on Bethan. 'And?' she asked simply.

'And,' Bethan's face lit up, 'she's offered me a job!'

'Wow, that's fantastic!' Sylvia smiled.

Katie looked concerned. 'But you've got a job, an apprenticeship. Aren't you committed for a year?'

'Yes, Mum, I know. That's okay, Carol understands that I won't be free until November.'

'Will you have to make cup cakes, if you work for her?' Alice asked looking doubtfully at her sister.

'Yes,' she replied uncertainly. 'Well, not much, but occasionally when we get extra busy but I'm mainly there to do the website and online marketing.'

'Sounds impressive,' Sylvia said.

'But you can't bake,' Katie let out what she was thinking but then wished she hadn't.

'Carol will teach me.'

'Yes, cup cakes are easy. I'll show you if you like?' Sylvia came to her rescue.

'Would you? That would be brilliant!'

'Oh Sylvia you don't have to do that.' Katie dismissed the idea.

'Providing we can squeeze it in soon. I don't want to outstay my welcome.'

Now Katie rushed to say, 'you'll never do that. We love having you here.' There was a general consensus round the table. 'You are welcome any time,' she added to be absolutely sure.

'Thank you Katie.' They both looked at Birch who was deep in thought on some other planet, perhaps.

'Now Katie and Birch, you go and relax in the living room and we girls will clear up.' Sylvia took charge of the situation.

'Oh but you did the cooking,' Katie objected.

'No matter,' Sylvia looked directly at Katie and nodded pointedly to her son.

'Yes, okay then.'

'I'll bring coffee through in a bit.'


Katie shut the lounge door and sat next to Birch on the sofa.

'So,' she said simply, turning his head gently in her hands to face her.

'So... I've had rather a bad day.'

'And?' Katie showed some frustration at his reluctance to explain his unusual mood.

'I don't quite know how to tell you.'

'How about now. Just tell me. Whatever it is, it's worse not knowing.'

'Okay, Celia came round this morning.'

'Right, so did you talk about the divorce?'

'I wish,' he said staring down at his hands in his lap.

'What?'

'She was full of remorse, wants me back apparently. All that ranting at New Year; it turns out to be true. Not just an alcoholic fuelled declaration.'

Katie went very pale and her meal now sat uncomfortably in her stomach. 'I see,' she said as she moved away from him. He didn't seem to notice.

'Oh yes and the really good news is that she's seeing a therapist, at my expense, of course.' He adopted a sarcastic tone. 'She was spouting all this stuff about just repeating the same mistakes in

86

new relationships. And she's got some interior designer in to refurbish the house! She's going to bankrupt me at this rate!'

'Oh my God.' Katie suddenly felt very unsure of her ground. 'So what does this mean?'

Birch turned to look at her, 'I just don't know... yet, anyway. I called Jonathan back this afternoon but he was out. I mean I don't know where I stand if she really doesn't want a divorce. It rather scuppers things.'

Katie didn't hide her horror. Was her world really falling apart? She had to ask the obvious question. 'So where does that leave me? I mean, us?'

'Waiting for five years maybe. Until I can divorce her without her consent.' He sounded disheartened by the whole thing, defeated even.

'So is that what you still want? I mean, a divorce. Do you still want to divorce Celia?'

'Of course I do, oh my love...' Finally he was taking notice of her. 'Oh I'm so sorry, I've been really selfish, wrapped up in my own problems. Of course I want to divorce her. I love you.'

'That's good,' she said and forced a smile. He went to kiss her but she struggled to respond. Just then there was a quiet knock on the door and it was opened.

'It's alright,' Sylvia said, 'only me,' and she put two coffees in front of them. She was looking at their faces as if searching for clues. With a serious expression she crept back towards the door.

'Sylvia, do come and join us,' Katie called after her.

She turned back to say, 'No, no, the girls and I are making cup cakes. Chocolate. Bethan insisted. It's a terrible mess at the moment but don't worry it will all be cleared up.' She closed the door behind her and Birch and Katie looked at each other.

Katie was laughing. 'Your mother's a real marvel; I really like her.'

'I'm pleased,' Birch said trying to move closer to her with subtlety. 'I'm really sorry about all this Celia debacle; the woman's nuts; she has no sense of reality.'

Katie was thoughtful. 'It's worrying the amount of money she's spending, I mean...'

'You're right. I need to find a way to...'

'Contribute more?' Katie interrupted with exactly what she wanted to hear.

'Yes, well I've talked to Harry and he's set up an offshore account for me. The money from this new job I've got, the London guide, is going in there.'

Katie looked unimpressed. What did that actually mean? 'I hate having to ask but you know the situation.'

'I will get some money to you in the next week or so, I promise.'

'Right.' She had some hope now but there was still a tension between them.

# Chapter 9

'That woman needs sorting out!' Julia's voice was undoubtedly loud now and could be heard above the general hubbub of the cafe. A young couple on the next table were moved to stop their conversation in its tracks and peer round at her. Julia smiled apologetically.

'Careful,' Katie said, trying to calm her friend down. 'Celia lives in this village too, you know,' she whispered.

'Good!' Julia flung an arm carelessly away from her. 'She needs to know what a divisive little arrrrgh... she is!'

Katie laughed, but then sighed deeply. 'I just don't know what we're going to do.'

Julia leant in towards her friend, 'you need a plan,' she said with emphasis.

'Ah, the famous plan.'

'You may mock me darling, but the last plan worked out pretty well, didn't it?'

'Remind me,' Katie was playful now, 'was that the plan to avoid financial ruin by taking in a lodger, who turned out to be Birch, who turned out to be married to a psychopath?'

'Listen, it was all going swimmingly until Alistair didn't measure up to much and Celia selfishly decided she wanted her husband back.'

Another sigh from Katie.

'Sorry darling,' Julia continued, 'but really, you've got nothing to worry about, Birch is totally smitten with you.'

Katie looked doubtful. 'So, what's the plan going to be this time?' she asked half-heartedly.

'Well....' Julia's mind searched frantically. Eventually she only managed, 'not sure...'

Katie raised her eyebrows.

'Yet! Not sure yet!' she said hurriedly. 'Oh, it's so frustrating isn't it?' Then suddenly it came to her. 'listen, what you need to do is get onto this what's-his-name-lawyer-chap. He's far too passive. It's time he got the big guns out!'

Katie stifled a laugh and Julia smiled and said, 'well it's good to see you looking a little brighter at last.'

'I can always rely on you to cheer me up,' Katie said. 'I must admit, I do think he's being rather pathetic. He even suggested that Birch move back in with her to try and unnerve her.'

'What?! This man needs to have some sense knocked into him! How about you and me take a trip down to... where did you say he is?'

'Sandgate.'

'Crikey, where's that?'

'Near Folkestone in Kent, on the coast.'

'Sounds like a long way. Well, needs must. When are you free?'

Ross came through the door of Fegos wearing chinos and a smart navy blue crew neck jumper and carrying a large white envelope. He spotted Katie and walked over to her table.

'Hello there,' he said cheerfully.

'Hi Ross, this is my friend Julia, I don't think you've met.'

He shook her hand and she looked puzzled.

'Ross knew David,' she said leaving it there.

Ross smiled apologetically. 'Sorry, if I'm interrupting but..'

'No, no,' Katie said, 'just putting the world to rights as usual.'

'You women do that sort of thing so well.' He bowed to each one of them pulling an imaginary forelock from his forehead.

They looked at each other, slightly bemused. Katie changed the subject, 'what brings you here?'

'Ah well, would you believe, I'm hoping to buy this place.'

Harry walked from the station at Guildford and following Charles Steer's directions he found Cordell Moss & Steer on the second floor of a large office block. The receptionist wore a smart navy suit, had soft chestnut hair framing a pretty face and tortoiseshell spectacles on the end of her nose. She glanced up at Harry.

'May I help you?'

'Yes, I'm here to see Charles Steer.' He smiled as his eyes lingered; she was an attractive woman.

'I'll just tell him you're here,' she said avoiding eye contact.

Charles appeared and showed him into his office which was piled high with files, his desk covered in papers. One could only hope that it was organised chaos. His hair was curly and unkempt and his open neck shirt scruffily tucked into a pair of trousers. Harry picked up a file from the only chair on his side of the desk and waved it questioningly at Charles.

'Ah, yes, the very file,' he took it from Harry gratefully. 'Julie always puts the file for the visiting client on that chair. It's a system that most of the legal profession would frown upon but, ever since it took us an embarrassing half hour to find the right paperwork for an important client, we've adopted it.'

Harry was amused and sat down. He realised that this man was just the sort his uncle would have employed to deal with his legal affairs.

'Now,' Charles opened the file and started flicking through it. He pulled out one particular sheet of paper, 'ah yes, this is it. Yep.'

Harry looked on expectantly.

'Yes, there's the property owned by James Liversage which is probably worth around four fifty and then there's about one hundred thousand in savings, investments etc..' He looked up. 'That's your bag, isn't it?'

'Investment management, yes.'

He scanned the rest of the document. 'And then there's some assets, a car, some antique furniture etc..'

'Right,' Harry was trying to take it all in.

'You're probably talking six hundred thousand all in. Of course there's a bit of inheritance tax to go on that.'

'Yes, still,' Harry was now fully realising what this meant, 'it's a tidy sum. And I have to say totally unexpected.'

'Your uncle didn't tell you then?'

'No, no, not a word.' He thought back to the exchanges he and his uncle had had. Jimmy was certainly proud of him and on more than one occasion he'd said something on the lines of, 'you and I, Harry, we're two of a kind.'

'I see,' Charles interrupted his thoughts, 'well he didn't have any children, did he? And he never married so...'

'It was me or Battersea Dogs Home.'

'Indeed.'

Sylvia knocked on the door to the attic room and walked in. 'I've brought you a drink,' she said in a no nonsense fashion placing the mug on Birch's desk.

'Thanks,' he said looking surprised. There had always been some sort of unwritten rule between them about her not disturbing him while he was working, whether they were in the same house or not.

Sylvia sat in the armchair in the corner of the room, crossed her legs and placed the finger tips of each hand together to create a pyramid. Birch turned to look at her. He knew this expression well. 'You have something to say, Mother?'

'Yes, yes I do. And I don't think it can wait. Poor Katie is not in a good place. Even I can tell that. Something needs to be done to stop Celia causing havoc.'

'Mum, I agree. Totally. But tell me what? I'm still waiting for a call back from Jonathan.'

'I thought you had your mobile on silent when you're working.'

'Oh!' he picked up his phone and looked at it. 'Ah, yes, you're right. He has called. Twice it would seem.'

Sylvia didn't take her eyes of him. He shuffled awkwardly in his chair. He was trying to brush off her gaze but it was drilling into him. She raised her eyebrows.

'Look Mum, I will phone him back. Okay?'

'Now?'

'Well yes, now.'

She didn't move. Eventually he realised she wasn't going to move. 'Mum, some privacy maybe?'

'What have you got to say to Jonathan that I can't hear?'

92

He sighed with exasperation. 'Look, I promise I will call him and then report back to you. How's that?'

'Oh, if you must.' Sylvia sprung from her chair and made her way over to the door. She turned and said, 'now!' before closing the door and heading down the stairs.

Birch called Jonathan's number.

'So you see it would be perfect for myself and Elaine but we're not sure how to raise the money,' Ross sat back in his chair.

Katie considered how kind he had been to her, giving her free adverts in My Mag to help her promote her business. She had had a call only that morning from a potential new client who had seen the latest promotion.

'What about Harry?' Julia suggested. 'He knows people with money to invest, doesn't he?'

'Yes, I suppose he does. That's not a bad idea.'

'Who's Harry?'

'Harry Liversage, he's an investment fund manager based in Hampstead,' Katie explained. 'I'm his VA actually,' she added by way of explanation as to how she knew him even though the truth was a much longer story.

'I see. Well I suppose it's worth a shot,' Ross looked hopeful but daunted by the prospect.

'I tell you what,' Katie said helpfully, 'I'll explain the situation to Harry and see what he thinks, if he can advise you. That might be a better way to approach things.'

'Oh that would be great.' The tension in Ross's shoulders softened. 'Thanks Katie.'

'It's nothing; I'm happy to help.'

'It would be good to see this place under new management,' Julia said scanning the room, 'the service hasn't been up to much recently. I can see why now. And I love your idea about a deli too.'

Birch considered that a cup of tea would be welcome. He seemed to have stalled on his writing. The phone call with Jonathan had left him distracted, his words playing on his mind. But he knew as soon as he went downstairs his mother would start asking difficult questions. He considered that he could say that Jonathan wasn't available until tomorrow but telling lies to her had never been his strong point; she always saw straight through him. He paced the attic room like a lion in a cage, stopped to stare out of the window and then sank back into his chair and sighed. It was no good, he had to face the music.

He made it to the kitchen unscathed and put the kettle on. Maybe she'd gone for a walk down to the village. He noticed it had stopped raining and the sun was out. He was tempted to take a walk himself to try and clear his mind.

'Making tea?' Sylvia appeared at the doorway making him jump.

'Yes, Mum,' he quickly composed himself.

'Reggie rang,' she said as she smiled to herself.

'Reggie?'

'Yes, the gentleman who I drank G&Ts with on the train up from Folkestone.'

'Ah, that gentleman that got you squiffy at ten o'clock in the morning.'

'No need to judge,' Sylvia said with amusement.

'So, are you going to meet up with him?'

'Well,' she paused as she pulled out a kitchen chair, sat down, crossed her legs, swinging the top one back and forth carelessly. 'I don't think so.'

Birch looked puzzled but quickly put out of his mind any attempt to understand his mother. 'Up to you,' he handed her a mug of tea.

'But then again...' she cocked her head to one side.

Deep lines appeared on his forehead as he frowned in disbelief. 'I hope you're not stringing him along, playing with his feelings?'

'Of course not darling.' She looked up at her son with an expression of innocence. 'Anyway enough about me, how did it go with Jonathan?'

'Not brilliantly,' he said squirming and remained standing. At least he had a height advantage over his mother this way.

'So?'

'Well it's all rather difficult, as we suspected, I mean Celia not wanting to go ahead with the divorce and all that. It means I wait five years for what's called a "no fault" divorce or...'

'That's no good,' she interrupted him.

'Or we find grounds for divorce some other way,' he continued doggedly, 'which according to Jon leads to inflammatory accusations and it can all get very messy.' Birch looked as if he was exhausted by the whole thing.

'Am I missing something or is the fact that Celia has admitted to adultery just by the by?'

'She did admit it to me, verbally.' He pursed his lips. 'But there's no written evidence, so Jon says she could just deny it, if it came to it.'

'Typical! That woman has never faced any responsibility for her own actions!'

Birch was surprised now at his mother's fervour. 'Where did that come from?'

'Oh I'm sorry. I know I kept quiet in the past.'

'Hardly!'

'Well, I didn't explicitly say I hated the woman even if I heavily implied it.'

Birch allowed himself to let go for a moment and laughed. 'Ah the passive aggressive approach you women love so much.'

'Now now, darling, you know I only want the best for you.' She looked straight at him and added quickly, 'and Katie, of course! I like Katie; you're good together. You don't want to do anything to upset her, do you?' she was glaring at him.

'No Mum,' he agreed like a petulant child.


Charlie sped up Cholmeley Crescent in his open top MG, screeched to a halt and bounced out of the car. 'Katie! I'm not late am I?'

He was late but Katie hadn't minded pacing up and down a few times outside number eight now that the sun had come out. 'No matter,' she replied. She waved the keys in front of him.

'Great doll, well let's go to it then.'

Katie negotiated the locks on the door efficiently and they walked carefully in taking in the general dilapidation of the place. 'I wonder how it got like this, I mean on a lovely crescent in Highgate village?'

'Oh you'd be surprised how bad some of these buildings get. Usually after letting them out for a long time and then not being bothered to refurbish.' He was sizing up the place, checking walls for damp and knocking on internal walls as he went through the ground floor. 'Mm, yep, not bad. Nothing too dreadful. Wouldn't hurt to rip out this wall here and move it over there,' he waved his arms about to illustrate his point.

'So there'd be a smaller kitchen?' Katie grabbed a note pad and pen and started jotting down his thoughts.

'Yeah, we're turning this into flats, so we want to get a second bedroom on this floor ideally. Should be okay as this is a stud wall here, so we won't have a problem with building regs.'

'Are you getting plans drawn up by an architect?'

'Yeah, course, that chap Jeremy we used before. He's good and not too expensive. He dealt with the regs guy as well, saves me the bother.' He turned round and grinned at Katie. 'Still I've got you now. I'm sure you could get him to sign everything off no trouble.'

Katie looked at him with mock astonishment. 'Let's keep this professional shall we?'

'Of course, doll. Absolutely. Professional until me dying breath. Well, that or until I hit the wine bar!'

'Shall we move on?' she led the way up the dusty stairs.

Birch had made a second call to Jon, this time determined to be more assertive and to attempt to get him to suggest an alternative to the 'no fault' route and a five-year wait.

'But if five years isn't acceptable to me, or indeed Katie, then what do you suggest?' he had asked trying not to raise his voice.

'Birch, if she wants you back she's not going to make life easy for you.' He had every argument off pat and kept a calm, measured approach to every sentence whilst Birch was getting more and more agitated. So in the end it was Birch who ended the call lest he should explode.

Sylvia knocked on his door and opened it. She had her hand over the mouthpiece of the telephone and whispered, 'Sorry to interrupt again but there's a PC Blackwell on the phone.'

'What? And he wants to talk to me? Are you sure?'

'Yes,' she said quietly and nodded her head to leave him in no doubt.

'What on earth about?' he mouthed.

'He didn't say.' She passed the handset to him and closed the door.

'Hello?'

'Is that Birch?'

'Yes, yes that's me.'

'Ah good. PC Blackwell here. I need to talk to you, your wife has made a complaint about you.'

'What? I don't understand.'

'She is claiming that you assaulted her when she visited you last Tuesday.'

'Assaulted her? I don't believe it!' Birch ran his hand through his hair and started pacing the room.

'Yes, that is what she's saying. We do need to interview you under caution Mr Birch so I have to advise you that you are entitled to have a solicitor present.'

'Solicitor? But I didn't assault her. This is ridiculous.' He hated it when people called him Mr Birch but was too outraged by the allegation against him to correct him.

'Even so, sir, we do have to investigate.'

He collapsed into his chair in despair. 'So when do you want to do this?'

'I could come round to 12 Bisham Gardens at the start of my shift tomorrow, say about nine o'clock.'

Birch found the fact that he knew where he lived even more unnerving. 'Right,' he said, the wind banished from his sails, the endless dreadful possible outcomes whirring around in his mind.

The call ended and now he remembered how Celia had fluttered her eyelids at him and exuded profuse apologies for her affair. Anger welled up inside him as he thought about the injustice of it all. It was not long before he sprang from his chair and stormed noisily down the stairs. Sylvia emerged from the kitchen into the hallway wondering what was going on and upon seeing him her jaw dropped. He didn't even turn to notice her but grabbed a jacket and some house keys and went straight out, headed for the park.

# Chapter 10

'Assault? Why on earth?' Katie was confused. 'But... but.. how?' She was sat at her dressing table in a silk kimono looking at him in the glass as he stood behind her. 'No wonder you've not been yourself this evening.'

Birch was pale and held a troubled expression. He took a deep breath, 'I've thought long and hard about it and I can only think that I really upset her when I didn't fall back into her arms after her pathetic performance when she came round the other day.'

'But it's so vindictive. If she really wants you back, surely she realises that this isn't going to advance her cause?'

'It's certainly irrational behaviour, but then looking back at the last year, why am I surprised? She's turned up drunk, led me up the garden path with this divorce, cost me a fortune and now this!'

Katie turned to him now and stood up to meet him. 'Darling, I'm so sorry.'

'I couldn't say anything earlier, not with Mum still here and Alice around,' Birch explained.

She put her arms around his neck, and kissed him lightly. 'If it's just your word against hers, I don't see how the police can take it any further.'

'Exactly. I rang Jon and told him; I wanted to see how I should play it when PC Blackwell turns up.'

'And he said?'

'He sounded quite worried about the whole thing, said she's a loose cannon and I really need to be careful how I handle it.'

'That's not very reassuring. So how do you play it?'

'Well, he said I should be very matter of fact when answering his questions and not to get riled even if they are really emotive. And well...' There was an uncertain pause.

'What?'

'Nothing really. But obviously I'll have to deny anything she's told him about what I supposedly did that led her to put me through this ridiculous charade.'

'Of course.'

'Listen, I know this is a big ask but I was wondering if you could be there. At the interview, I mean. Jon said it might help.'

'Yes, of course, but will that be okay? And what about Sylvia? Earlier you were suggesting that we go to that farmers' market at Hampstead.'

'Yes, well I was trying to think of ways of getting her out of the house. But she said she'll be going out first thing anyway; into central London apparently. It's a bit odd, she wasn't specific.'

'Oh?'

'Yes, I think she might be meeting this Reggie chap she met on the train.'

'Well that's okay then. But will the police officer mind me being there?'

'Jon thinks he'll be okay with it. The fact that he's coming here and not hauling me down the police station is a good sign.'

'Oh God that doesn't bear thinking about.'

He drew her close and said, 'Thank you,' as he kissed her nose. 'Thank you for believing in me.'

'Don't be silly. Of course I do. And I want to help.'

***

Sylvia had arranged for a black cab to pick her up at nine o'clock that morning and it had arrived a little early. She opened the front door and waved to the driver before looking up to the sky. It looked like rain. She hurriedly put on a cream Mac, slung a pretty floral scarf round her neck and grabbed her gold tote bag. 'See you later!' she shouted to no one in particular as she went out of the front door.

'Royal Academy of Arts,' she said simply to the driver and climbed into the back. And then she sat back and took a deep

100

breath. She'd made it, this far at least. Birch had assumed she was meeting Reggie and she let him. Now she had the space and time to dare to think beyond her wildest dreams. What if it really was him? What would she say to him? Would he even recognise her? Of course, just because he was exhibiting there didn't mean he would be there. He might not even be in London. The last she had heard was that he was in the south of France and that was decades ago. But perhaps, at the very least, she would find out what had become of him.

She stared out of the window watching row upon row of Victorian terraced houses go by until they hit a main road and the housing got shabbier and there were dingier looking blocks of flats put up in the sixties. She hooked her wallet out of her bag and found the faded photograph that was hidden behind all her credit and loyalty cards. She looked at it and this time she didn't try to quell the frisson it gave her. She was excited and why shouldn't she be? Even if she was risking grave disappointment, she was going to indulge in this moment and delight in it. Maybe, just maybe, after five decades she was going to find her Jack.

PC Blackwell was very young and polite in his manner and Birch was at least thankful for that. He let his inexperience show at the outset.

'You're the author, aren't you?'

'Er, yes. Yes, that's right.'

'I'm a massive fan.'

'Right.'

'Sorry, shouldn't have said that. Not part of my training.' He rolled his eyes at his faux pas.

'Don't worry.'

Katie appeared and smiled. 'Would you like some coffee?'

'If it's not too much trouble.'

'Not at all.' She went off to the kitchen and Birch showed him into the living room. He sat on an armchair, took out his notebook and looked for a blank page where he wrote the date and a heading for the interview.

'Is Birch your surname? Only I see your wife goes by the name of Celia Nicolson.'

'Yes, that's her maiden name,' he replied not offering to explain that she had never changed it.

'So your full name is?'

'Wayland Birch,' he muttered under his breath and then added, 'it's not something I advertise.'

The police officer struggled to keep a straight face.

Katie appeared with a tray of drinks. 'Milk and sugar?'

'Milk, three sugars please,' the PC replied looking embarrassed.

Katie obliged, handed out the mugs and then furtively sat down. The PC regarded her and said nothing. Birch was pleased, seeing this as a small victory in a major war. He was tired after a restless night during which the only sleep he had had seemed to be beset with nightmares starring Celia as a deranged Cruella de Vil strangling Dalmation puppies.

'Now I do have to caution you, but first, are you sure you are happy to go ahead without legal representation?'

Birch and Katie exchanged glances, she looking horrified, him somehow holding it together.

'I'm sure,' he said and looked straight at PC Blackwell to add conviction even though inside he was a bundle of nerves.

Sylvia stopped to read the posters promoting the exhibition by Jack Harvey which she noted had only just begun but was running until the end of May. She composed herself and walked through the archway of Burlington House and across the courtyard where there was a queue for tickets spilling out of the gallery. She opened up her bag and found the print out she had made when she booked online, with the help of Alice, and was reassured to see there was a separate entrance for ticket holders.

As she entered and showed her ticket her heart fluttered. 'Thank you Madam. This way,' the man added waving his hand in the direction she should take from the entrance hall. She went along the corridor with a spring in her step until she found herself in the first room of paintings. The writing on the wall began to tell the story of Jack Harvey. It talked about the artist's early life growing up in North London - that fitted - but not being able to settle as an adult when he discovered he could paint. He had headed off to Paris, where his bohemian lifestyle fitted in well; he was amongst like-minded individuals at last. Sylvia gasped with excitement. So far, so good. This was the story of her Jack. There was no mention of marriage. Not in room one, anyway. Sylvia perused the works devouring everything that was written about him, desperate for affirmation. She loved the paintings which transported her to the summer heat of the Amalfi coast and the lavender fields of Provence. So he must have travelled around, she thought to herself. He painted in oil on board and every image captured the gold effect of sunlight on the Mediterranean.

Room two brought warming landscapes full of oranges, yellows and turquoise blue seas. The walls told her that he settled in Provence for a time and eventually spoke fluent French. It was here he met Abella and they had a long and torrid affair it seemed. There was a painting of her, the only portrait so far; the only person in his life important enough to capture. Sylvia examined the image before her. Her long dark hair was piled up messily on her head and her elfin like face held a seductive smile. Her skin was like porcelain and she was petite and perfectly formed; slim as many French women are. She glanced around the rest of the room. This really was the only portrait. It didn't even fit the theme of the exhibition and so she was clearly a significant influence on him. Sylvia braced herself and marched on into the next room deciding never to return to this one.

In the third room she learnt of the demise of Abella; leukaemia at the young age of forty-two. She had to feel sorry for her now; this was not a fate you would wish on anyone. She read of how distraught Jack became and the paintings now took on a darkness with atmospheric skies, turbulent seas and landscapes fighting the mistral winds of Provence. She moved on from this room hoping for something better. How wonderful it would be to find an image of the artist himself, surely a self-portrait at some point? Or maybe a photograph? She needed to know for sure. Was this her long lost Jack or was it just a cruel coincidence?

She reached the end of the exhibition unfulfilled in her mission and found herself back in the entrance hall. She gave herself a talking to; she must not let this get the better of her. She had been content enough with her lot up until now, she would go on in the same vein. But then she thought of Reggie and how he'd amused her and entertained her on the way up from Folkestone, but the absence of any chemistry between them had been stark. 'Is this as good as it gets?' she asked out loud. The man who had shown her the way in approached her. 'Everything alright, Madam?'

'I don't suppose you can tell me where I can find out more about the artist, Jack Harvey, by any chance?'

'Ah, you may be interested in the talk he's giving here tomorrow evening. It's about his life and the influences on his work. I'm not sure if there are any tickets left but you could ask at the information desk.'

'Thank you,' she said, her heart skipping a beat. So he was in London. She rushed over to the desk, fearful they might have sold out. A Chinese woman, no taller than five feet, was trying to explain something to the man behind the desk and he was struggling to understand her. He looked pompous enough to wave her away, rather than bother to work out what she was saying, but still he persevered. Eventually he managed to give the woman the information she sought and she was profusely grateful, virtually kowtowing her way away from the desk. At last it was Sylvia's turn.

'Hello.' She put on a sickly sweet smile. 'Would you be able to sell me a ticket for tomorrow's talk with Jack Harvey, please?'

'I think we're sold out Madam,' he said with an air of finality which made Sylvia want to punch him.

'Would you double check, please?' She decided she would gate crash if necessary.

He reluctantly turned to his computer and clicked on a few buttons with his mouse. 'Yes, as I suspected, fully booked apart from,' he peered at the screen, 'just one seat at the back. Presumably you want more than one?'

'No! No! One is good. Please may I buy it?'

He looked at her like a teacher might look at a truant child.

'Now!' Sylvia added with emphasis.

'Of course Madam,' he said looking bored by the whole experience.

Birch had shown PC Blackwell the kitchen where he'd sat opposite Celia, as she had spouted her profuse apology, and they were now in the hallway.

'So you suggested she leave at this juncture?'

'Yes, that's right.' Birch was managing to stick to the brief he had had from Jonathan to the letter.

'And did she?'

'Yes, I opened the door for her and she went.'

'Was anything said at this juncture?' the PC asked looking puzzled.

'She wanted me to think about what she had suggested regarding our divorce.'

'And how did you respond to that?'

'I didn't really.' Birch was pleased with that answer.

The PC looked up from his notepad. 'Shall we return to the living room?'

'Of course.'

They both sat back down. Katie hadn't moved from her chair.

'Did you at any time during your wife's visit touch her?'

'No,' he said, quickly but without emotion.

'Did you push her?'

'No.' the same tone was applied.

The PC finished writing and looked up. His face wore a frown. 'I'll just read your statement back to you.'

Katie stood up. 'More coffee?' she asked.

'No thank you.'

'I'll just clear these away,' she said loading the tray and went down to the kitchen where she took a deep breath. She put the mugs in the dishwasher and tidied up an already tidy kitchen.

Eventually Birch appeared.

'Alright?' she asked him.

'As alright as I could be, I suppose.' He still looked strained.

'What did he say at the end?' Katie asked with hope in her voice.

'He said that my statement doesn't fit with what Celia had to say and he has to discuss the case with his superior officer.'

Katie went to him. 'Do you know how long it will be before you hear anything?' She still sounded upbeat.

'A few days, he said.' He was close to tears. She hugged him and he kissed her.

'Thank you for being so supportive,' he said.

'It's nothing. Now, how about I take you out for lunch at The Flask?'

'What, while I'm still a free man?'

'It's not going to come to that,' Katie said tapping his nose gently with her forefinger.

'I'm probably being melodramatic but anyway, aren't we penniless?'

'Possibly, but I've just taken on a new client and Charlie's invoice is nice and big this month so things are looking up on that front.'

'Gosh, I'm going to be a kept man at this rate,' he said as he looked into her eyes and considered he was a very lucky man.

'So, steak sandwich and a glass of red wine?'

'Make that a bottle.'


Sylvia had an air of wonderment about her as she walked back on to a busy Piccadilly. Today had been a momentous day and she decided to treat herself to coffee at Fortnam and Mason as it was just on the other side of the street. She needed to sit alone and take it all in.

The maitre d' showed her to a corner table where she could look out on to the finest of tea rooms, which were the height of Regency elegance, and watch the world about its business. But Sylvia was far too engrossed in her own world to take in the ambiance.

'Just a latte,' she said to the waiter, waving the menu away.

So, tomorrow evening she was going to meet the successful artist, Jack Harvey. This conjured up an image far from the Jack she had known back in the sixties. What was it her mother had said about him? 'Self-obsessed, unkempt, good-for-nothing idiot who frittered away every penny he made,' and of course, that wasn't much as a struggling artist. Little did her mother know that her daughter was sharing flights of fantasy with this man. At a moment's notice they would be swanning into central London to the King's Road to meet up with the rest of Bohemia and drink red wine until their wallets were empty. These people lived in the moment without a thought for tomorrow, let alone next week.

Jack adopted the artist's uniform of a wide brimmed, felt hat and his hair flowed down his neck in soft curls. With his dark eyes and his moustache he was devilishly handsome and turned many a head. These thoughts brought a wave of emotion over Sylvia and a tear came to the corner of her eye. She blinked it away, but others around her had noticed so she pulled herself together momentarily. She contemplated different scenarios for the following evening. Would she discover he was now happily married and their exchange be brief and disappointing? Would their eyes meet across a crowded room and...

'Latte, Madam.'

'Thank you,' she said as she dragged herself back to reality. She really needed to stop fantasising. She was seventy-five, not twenty-five. He probably wouldn't even recognise her. 'Hello, I'm the woman you wooed and made love to way back in the sixties before you decided to flee to Paris, where you would be really at home, without even telling me.' But then she had married Arthur. He must have known about Arthur even though they never spoke about it. To think she was in a mind-numbing marriage while he was having a passionate affair with Abella; it was heart breaking. Even her name sounded beautiful.

She reached the bottom of her cup, placed it back on its saucer, and looked at her watch. It was nearly midday. Thirty-one hours to go until she was in the same room as Jack Harvey.

# Chapter 11

Alice was sure she recognised the woman at table seven but she was struggling to place her. She'd caught her eye once and the woman had stared back at her in a rather alarming way, so she was keeping her head down now and getting on with her job.

She reached the kitchen door at the same time as Marcus. 'Will you do me a favour and serve table seven? I'll take one of yours.'

'What you mean those two women, what's wrong with them?'

'Nothing. It's just that I think I know one of them and I'd rather avoid her.'

Margaret appeared and approached them. 'What's going on here? There's no time to chat; we've got a full house.'

'Sorry, yes,' Alice said quickly as she moved away. Marcus followed her. 'Okay, if you take table nine.'

'Done. Thanks Marcus.'

Table nine housed a mother and four restless children who would definitely be demanding but Alice didn't mind that. She went straight over to them.

'What can I get you?' she asked smiling sweetly. The youngest child said simply, 'chips,' and Alice looked at the mother.

'No darling, not chips. You can have some nice cod. There aren't any bones in it, are there?'

'There shouldn't be,' Alice replied honestly. The mother looked unimpressed and sighed. She put her hand on the head of the small child next to her. 'Now, this one's got a peanut allergy, so what do you recommend?'

An hour had passed and Alice dared to look over to table seven where she fully expected to see two new diners, but no. The two female friends were still chatting away as they sat in front of empty coffee cups.

'Excuse me,' one said beckoning Alice over. She pretended not to notice and frantically looked for Marcus. He wasn't around but Margaret was and she was staring at her and looking appalled. Alice had no alternative but to go over to them.

'You're Katie Green's daughter aren't you? You came round to my house with my husband one day to ransack my living room!' Celia was looking very pleased with herself.

'I am Katie's daughter, yes.' The penny dropped.

'And I'm Birch's wife,' she said with a sarcastic grin across her face.

'May I get you anything? The bill, perhaps?' Alice knew she was pushing her luck, but what else could she say to them?

'No, I think I'm going to have another coffee. Complimentary,' she said with an air of triumph, 'on the house. I'm sure you can arrange that for us. Or are you one of these minimum wage workers with no clout and lucky to have any job at all?'

Alice looked distressed. Margaret appeared by her side. 'Everything all right here?' she asked breezily.

'Your waitress has just said that we can have another coffee, free of charge.'

Margaret maintained an air of professionalism. 'Coming up,' she said, and led Alice to the back of the restaurant. 'What's going on?' she said firmly but quietly.

'She is demanding a free coffee; I didn't say she could have it.'

'But why? Are they not happy with the service they've had, or is it the food?'

'I don't know; Marcus was serving them.'

Margaret looked over both her shoulders as if expecting to find Marcus. 'Really. Where is he now?'

'I don't know.'

'Right, well, we better get them some more coffees and deliver them with the bill.'

'Okay,' Alice said shakily.

'Are you all right?'

'Yes.' Alice gulped back a tear. 'It's just that she was being really horrible to me.'

Margaret looked concerned. 'But why?'

'I... I can't...'

'Okay, don't worry, you get the coffees and the bill, and I will deliver them.'

'Thanks Margaret,' Alice said with massive relief.


Sylvia looked up at the high ceiling of the elegant Reynolds room, a white dome covered with an ornate and elaborate gold pattern. Some of Jack's paintings were hung around the room including the portrait of Abella, which was just to the right of Sylvia's chair. If she kept her gaze forward, she could not see it. She smoothed the fabric of her orange jersey shift dress over her crossed legs for the umpteenth time and thought about checking her mobile phone for messages. She then considered that there certainly wouldn't be a message from Jack, possibly the only person she'd love to hear from right now, so she would leave it in her handbag. The audience waited in a state of relaxed anticipation for the artist to arrive and were looking at two empty chairs at the front of the room. As Sylvia was right at the back of the room she had to sit tall to see where it was all going to happen.

She had been excited all day leading up to this event, and it had been difficult to be around Birch and Katie without saying something. It was obvious that Katie had sensed her heightened state when she asked over lunch, 'Everything alright?'

'Oh yes, of course,' she'd replied trying to sound casual.

Katie had a knowing look about her. 'Any plans for today?'

'Yes, actually, I'm out this evening.'

This had led to the inevitable queries and Sylvia had lied in as much as she said she was going to the Royal Academy with a friend. Somehow this had made her feel guilty and so she had quickly added, 'I'll be going home soon, back to Sandgate; I don't want to outstay my welcome here.'

'Don't be silly, we love having you here; please stay as long as you wish,' Katie had responded.

'Yes, Mum,' Birch added, 'you're having an amazingly positive effect on Bethan, something I've never managed.'

It had been the lightest moment of the day so far. Otherwise she had contemplated every possible scenario from the artist not being the man she thought he was through to her falling head over heels in love again.

A man in a formal suit appeared now and addressed the room, which obediently fell quiet. Sylvia's heart leapt in to her mouth. This was not Jack.

'Good evening ladies and gentlemen, it's lovely to see so many of you here this evening at the Royal Academy. I'm Mike Tyndall, a Royal Academician here at the Academy, and I am very much looking forward to interviewing the artist, Jack Harvey, before hosting a drinks reception where Jack will be able to answer some of your questions.' He looked nervously to the door and then nodded before adding, 'So, please may I introduce, Mr Jack Harvey.'

Everyone clapped except Sylvia. Her whole body seemed to have turned to jelly. It was all she could do to stay upright on her chair. Jack appeared wearing a slightly crumpled ivory linen suit over a dark navy blue T-shirt. His grey wavy hair was swept back from his Mediterranean tanned face and was cropped just below his neck. His eyes were as big, dark and seductive, as Sylvia had remembered and his smile was as infectious as ever, as he lapped up the applause from his audience. A tear appeared in the corner of Sylvia's eye, and the man sitting next to her turned to her looking puzzled. She pulled a tissue from her handbag and used it discreetly.

Jack started to speak and it was amazing to hear his voice. She realised instantly that he had made his life in southern France. His English now had a strong French accent, and occasionally he used a French word instead, not taking the trouble to translate. His story seemed to start in Paris when he was twenty-five years old, but the interviewer pointed out that he was born and brought up in London.

'Yes, I was, around Camden Town in fact, but unfortunately you English were not ready for me then.' There was a general murmur of laughter around the room before he continued, 'I think I was a bit too bohemian for your middle classes. You didn't seem to appreciate my work at that stage, but then I had a lot to learn.' He had a mischievous glint in his eye.

The audience were warming to him and Sylvia was in some kind of dream world not quite believing her eyes and her ears. She had a serene look on her face and lapped up every word, heaving up in her chair to ensure she didn't miss a thing. This was her Jack.

'Shall we get a bottle?' Alice asked her sister. The Flask was busy with workers enjoying an after work drink.

'Yeah, let's. Shall we sit over there by the window?'

'Good spot, you nab those seats and I'll bring the wine over.'

Bethan threw her bag on one chair and sat on the other. Alice appeared with a bottle of house white in an ice bucket, and two glasses. She collapsed down into a chair. 'God, what a day!'

'I thought, you sounded a bit desperate in that text you sent me.'

'Yeah, well, you'll never believe who turned up at the restaurant this lunchtime?'

'Who?' Bethan started pouring the wine out.

'Only Birch's wife, Celia. And what a bitch she is!'

'Really? What did she do?' Bethan took a large gulp of her wine.

'Well first of all, she was glaring at me in this weird kind of way. So I got Marcus to wait on her table but he disappeared before the end of his shift.'

'That's not good. He should try working at Web Dreams; they have you there all hours.'

'At least they're nice to you there, though.'

'Well, on the whole. Matt's still in a sulk.' Bethan said with disdain.

'Have you heard from Harry?' Alice asked gently.

'What do you think?' she started fiddling with a beer mat, eyes down. 'I suppose I always knew he was too good for me.'

'Don't be silly. You're too good for him.'

'Thanks, but well, if I was we'd still be together, surely?'

'No! It doesn't work like that.'

'There speaks the voice of experience!'

'Listen, I might only be a couple of years older than you, but I know Harry's type. They just aren't interested in any kind of commitment. Anyway Mum said..'

'Mum? What does she know?'

'She said that Harry told her he didn't like to get involved with any business associates.'

Bethan looked doubtful.

'Or their relatives,' Alice added by way of explanation.

'But Mum's not a business associate.'

'Well she kind of is, I mean she's his VA, so..'

'Well that doesn't bother me.' Bethan looked confused.

'Listen,' Alice tried another tact, 'you know what Dad would have said?'

'Yeah, I'm the best,' she smiled at his memory and added, 'no man is good enough for me...' as she flitted her eyes heaven wards.

Alice smiled at her sister admiringly. 'Something like that.'

'God, I miss him,' Bethan swallowed hard.

'I know. Me too.'

There was a reflective pause before Bethan said, 'Anyway, we were talking about how horrible Celia was to you. So are you in trouble with Margaret?'

'Well, she wanted to know why Celia was demanding free coffee after they'd sat there nursing two empty cups for ages. We were really busy this lunch time as well.'

'Makes you wonder, doesn't it? Birch was with that silly cow for ages and now he's with our Mum.' Bethan ran her middle finger around the rim of her glass.

'I don't mind Birch, actually.' Alice swept her hair back from her face.

'I know you don't,' Bethan said as she refilled both their glasses even though they were still half full and then she added, 'I like Sylvia, she's fun.'

'Yes, she is, but I think she's going home tomorrow.'

'Oh no! I think I'll try and persuade her to stay,' Bethan said with a mischievous smile on her face, 'I need to practice my cup cakes!'

'Mm.. they were yummy. I'm happy to test them for you if you make some more.'

'I bet you are!'

They both took a sip of wine, and there was an amiable pause in their conversation.

'Perhaps you should suggest that Celia is banned from The Lemon Tree,' Bethan said and they both laughed.

'I can see that happening!'

The talk was over and there was a general movement of people, led by Jack and his host, into a side room where a glass of wine was promised. Sylvia didn't move. Her heart was aching and she wondered what good could possibly come of her following them. What if he didn't remember her? What if he would rather avoid her? She now knew some of what path his life had taken. Perhaps that was enough and she should simply slip away and go home. She was the only one left in the room now, and one of the staff, an East European woman, was looking at her awkwardly. She waved her left arm in the direction the others had gone inviting Sylvia to join them. Should she face her moment of truth or should she run scared?

The woman now approached her. 'You need some help, madam?'

'Ha!' Sylvia yelped, now seeing the ridiculous side of this situation.

The woman looked confused.

'Sorry darling, it's just that I used to know Jack Harvey, intimately I mean, but I haven't seen him for so long, I mean decades.'

The response was simple, 'Well, why don't you go and say hello to him?'

Sylvia collected herself, rose to her feet, and said, 'why not?' She walked towards the door, turned to say, 'thank you,' and walked into the crowd.

The wine was being served from a table at the far end. Sylvia expected it would be cheap plonk and probably too warm but she decided a bit of Dutch courage was not a bad idea. She chose the red, a Cabernet Sauvignon, and after the first two sips it started to slip down nicely.

Jack was surrounded by people eager to rub shoulders with him. There was one woman in particular, who looked like she was in her fifties. She was obviously French and cut a neat, diminutive figure in a steel grey suit. Sylvia watched as the woman fussed around him, touching him lightly at every opportunity. She even seemed to be answering some of the questions for him. But then, despite the decades that had separated them, she knew only too well that look on Jack's face, which gave away the fact that he was tolerating her and not at one with her. Surely he hadn't trapped himself in a hapless relationship?

Sylvia was getting nearer to him as the crowd subsided. She heard her phone bleep and saw that Reggie had sent her a text message, which said simply, fancy dinner? She put her phone away.

A man in a blazer and chinos came over to her. He had blue eyes and a very obvious comb over. 'Splendid talk, wasn't it?'

'Yes, yes. Great. Excellent,' Sylvia was in no mood for small talk.

'Have you seen much of Harvey's work?'

'Not really,' she replied vaguely.

'Yes, he doesn't come to London much. As he said, he prefers the Languedoc these days.' The man put on his most pleasing smile.

Sylvia realised that she must have missed that bit of the talk. But it had been so difficult to concentrate. Every answer he gave had her wondering about all sorts of scenarios. She had been trying to get an up-to-date picture of his life but he had been quite reserved when his private affairs were touched upon.

People started to leave, the circle around Jack was diminished and Sylvia was able to get close enough to be noticed. Finally she stood there feeling exposed, nowhere to hide. His eyes met hers. They seemed to linger. Was that a look of recognition on his face? The French woman turned him around to answer yet another question. She had him in her grasp. Sylvia felt defeated. She had no energy to fight this woman off. She decided to slip away and walked quietly out of the room, her head bowed low. As she made her way down the corridor she felt wretched. Should she turn back? She was approaching the main entrance hall when he called her name.

'Sylvie?'

She turned to face him. 'Jack,' she said and smiled.

'Sylvie! Is it really you?' he cried excitedly.

'Yes, Jack. Yes, it's really me.'

Alice and Bethan were both quite tipsy when they got back to Bisham Gardens. They were giggling loudly as they fell through the front door. Birch smiled at Katie as they sat together on the sofa watching a film.

'I think your daughters have been drinking. Together.'

'Good,' Katie said simply, 'It's nice when they get on. David always insisted they were nice to each other.'

Birch crossed his arms. 'I make a poor substitute, clearly.'

'Don't be silly. You're not trying to replace him, and that's how it should be.'

Bethan burst into the room. 'Hi Mum!' She noticed Birch and subdued her tone before saying, 'Hi Birch. Anything for supper, Mum? I'm starving.'

'There's bolognese sauce on the hob. You just need to cook the pasta.'

'Excellent!' She turned to go, but then turned back. 'Is Sylvia in by any chance?'

'No, darling, she's out.'

'Oh, bad luck. Is it true she's going home tomorrow?'

'Possibly. I'm not sure.'

'I hope not. I'll talk her out of it when she gets in.'

Katie looked puzzled in a happy kind of way. Alice appeared and said, 'your wife was truly horrible to me today.'

Birch sat up. 'Oh Alice, I'm so sorry.'

'Not your fault, but she nearly got me sacked from The Lemon Tree.'

'Oh God, I'll go and see Margaret if you like and explain.'

'Well, might not be necessary, but thanks anyway.'

'Come on sis, there's spag' bol' in the kitchen,' Bethan beckoned her sister.

'Brilliant!'

# Chapter 12

From the moment he called her name and Sylvia knew, that Jack knew it was actually her, all her fears of disappointment were gone. He looked at her as if enchanted by her presence, it was a look that she remembered well. Words didn't seem necessary for those first few moments. It was enough to take in the enormity of what was happening.

He took both her hands in his. 'Sylvie, my adorable Sylvie. You came at last. I've missed you so much.'

She loved the way he used the French version of her name. 'But... ,' there were so many questions but where did she start, perhaps not with why did you disappear?

'Well, I'm here now,' she said instead.

'This calls for Champagne!'

'You haven't changed!'

They laughed together and he led her out of the building and hailed a cab immediately. Before she knew it they were walking up to the Opera Terrace in Covent Garden and sitting in the romantic Parisian style conservatory with views across the piazza which was bathed in white lights in the cold night air. The restaurant was busy with diners and they were shown to the only remaining table.

'That was lucky,' Sylvia said.

'No, this is lucky,' he smothered her hands with his across the table. His face was the epitome of contentment; he looked like he had arrived after some long arduous journey.

'You're right because I don't live in London any more. I just happen to be visiting my son.' She was almost reprimanding him, but how could she?

'You have a son. How wonderful.' His calm, self-assured demeanour had stayed with him through the years.

The waiter presented them with menus. Neither of them looked.

'May I order a bottle of your finest Champagne?'

'Of course, sir. Would you like the Veuve Clicquot or perhaps the Bollinger Special Cuvée?'

'Anything, just bring it. We're in a hurry, we have a lot of time to make up.'

They stared into each other's eyes. There was a lot to take in. The years had been kind to them both but still five decades had made their mark. It was only then that Sylvia realised he had simply walked away from the event he was hosting at the Royal Academy.

'Did you just walk out? Will they not be wondering where you are?'

'Yes I did just walk out, and I'm sure they will be flapping around like gros poulets!'

'Typical Jack! No responsibilities.'

'You know me so well.'

A waiter appeared with a bottle of Champagne and opened it in front of them. A nod from Jack, and he simply poured two glasses.

'Santé,' Sylvia said as they clinked flutes.

'Santé,' Jack looked impressed.

They both quaffed their drinks readily and for Sylvia it was very welcome. Another waiter was hovering near their table. Jack picked up his menu and handed it to him without so much as glancing at it.

'So, erm, er.. what is your finest dish this evening?'

The waiter looked surprised, but then said 'confit duck with dauphinoise potatoes and...'

'This is good for you?' he asked Sylvia, interrupting the waiter.

'Sounds lovely.'

'Deux, s'il vous plait,' he said waving him away and leaned back in his chair. 'So, you have seen my paintings?'

'Of course, I came up yesterday to the exhibition but you know, I wasn't absolutely sure. I mean, I couldn't be absolutely certain that it was you.'

'But you came back for the talk this evening?'

'Yes, of course.'

'But I didn't see you in there.'

'There was only one seat left, right at the back.'

'Ah, so you were hiding from me. Checking me out before you revealed yourself to me.' His eyes twinkled.

'Well, I didn't know what to expect; it's been so long.'

'Of course, I understand. But you nearly ran away.'

Sylvia's cheeks blushed. 'I didn't like the look of the competition.' There she'd said it. It had to be said.

'What? Oh Chantal! That woman does fuss around me. She's my agent. I'm sure she'd like to be more than that, but still she gets on my nerves.'

Sylvia tried not to look too relieved. 'Oh, I see.'

Their meals arrived and she wondered how on earth she was going to eat it. She could happily drink champagne all night but had little appetite for food.

'C'est énorme, n'est pas?' It was as if he could read her mind.

'Mais oui, il sent bon, mais je dois d'yeux que pour tu ..' It felt safe, saying it in French.

'Ah, tu parles français mon amour,' his eyes were admiring.

'Yes, I did a degree in French after..' She wasn't sure if she should mention Arthur this early on.

'After?'

It was no good. 'After Arthur died.'

'Ah, he died. I wondered. So sorry to hear that.'

Sylvia was thoughtful. She needed to express to him something of how her marriage had been. 'He didn't make me happy.'

'But he did please your mother. I know she hated me.'

'I was never sure how much you knew about Arthur.'

'Your mother didn't tell you?'

'Tell me what?' Sylvia looked worried. Was there some dark secret from her past that had been kept from her all these years?

'Ah, that explains a lot,' Jack said.

'Tell me, what did my mother do?' She needed to know urgently now.

'It's all in the past now. We have to let go.' He clearly was dealing with this better than her.

'But still, I want to know,' she said firmly. 'Did she tell you to leave me alone?'

'Well, yes, but you don't think a little thing like that would put me off, do you?' His eyes were playful.

'So, something worse? Oh, Jack you have me worried now. What did she do?'

He took a deep breath. 'I rang up one day and she said you were marrying Arthur. I asked her if you loved him and she said yes. She made out that that was the reason you didn't talk about him to me.'

'Oh but Jack, you know why I married Arthur. I didn't love him, I just..'

'You just had to please your parents.'

'Oh God that makes me sound so feeble.'

'You were twenty-five, for goodness sake. Your mother was a formidable woman. I don't blame you.'

Sylvia was piecing together the events of the past in her mind. 'That was the day you disappeared, wasn't it?'

He bowed his head in shame. 'Yes, that was the day I went to Paris. I was ringing to see if you would come with me. Crazy idea I know.'

'No more crazy than your usual ideas,' Sylvia added and it lightened the mood for a moment.

'Anyway, your mother said you were out with Arthur and that I should never darken your door again.'

A wave of realisation came over her. Her mother had changed the course of her life dramatically that day. Suddenly she wanted to bring her back from the dead to shout and scream at her.

'You can't blame her,' Jack said quietly. 'I did for years and it didn't help. You have to forgive her. She knew Arthur would provide a good home for you.'

Sylvia tried to let it go but to think of all those years she had wondered why Jack had up and left without saying goodbye. She slugged back more Champagne before the waiter refilled their glasses for a second time.

'Now, let us be thankful for this evening,' Jack said grinning, 'and try and eat at least some of this canard. I don't want the chef spitting in my coffee!'

Back at Bisham Gardens, Bethan was the last one up as she had fallen asleep in front of the DVD of the film, Les Petits Mouchoirs. Alice had mocked her choice earlier.

'You'll never stick with that.'

'But there are subtitles, aren't there? And you're always saying what a good film it is.'

'Oh yes, of course, but still...'

She woke up now and realised it was half past eleven and the film was still running. The house was quiet. She considered that either Sylvia was still out or she had crept in and up the stairs without waking her. Knowing she had to be up early for work the next day, she decided to write her a note and leave it in her bedroom.

She found a scrap of paper in the kitchen and a pen, which didn't work. She was going to take the paper up to her room, but as she passed her mother's study, she decided to go in and find something better. There was a smart notepad and pen to the right of her keyboard. She recognised it as the one her mother took to meetings. Bethan opened it up and saw her mother's handwriting. It looked like she had been getting quotes from various electricians to re-wire Cholmeley Crescent. Bethan suddenly felt immensely proud of her mother. She thought back to the awful moment when they had been thinking they would have to sell their home; the very thought was heart-breaking. And now her mother had set herself up as a VA and financial disaster was averted. She tore off a clean sheet from the notepad and started to write.

Hi Sylvia,

It's been great having you to stay. I'm not sure what your plans are, but I hope you're not going back to Sandgate just yet. Let's make more cupcakes tomorrow evening!

Bethan x

She folded the sheet in half and wrote Sylvia's name on the outside before taking it all the way up to the attic room, where the door was closed, so she slid it underneath feeling pleased with herself.

They were the last to leave the restaurant and as they roamed the streets, despite the chilly night air, Sylvia felt warm inside. She thought about hailing a taxi to take her back to Highgate but didn't want the night to end.

'I suppose Birch will be wondering where I am. I should think about..' She looked at his face and wondered if he was even listening to her.

He took her by the arm and seemed to be walking in a particular direction.

'I'm staying at the Hazlitt's Hotel. It's just a few minutes further from here.'

She mocked surprise that he might presume she would go back with him and then laughed and rested her head on his shoulder. This was definitely a moment to throw caution to the wind; this was going to be the night of her life.

# Chapter 13

Bethan was already running late for work. 'Mum, have you seen Sylvia?' Her expression was deadly serious.

'No darling, maybe she's having a lie in after her evening out.'

Bethan looked worried. 'Have you checked on her?' she asked.

Katie assumed she was being melodramatic. 'Of course not. She's a grown woman.'

'But Mum, she went out last night and who knows if she made it back?'

'Well you were going to stay up until she got in...'

'Yes, exactly! I didn't hear her come in.'

Katie decided it was worth checking her room and without saying anything they both headed up the stairs. Katie knocked. Nothing. She knocked again. 'Sylvia,' she said gently.

They looked at each other. 'Let's go in, Mum.'

Katie opened the door slowly repeating her name, 'Sylvia?'

The note Bethan had written was still on the floor and the bed had not been slept in.

'Oh my God!' Katie rushed down stairs and found Birch in the kitchen.

'Your mum's not there. She's not in her room.'

'What?!'

'I just assumed..'

'Yes, me too,' Birch looked puzzled.

'Shall we call the police?' Bethan said causing everyone to spring into action.

'Well, let's see if she's called first.' Birch grabbed his mobile from the table. 'Damn! The battery's flat.'

'Here.' Bethan pointed to a charger on the kitchen worktop. She took the phone from him and plugged it in. 'It should work in a minute or so.'

'Hang on, I've got her number in my phone,' Katie said going off to her study. She returned checking her messages. 'Nothing from Sylvia,' she said biting her bottom lip and then asked Bethan, 'Aren't you late for work?'

'Sod that! I need to know she's okay.' Katie looked surprised but didn't say anything. She was touched that her daughter cared so much.

After a couple of long minutes Birch's phone sprang to life. He stared at the screen. Nothing. 'I'll call her,' he said and found her number.

It rang eight times before Sylvia answered. 'Birch,' she said hazily.

'Mum? Are you okay?'

'Oh yes darling, I'm just wonderful apart from a dreadful headache; Champagne always does that to me.'

'Where are you?'

'I'm not sure I can divulge that right now but don't worry about me, I'm absolutely fine.'

'What are you talking about? You've had us worried sick!'

'Us?'

'Yes, me Katie and Bethan.'

'Oh bless you all. I'm so sorry, but tell them I've just had the most amazing night!'

Birch's face was one of shocked embarrassment. 'Right Mum. Will we be seeing you later?'

'Oh I should think so. Listen, I'll call you in a while but are you doing anything today?'

'Nothing special.'

'Right, well keep it that way; I'll call you soon.'

'Okay Mum.' He ended the call still looking perplexed.

'So?' Katie asked.

Birch looked lost for words. 'So she's alright, more than alright, apparently.'

'Oh, thank God.' Bethan looked happy. She looked at her watch. 'I suppose I better go to work.' She looked at Birch as she asked, 'will you tell her not to go home today, please?'

'Yes, of course.' He smiled at her. 'Listen, would you like a lift?' It just slipped out and there was an awkward pause hanging in the air.

'Oh thanks. Yes please, I'm late enough as it is.' Bethan had picked up her bag and was half way down the hallway.

Katie and Birch looked at each stunned by her response.

'Why don't you call your work on the way?' Katie shouted towards the front door.

'Yes, I will Mum.'

Birch wore a deep frown as he drove Bethan to work. The car was filled with silence and he considered putting the radio on but knowing it was tuned in to Radio 4 he decided against it. Realising he didn't know exactly where Bethan worked he said, 'Sorry, you'll have to direct me from here.'

'Oh, yeah, of course, it's right at the lights.'

He was in the left hand lane and had to signal and wait for a gap before he could get over to the correct lane. The other commuters were not in a forgiving mood and by the time he made it, the lights had turned red again. He said nothing, didn't even breath.

'Sorry,' Bethan said.

Birch looked over to her. 'No prob's,' he said as lightly as he could manage. He was only too aware that when Bethan agreed to this lift it was a significant breakthrough in their relationship.

The lights turned green.

'It's second left down here.'

'Thanks,' Birch said simply.

As they turned into the road she said, 'You can drop me here, if you like?'

Birch pulled over and stopped the car. He looked up and could only see residential houses. 'Is this it?'

'Yeah, it's just up the road actually but the parking is difficult further up.'

126

'Oh, I see.'

She picked up her bag.

'Not that you're too embarrassed to be seen with me?' he joked praying she would take it the right way.

She let out a small laugh. 'Well, yes, that as well,' Her eyes smiled at him. 'Don't forget to tell Sylvia,' she added.

'No, no I won't.'

'Thanks for the lift,' she said as she got out of the car and as soon as she was out of earshot Birch sighed with enormous relief.

Katie was trying to compose an email to Harry but decided it would be easier to speak with him direct on this particular matter. She grabbed her mobile and found his number.

'Katie, what can I do for you?'

'Hi Harry, everything okay?' Why didn't she just get to the point?

'Great, thanks,' he sounded bored.

'Good, erm, I'm calling about a friend of mine, well when I say friend..'

'You're really talking about yourself but it's rather embarrassing!' he joked.

'No! Definitely not. I'm talking about Ross. I think I may have mentioned him to you; he's the guy that befriended my husband before he died.'

'Right. Not ringing any bells but carry on.'

'Well, Ross has partnered up with Elaine who manages Le Bistro in the village and they are looking to buy Fegos and turn it around.'

'That sounds good. That place really needs new management. I mean, it's in a great location and yet it's really gone downhill recently. The décor's tired, the staff are tired...'

'Exactly, yes. And Ross and Elaine have some good ideas too, like turning it into part café, part deli.'

'Even better. Take away food, I like it!'

'Yes, definitely your kind of thing. Anyway the thing is..'

'They need some finance.'

'Yes Harry, you're quick off the mark today.'

'Oh just having a run of good luck, I guess. Garcia's investment has certainly made a difference to my portfolio.'

'I bet it has. Puts my five thousand to shame.'

'Hey, no longer five thousand, it's nearer six now, thanks to my expert management.'

'Yes Harry, you are a genius.'

'I know. So where do I come in with this Ross chap?'

'Well it was a long shot really, I mean you might know someone who'd be interested in investing. They wouldn't have to do any of the work, well not the legwork so to speak.'

'Mmm.. let me think about this. How much are they looking for?'

'It's up for four hundred and fifty thousand but that includes a two bedroomed flat above it and the owners are desperate to sell according to Ross. There's been a death in the family.'

Harry went quiet. To break an awkward silence Katie said, 'Shall I leave it with you?'

'I'd like to meet with the guy. And Elaine. See what they're made of.'

Katie quietly punched the air. 'Of course, I can arrange that.'

'What does Ross currently do?'

'He runs the local magazine, My Mag, the one that comes through the door.'

'Oh yes, I know. And he owns that, does he?'

'Yes, that's right.'

'Mmm.. okay set the meeting up.'

'Thanks Harry, I appreciate that.'

Birch had just got back to Bisham Gardens when his mobile rang.

'Hi Mum,' he said trying be upbeat.

'You alright darling? You've been sounding a bit down recently.'

'Yes, well, Celia is single-handedly making my life hell.'

'Oh dear,' Sylvia still sounded deliriously happy despite this declaration. 'Well anyway, I was wondering if you fancied popping down to Covent Garden this lunch time?'

Birch immediately wanted to say no. 'Nice idea Mum, but..'

'There's someone I'd like you to meet,' she interrupted him.

'What... Reggie? Surely not Mum.'

'No, I'd like you to meet Jack Harvey, the artist.'

Birch was confused. 'What are you talking about Mother?'

'I knew Jack many years ago before I met your father and well, he's been living in France all these years but he happens to be..'

'That's why you went to that talk. Why didn't you say?'

'Yes, well there's a bit more to it than that.'

'Really? Like what?'

'Why don't you come down and we'll meet at Browns on St. Martin's Lane at one o'clock? Lunch on me, of course.'

'Is it that important? I should really be writing.' He knew the truth was that his writing was not going well at the moment. 'Oh darling, I wish I could help you, you sound so drained. When I get back to Sandgate I'm going to give that lawyer of yours a stern talking to!'

'Really Mum, I'm sure that will help.' Even his sarcasm was deflated.

'Why don't you bring Katie too?'

'Oh, she's busy working. One of us has to earn some money.'

'Come. Just come. Please?'

'Okay Mum. Where did you say again?'


Birch walked in to Browns restaurant to be confronted with Sylvia waving at him from behind a Kentia palm. He couldn't help noticing the man next to her who stood out with his Mediterranean tan, cream linen suit and panama hat as he sat amongst a wrapped up British crowd.

'Darling!' Sylvia sounded to him as if she was on ecstasy.

'Mum,' he said almost mocking her.

'This is Jack. Jack Harvey.'

'Hello Jack, good to meet you,' he said using every ounce of his energy to portray a pleasant demeanour.

'Birch, your mother has told me so much about you.' He stood up to shake his hand warmly.

'Oh dear.' Birch half smiled indicating he wasn't to be taken too seriously.

'Not at all. I'm very impressed by what you've achieved and, yes,' he said as he stood back to get a better look at a tall, lanky, Birch. 'You've inherited your mother's good looks!'

'Lucky me,' he replied through gritted teeth.

They both sat down and Jack said, 'but you have a look of a man with much weight on your shoulders; this is not good.'

'Yes, well if you can describe my ex-wife as heavy you'd be right there.'

'Now darling, let's order some food.' Sylvia handed him a menu and gave him a look that implored him to behave.

'And pour you a glass of wine.' Jack filled a third glass from the bottle of Rioja they had already started.

'Well there's a good idea.' Birch raised his glass before taking a large gulp of the spicy wine.

'And then I want to tell you how Jack and I know each other,' Sylvia said like an excited school girl.

'Not a dating site, surely?' Birch mocked but they both laughed and looked into each other's eyes like two people in love. Birch couldn't believe the sight before him.

Ross was stood at the door of Le Bistro and a waiter was trying to seat him. 'Actually I'm here to see Elaine.'

'Well she's busy at the moment,' the young man said brushing him off with an air of authority.

'I'm sure she is but would you mind telling her that Ross is here.'

'I'll see what I can do,' he said but then went on to clear a large table, obviously in no hurry to meet his request.

Emma appeared and recognised Ross. She went straight over to him. 'Hi Ross, are you here to see Elaine?'

'Yes, that's right.'

She hesitated before she said, 'we've had a rather difficult morning; Elaine has asked not to be disturbed.' She read the disappointment on his face, 'but as it's you...'

Ross was immediately concerned. What had Adrien Moreau done now? 'I take it she's in her office upstairs? May I go to her?'

'Er, well, yes, I suppose,' she agreed reluctantly.

'Adrien's not here, is he?'

'Well he's in London and was here earlier but he's gone now.'

'I see. I'll go straight up then.'

He found her slumped over her desk in tears.

'Ross? What are you doing here?' she took another tissue from the box on her desk and blew her nose. Her face was red and her eye make-up was smudged.

'Oh darling, thank God I am here! What's happened?' He put an arm around her shoulder and kissed the top of her head. 'I hear Adrien's been here, I suppose he's behind this?'

'Yes, it was truly awful. I really don't think I can take anymore. I was so close to telling him where he could stick his stupid job! You know he blames me for everything?'

'You poor thing. Perhaps you should resign?'

'I can't afford to. There's the mortgage to pay; Jessica's already grown out of her school uniform and..'

'I know. But I do have a bit of good news.'

'What's that then?'

'You know I told you that Katie knows this investment man, Harry Liversage his name is, well anyway he's agreed to meet with us about finding someone to fund the purchase of Fegos.'

'Oh, that's good. Well a step in the right direction, I suppose?'

'Listen, I know it's not definite or anything but Katie said he sounded really interested. He wants to meet both of us. I'm going to go through the business plan again this evening and make sure it's top notch.'

'Okay,' Elaine said as she sighed.

'Hey, I promise we'll have something sorted soon. I have a good feeling about this.'

She put on a brave face and smiled at him.

'Listen, are you due to be here tomorrow morning because that's when Harry wants to meet us. Katie said we can meet at her place.'

'That's kind of her.'

'Yes, it is.'

'But I'm supposed to be working.' Elaine looked frustrated.

'Why don't you see if Emma can cover for you?'

Elaine looked doubtful. 'I'm always asking her. You know I've been trying to do more school runs recently and she's been so good about it.'

'It's just one more morning. It's important.'

'Yes, you're right. I'll ask her.'

'And can I come round to your's this evening, after Jessica is in bed, so we can go through the business plan together?'

'Oh I suppose so,' she looked exhausted at the thought.

'Don't worry, I'll make sure it's all as good as I can make it and then I'll just go through it with you so you know what's what.'

Elaine pulled herself together, straightened herself out and stood up. 'Okay, let's do this.'

Birch was stunned by the story his mother told. If the man himself, Jack Harvey, had not been sat at the table looking like a fish out of water, he would not have believed her. Sylvia had, of course, been careful how she related events with regard to his father, but he only had to look at her radiant face to realise that this was the man she had loved all along. His own relationship with his father had been far from close; he had disapproved of Birch's career choice of journalism over accountancy. Sadly his father hadn't lived to see his first novel published but still, he doubted whether that would have been affirmation enough to please him. The couple before him were clearly besotted with each other and he had to admit that it was great to see his mother so happy.

He measured out the end of the bottle of wine into the three glasses, raised his own glass to them both and said, 'Thank you for inviting me to lunch. Jack, it's been wonderful to meet you and I sincerely hope you and my mother have many happy adventures together.' At last he could be magnanimous despite his own troubles.

'Thank you, Birch,' Sylvia wiped a tear from her eye.

'Oh and I nearly forgot,' Birch added. 'Bethan is very keen that you come back to Highgate before you return home, something about making more cupcakes?'

'Bless her,' Sylvia said.
'Cupcakes?' Jack looked confused.

# Chapter 14

Ross had worked out, using Google maps, that it would take him fifteen minutes to walk round to Katie's house. He had put on a navy jacket with his chinos, having considered a suit was a bit over the top for this type of meeting. He checked and double checked that he had the two copies of the business plan in his document wallet. He had made a third copy but Elaine had asked him to leave it with her last night when he went round. He couldn't help hoping that she wouldn't crease the pages in case Harry wanted that copy as well.

'I'm just too tired to take it in now,' she had said last night sinking into her sofa. He felt a little deflated even though he did understand. He'd put so much work into it and she didn't seem to share his enthusiasm.

'Well, if you're sure. Shall I come round in the morning and we can go to Katie's together?'

'No,' she said too abruptly, 'No, I mean I'll be dropping Jess at school first so...'

'Okay I'll see you there. That way it won't matter if you're a little bit late.' He was trying to be kind but it back fired.

'I won't be late,' Elaine said, tetchy now.

'Sorry, I didn't mean to imply you would be.'

She said nothing. He felt awful.

'Right, well then, I suppose I'll go now,' he said saddened by her response; she had seemed glad to see him go. He had not slept well, more concerned about his relationship with Elaine than the meeting with Harry. He'd obviously pushed her too far. Why did he do that? If only he had the money to support her and Jessica, he could free her from the dreadful Adrien Moreau. But he didn't.

He got to Katie's ten minutes early. It took a couple of minutes for her to answer the door.

'Ross, do come in.'

'Thanks Katie, sorry I'm early.'

'No problem.' She looked at him, 'You okay?'

'Yes, yes, fine,' he put on his bravest smile.

'Don't worry about Harry, he's a lamb.'

'Well that's good to know.'

Birch appeared, 'Hi Ross, you look like you need a double espresso.'

'Oh do I? Oh no!'

'Only joking, but some caffeine wouldn't go a miss, maybe?'

'Lovely, yes, please.'

Katie showed him through to the living room. 'Make yourself comfortable. Is Elaine coming?'

'Yes, she'll be here soon.'

'Oh good.' She placed a hand gently on his arm, 'don't worry about this, it's just a friendly chat.'

'Of course.' He placed two copies of the business plan on the coffee table.

'Impressive,' Katie said and smiled at him. The doorbell rang. 'I'll get that,' Katie said. She returned with Elaine who smiled at him, went over and kissed him lightly.

Ross looked at her adoringly.

'I'll just chase up the coffee,' Katie said with a strong inclination to leave this couple alone for a moment.

'Do you think you'll need to buy new kitchen equipment?' Harry asked as he looked up from the business plan on his lap.

'Actually, what's there already seems to be in pretty good shape. They installed a new, state of the art coffee machine only last year but it's at the back in the kitchen. I would suggest we create a self-service counter and have the machine on display like they do in the chains.'

'Yes, I'm sure you're right. And the deli idea, would you need planning permission for that as it would be a change of use?'

'Well, that's the strange thing, they already have it. It seems one of the sons got very involved a couple of years ago and persuaded his father to make a few changes. He did the groundwork but then met an American woman on holiday in Italy and now lives with her in New York with no interest at all in the business.'

'You've really done your homework.' Harry looked impressed.

'He's worked really hard on this plan,' Elaine said.

'I can see that.' Harry was leafing through his copy. 'And you manage Le Bistro, I hear?'

'Yes, that's right. We have fifty covers, a French chef; it's high end gourmet dining. I would, of course, leave there to work full-time on this project.'

Harry was thoughtful and looking at the financial projections on the back page. 'This turnover figure, is that based on what they are currently doing?'

'It's based on last year, so before the owner died. Things have gone downhill a bit since then,' Ross explained.

'Yes, I've seen that for myself.'

'I've assumed we will improve on last year's turnover by about ten per cent which I don't think is too ambitious.'

'Given what you have planned, including the marketing, I think that could be conservative. Yes, I think this has the makings of being a nice little earner.' Harry sat back in his chair before he asked, 'have you seen the flat upstairs; two bedrooms is it?'

'Yes, I have actually,' Ross replied. 'it's not bad. I was thinking of moving in myself and using one bedroom as an office.'

'Makes sense. Of course there will be a rental value on the flat alone.'

'Yes, well I currently pay rent elsewhere anyway.'

'I see.'

They sat in silence as Harry pondered the figures further. The big question hung in the air. Ross decided to go for it. 'So do you think you might know someone who would be interested in investing in this?'

'Yes,' Harry said nodding his head, 'yes, I do.'

'Oh?'

'Yes, me.' He looked up at them both and smiled, 'I think I might be your dragon!'

'Really?' Ross couldn't believe his ears. He looked at Elaine who was beaming.

'I just need to run the figures past my accountant, so I'll give you a definitive answer in the next few days if that's all right? But I can't see any problems; it looks like a very sound venture.'

Ross looked like a kid in a sweet shop. 'Thank you Harry,' he said sincerely and breathed a huge sigh of relief.

Birch had been staring at his laptop screen for some time. The page remained empty. He'd tried his usual ploy of reading through yesterday's work to help spark ideas but he'd just been disappointed with what he'd found. He couldn't bring himself to re-write it and so there he sat. He was going over the interview with PC Blackwell in his mind and trying to second guess the outcome. It was a few days now since it had happened and there was no word from the constabulary. He had taken Birch's email address and had promised an email as soon as he had spoken with his superior. It had sounded as if it would be quite soon. Maybe Celia had made further accusations? Maybe they would come round and haul him to the police station for further questioning? Maybe they would arrest him?

He decided that he would put an end to this ridiculous deliberating and call PC Blackwell for an update. Surely that would be a reasonable thing to do? He would make it sound casual. But then, wasn't that tantamount to admitting that he was worried which would suggest he was guilty. He thought about calling Jonathan to see what his view would be. He could hear Jon's voice in his head; he knew him too well. 'Just sit tight and try not to worry,' he'd say. Huh! Easy for him.

It was torture. He couldn't write. He couldn't do anything. In a desperate and mindless act he found himself calling his publisher.

'Birch, how's it going?'

'Dreadful. Couldn't be worse.' Birch knew only too well this was something you never said to your publisher. If things were going badly you lied. They only want to hear good news.

'But I thought you were about thirty thousand words in?' Henry sounded confused.

'I was. I am.'

'So you're stuck?'

'Probably not. I've just got my ex-wife making my life hell.'

'Are you divorced now?'

'If only. No, it's all proving rather difficult. Make that impossible. I think for the first time in my life I can see why people are driven to murder.'

'Oh Birch, for goodness sake. I thought adversity was good for writers?'

'This is beyond adversity. This is Armageddon!'

Henry laughed. 'Dear chap, I'm taking you out for lunch. Get yourself down to Browns in Covent Garden say by..'

'Ah yes! Funny you should mention that place. I was there just a couple of days ago watching my mother and her first love, fresh from the Mediterranean, practically fawning over each other!'

'Your mother must be... seventy odd? How wonderful for her to have found love again.'

'Don't you start!'

'I hope you behaved yourself.'

'It was difficult but in the end I could see they were both genuine and there was nothing for it but to wish them well. Anyway he's coming for Sunday lunch this weekend. Not so much meet-the-parents, but a sort of meet-the-son-and-his-dysfunctional-family event.'

'Sounds great! Now are you coming this way or not? We can make it the Palm Court instead if you would prefer?'

'You're on. Palm Court it is.'

'Good. One o'clock. Don't be any later than you usually are.'

'Ha ha! And Henry..'

'What?'

'Thanks.'

Jeremy Knight was early for his appointment with Katie and was sizing up number four, Cholmeley Crescent from the outside. He used a pair of binoculars to get a better look at the roof and noticed some loose tiles.

'Hi there.' Katie got out of her car and greeted Jeremy warmly. 'I hope you haven't spotted anything too dreadful,' she said nodding at his binoculars.

'Katie, isn't it?' he shook her hand.

'Yes, I'm Charlie's assistant. I have the keys so...' They went inside.

'Charlie tells me he wants to get four flats in here,' he said peering at his surroundings.

'Yes, that's the plan. Two with two bedrooms on their own floors and then two, one bedroomed flats on the middle floor.'

'And all accessed from the existing stairwell?'

'He wasn't specific on that. I think he'd like your view.'

'Has this been rented out for a long time?'

'We think so,' Katie said feeling inadequate and wishing Charlie was there. She followed him as he walked into the kitchen.

'Yes, well that would account for the problems.'

'Oh. And they are?'

'Well for a start off someone's injected a chemical damp course into this back wall which has just made matters worse. Also the dank smell suggests a lack of ventilation.' He walked quickly through the ground floor checking each room. 'Yes, there aren't any vents down here apart from this one.' He pointed to a vent in the kitchen which had been blocked up with screwed up newspaper.

'Why would anyone do that?' Katie asked pulling the paper out. With it came a lot of black dust. She brushed her hands together to get rid of the dirt.

'Because they're renting and they care more about keeping their heating bills down than the fabric of the building,' he said as if he was personally affronted by this type of behaviour. He heaved open a sash window and chunks of wood flaked off as he did so. 'These

139

windows are wrecked. The woods rotten, see.' He easily shredded some of the frame away in his hand.

Katie pulled a 'help me' face. She knew Charlie was not unduly concerned about the state of the place when he had looked round. She distinctly remembered him using terms like, 'a lick of paint here and there' and 'sprucing it up.'

The surveyor made his way up the stairs and Katie followed him in silence, praying for good news.

'This is the floor where we need to squeeze two one bed flats in. Do you think it's feasible?' she asked and smiled at him as if it might help.

'Mmm..' He looked deep in thought and he wasn't giving anything away yet. Finally he said, 'squeeze is certainly a good word.'

'Perhaps if the living and kitchen area was open plan?' Katie offered remembering Charlie had mentioned this as an option when she had remarked on the lack of space.

'Yes, I think it will have to be. We'll need to try and get all the plumbing on that back wall otherwise it's going to be a lot more work.'

'Do you think we'll need to replace all the windows?'

'It would certainly be advisable. With PVC as well, they make some good imitations these days. It's not listed, is it?'

'No, no it's not.'

'There's one saving grace,' he said smiling at Katie. 'If I was going to live here I'd certainly change the windows,' he said nodding to himself.

'Charlie plans to do the conversion and then sell the flats on.'

'Yes, well he'll be looking for the lowest cost option then, if I know Charlie.'

Katie bit her lip as she followed him up to the top floor. She was walking into one of the bedrooms when he stopped her and looked up. 'Hang on a minute.'

They stood motionless and heard a scratching sound.

'Mice or maybe rats,' Jeremy said in a matter of fact way and Katie shuddered at the thought.

'Are you sure?'

'I'm afraid so. Another typical problem with an older property.'

Katie had been making notes as they walked round and it wasn't a happy story.

'Anything positive about this place?' she asked almost cheekily.

He turned to look at her. 'It's in Highgate village?'

Back in her study at Bisham Gardens, Katie couldn't settle. Her notes from the morning were still in her handbag hidden from sight. She was working on some graphs for Harry, part of a presentation he was giving to Garcia. She glanced at her handbag several times before sighing, closing down the document she was in and retrieving the condemning notes. She started typing them up, trying not to relive their full meaning, but getting it all down in what became a long list. She got to the end, scan read it for typos, there were none, and copied the whole lot into an email she addressed to Charlie.

She bit her lip as she thought about how she would introduce it. 'Oh well, here goes,' she said out loud before typing:

Dear Charlie,
Findings by the surveyor at 4 Cholmeley Crescent below.
Katie

Just thirty seconds later her mobile rang and Charlie's name appeared. Katie laughed nervously as she took the call.

'Charlie, how are you?' she asked in some vain hope he hadn't read the email yet.

'Katie my luv, this isn't good news is it?'

'Well no, but I'm just telling you what Jeremy said.'

'Mmm,' Charlie went quiet and Katie cringed as she waited.

'Surely all the windows don't need replacing! I thought the ones at the back weren't too bad.'

'He said that ideally you would replace them all.'

'Ideally! Ideally we'd knock the whole bloody thing down and start again! Does that man know what the budget would be for bleeding ideally!'

141

Katie stifled a laugh. 'Well, Charlie, perhaps we should meet at the property and you can tell me which of Jeremy's recommendations you'd like me to implement.'

'Yes.' Charlie sounded self-righteous now. 'Yes, that's a good idea. You and me, doll, we'll sort this out.'

'Fine,' Katie said desperately trying not to add any inflection to the word.

There was an awkward pause before Charlie asked, 'you do agree with me, don't you doll?'

# Chapter 15

Katie was ploughing through an old French cookery book getting more and more disheartened.

'What's that you're reading?' Sylvia appeared in the kitchen and sat opposite her.

Katie showed her the cover of the book.

'You're not worried about Sunday, when Jack comes, are you?'

'Well yes, I mean cooking's not my forte but I feel I should make an effort.'

'Don't be silly.' Sylvia took the book away from her as Katie looked bemused.

'But...'

'No buts, I'm cooking on Sunday. Jack's my guest and I have it all planned. It's a chicken dish which is easy to make and can be prepared in advance.'

'Oh,' Katie was smiling. 'Well if you insist.'

'I do and what's more I've enlisted the help of Bethan so you can put your feet up.'

'Bethan? What's your secret?' Katie's expression was quizzical.

Sylvia looked surprised by the question. 'I really don't know. I'm lucky. Perhaps it's because I don't pose any threat.'

'Mmm,' Katie was thoughtful, 'and even more than that you've managed to make friends with her. She clearly likes you a lot. Amazing considering the age gap.'

Sylvia laughed.

'Ooh, no offence,' Katie said not wishing to label this remarkable and spirited woman 'old'.

'None taken. I've never really paid much attention to my age. But you know when I was young I got up to all sorts of mischief behind my mother's back. Well at least I thought it was. But in the end I married Arthur to please her.

'So were you seeing Jack at the time?' Katie asked with raised eyebrows.

'I'm afraid so. Well actually no, I'm not! I was following my heart; I don't regret a moment of it.'

She reached across the table and held both Katie's hands in hers as she asked, 'tell me, does Birch make you very happy?'

Katie felt as if she'd been put on the spot. 'Yes, he does.' Was she saying this because she was talking to his mother? 'It's been a difficult time for my family and I don't know how I'd have got through it if it wasn't for him.' That much was true.

'Well, I'm pleased. It's lovely to have a daughter-in-law that I get on with.'

'Hey, whoa! We're not... and I don't know...'

'No, not yet. Not until the ghastly Celia has been removed from the scene!'

Birch was just getting back in his car when his mobile rang. He had taken to carrying it around with him all the time in the hope that he would hear from PC Blackwell. And now he was looking at the screen and it was the very man he was desperate to hear from. The man who had the power to put him out of his misery. But now the moment of truth had arrived he suddenly felt nauseas.

'Hello, Birch speaking,' he barely got the words out.

'PC Blackwell here. Is that you, Mr Birch?'

He coughed to kick his vocal cords back into action. 'Yes, that's right.'

'Oh good. Now, sorry to disturb you on a Sunday morning but..' his voice was slow and deliberate.

'No problem.' Birch was quick to interject.

'But I have to inform you that the allegation your wife made has been filed as N.F.A..'

Birch froze not knowing what to think.

'By that I mean, no further action,' the PC explained.

'I see,' Birch blinked his eyes wide open. As the tension lifted from his body, a tear surfaced. He swallowed hard. 'So that's it?'

'Yes, indeed.'

'Right.'

There was a lengthy pause while Birch took on the enormity of what this meant.

'So I'll wish you good day,' the PC said.

'You've informed Celia of this decision, I take it?' He blurted out as he imagined her reaction, as she found out she'd been thwarted in her mission to completely humiliate him, and it was not good.

'Of course, yes. That's all been taken care of.'

He was tempted to ask how she'd taken the news but thought better of it. 'Great. Well thanks for phoning.'

'No problem. Have a good day.'

Birch breathed a big sigh of relief and sat motionless in his car for a moment. Thank goodness this terrible episode was over. But then he thought about how cruel Celia had been to him after her sickly sweet smiles. He had to find a way to stop her throwing any more wicked blows at him. But how?

'So you just break the ends off where they naturally snap, like this,' Sylvia took an asparagus spear and broke it. 'This bit is too woody to eat. Now you try.'

Bethan picked up a spear and broke the end off. 'Oh yes, you can feel it, can't you?'

Sylvia smiled at her. 'Now, when you've done that we'll fry them in this griddle pan so they look delicious!'

Bethan laughed. 'I love the way you're so enthusiastic about everything.'

'Well darling, I'll let you into a secret; I haven't always been like this. But since I met up with Jack again...' Sylvia closed her eyes and imagined she was in his arms. 'I've been on cloud nine. I can't tell you how happy I am!'

'Is it the same?' Bethan asked. 'I mean is it the same when you're older and you fall in love and..'

'Actually, I think it's better. When you're my age you appreciate every single day. It all becomes so much more precious.'

'Good to know I've got something to look forward to! My love life's a disaster right now.'

'No, no no! It's not a disaster! You just haven't met anyone good enough for you so far. You'll know when you do. Anyway, you're only seventeen. For goodness sake!'

They laughed together and Birch walked into the kitchen and put some shopping on the table. 'Got everything you asked for,' he said cheerfully and Sylvia immediately noticed the change in him.

She studied his expression. 'Looks like you've offloaded something as well?'

He beamed and simply asked, 'Where's Katie?'

'Mum's in her study,' Bethan turned away from the asparagus to look at him as she replied.

'Thank you,' he said lightly and almost skipped down the hallway.

Jack was twenty minutes late arriving at Bisham Gardens. Sylvia had busied herself in the kitchen.

'Is he always late?' Katie asked sensing her agitation.

'Always.'

'So nothing to worry about,' she smiled but Sylvia was checking the chicken in the oven.

When he finally rang the bell, they looked at each other.

'Shall I go?' Sylvia asked.

'Of course,' Katie said and could not help grinning back at her. Her excitement was infectious and, after Birch's news about Celia, Katie had decided she was going to enjoy today come what may. After all, she'd hardly had to step foot in the kitchen all morning.

Jack appeared and Katie instantly liked him. He went straight over to her, taking in her features.

'Ah, your son is a very lucky man! So lovely to meet you Katie.' He kissed her on both cheeks and handed to her a neat bunch of dark purple tulips.

'Ooh, they are lovely but surely not for me?'

'Of course, you are my host.'

Sylvia was in her element and not at all bothered by the flowers. She led him through to the kitchen.

'Aren't we eating in the dining room?' Katie asked and then she saw that the kitchen table was laid up. 'Oh, I see.'

'This is lovely,' Jack said looking round. 'I'd far rather this than a formal dining room.'

Birch appeared with his new relaxed and jubilant demeanour, 'Jack, good to see you,' he said and shook his hand warmly. 'How's the exhibition going at the R.A.?'

Jack considered Birch and smiled. He flashed a knowing look at Sylvia. 'They tell me it's going well, practically sold out apart from a few tickets during the week. And how are things with you?'

'Good. Excellent, thanks.'

'So I see,' Jack winked at Birch.

Katie and Sylvia looked at each other in amiable silence. Alice and Bethan appeared and despite their casual jeans, both looked radiant.

'My goodness Birch, you are surrounded by beautiful women!' Jack's smile was contagious and the whole family laughed.


Ross was on his way to Elaine's house for lunch when he saw the words 'sale agreed' on the board outside the coffee shop he had set his heart on. Immediately he panicked. He had spoken to the agent only a few days ago and they had only mentioned another interested party. Surely they can't have sold in that short time. His first thought was to ring Harry, but as he hadn't heard back from him following their meeting, he still didn't know for sure if he would invest. Also it was Sunday morning and so it didn't feel like the right thing to do. But he had to do something or he would be delivering bad news to Elaine. They had both got very excited at the prospect of owning the Highgate Village coffee shop and had been madly making plans allowing themselves to get carried away. Elaine was desperate to hand her notice in at Le Bistro; that day could not come soon enough for her. Ross had felt so pleased with himself after the meeting with Harry. Elaine had been praising him to the skies. He felt that he had certainly gone up in her estimation. It was all going so well but now this!

He tried to calm himself and tapped the telephone number on the board of the agents, Knight Frank, into his mobile. It rang nine painful times before it was answered.

'Knight Frank, can I help you?' the voice was brusque but at least someone had answered.

'Er yes, is that John?'

'John speaking. Yes?'

'It's Ross, Ross Kirkdale here. We spoke about the coffee shop in Highgate Village a few days ago.'

'Ah yes, I remember. How can I help you?'

'Well the board says "sale agreed" so I was wondering what was happening. You see I was about to put an offer in myself.'

'Hang on a min. I'll just look it up.'

Ross heard him tapping on a keyboard.

'Yes. Yes, that's right. They've had an offer. A bit below the asking price but the owners are so keen to sell that they accepted it.'

'I see. Well I was going to offer the full asking price,' Ross said bravely whilst praying Harry would come good with the money.

'Right well I suppose we could put that to them. I mean make them aware that you are offering them the full four fifty.'

'Yes, please.' Ross's mind was whirring. Really he was in no position to offer anything but he was desperate.

'So you are definitely making an offer for the full asking price which is four hundred and fifty thousand pounds.'

Put like that it felt more scary. 'Well yes, I mean I was going to make the offer tomorrow, Monday. I mean I didn't realise you worked on Sundays.'

'But you called us?'

'Well yes, because I saw the sale agreed notice.'

'Okay, well do you want me to make the offer today if I can get hold of Mr Gimondo? Or should I wait until tomorrow?'

'Er...' Ross was pacing the pavement as he frantically tried to work out how best to play this. He decided he should at least try to call Harry before making the offer officially. He took a deep breath. 'Listen, I need to speak with my partner so would it be okay if I call you back later today?'

'Yes, that's okay. I'm here until one pm.'

Ross was still outside Fegos and it had started to rain. He found shelter in a doorway and looked for Harry's number in his mobile. He braced himself and made the call.

'Ross? Is that you?'

'Yes Harry, so sorry to call you on a Sunday.'

'Oh that's okay. Just easing myself into the day gently with a large espresso.'

'Right. Great. Erm the thing is..'

'Where are you? That sounds like traffic?'

'I'm actually outside Fegos.'

'But it's raining. Aren't they open?'

'No, they're not.'

'Listen why don't you come round to my flat; it's only ten minutes from there.'

Ross was pleased. It would be easier to talk face to face on such an important matter. 'Yes, I'll do that.'

If Harry was inviting him round to his flat surely he was intending to invest. But then he considered that Harry was so confident he would have no qualms about telling him he'd decided against it. He checked himself; it was important to stay positive. He looked at his watch. He was already overdue at Elaine's house. He would have to phone her and make some excuse as to why he was running late. It would be a white lie and far more preferable to worrying her sick and shattering her dreams.

'This food is delicious!' Jack enthused. 'Thank you so much.' He directed his comment at Katie.

'Oh don't thank me. Sylvia and Bethan were the cooks today.'

'Ah Bethan, you are a chef in the making!'

'Hardly,' Bethan blushed, 'I'm just learning from Sylvia.'

'Well I can report your lessons are going well.'

Bethan smiled and looked pleased with herself.

'That's good because she's going into the cup cake making business soon!' Alice teased her sister.

'I'm intrigued.' Jack turned to Sylvia before adding, 'Can I try one of these cup cakes?'

'Only if you're good,' Sylvia said with a broad grin on her face.

'So what's life like in the Languedoc?' Katie changed the subject away from her daughter who, whilst much improved in temperament, was still overly sensitive at times.

'You live in Pézenas, is that right?' Birch asked.

'Yes, it's a beautiful seventeenth century town full of artisans.'

'Do you get a lot of tourists in the summer?' Katie asked.

'Yes, but that's a good thing. We artists all open up our studios to the public, may even sell a few paintings. And the visitors bring life to the place. It's actually a bit too quiet in the winter. In fact, often I head up to Paris for a month or two. I have a little pied-à-terre there and since I spent quite a bit of time in Le Marais in the sixties I know a few people.'

'Sounds wonderful,' Alice said.

'Yes, well, being a French student,' Sylvia suggested, 'you could always go and spend some time there.'

Alice warmed to the idea. 'I might just do that.' She looked pleased with herself.

'What? Instead of your degree?' Bethan interrupted in her usual insensitive style.

'No! After my degree.' Alice looked annoyed and Katie looked pointedly at both of them sending them a clear message to behave in front of their guest.

'Why not do your degree in Paris?' Jack suggested.

'Brilliant idea!' Sylvia joined in.

Alice giggled. 'Sounds wonderful but I don't think I'd get the funding. But actually the course I'm going for at Nottingham includes a year teaching in a French school.'

'That is good.' Jack tapped the side of his nose with his forefinger as he added, 'keep me posted on that; I have a few contacts.'

'Good God man, you're soaked!' Harry made way for Ross to enter his home.

'Yes, I didn't see the forecast. I was on my way to Elaine's for lunch.'

'Do you not have a car?'

'Er no,' Ross looked embarrassed. 'Not at the moment.'

'I see. Well come in. Do you want me to hang your jacket in the airing cupboard for a bit?'

'Oh that's very kind.' He took the jacket off and handed it to Harry.

'Then I'll make you a coffee and you can tell me what you're doing here when you're supposed to be at Elaine's house.'

'Yes, it won't take long and I have phoned her.'

'Good.'

With a hot drink in his hands and sitting on the black leather sofa, Ross told Harry about the offer already on the table for Fegos.

'So you see I thought I better tell you as, if we were to stand any chance of securing it, we need to move fast.'

'Yes, I can see that.' Harry looked quite disturbed as he pondered the situation.

Ross decided to keep quiet at this point and he hoped with all his being that Harry would agree to put the offer in.

'Do you know, the more I think about this the more I like it. I like the idea of investing in something local and something I would be a part of. I didn't mention this the other day but I've actually come into a bit of money recently. My dear Uncle Jim sadly passed away and much to my surprise I'm the sole beneficiary of his estate.'

Ross's eyes widened but still he said nothing.

'So yes. Yes, I will invest.'

'Oh that's great news Harry. Thank you so much.' He leaned over to shake his hand. 'This means so much to me.'

'Ross, I'm rather chuffed about it myself. Now, as you say, there's no point discussing what we offer, it'll have to be the full asking price to knock these other chaps off the scene. Actually,

Adam, my accountant, said it was a very fair price. He said it was obvious they were keen to sell so let's go with four fifty.'

'I think that's safest.'

'I'll have to get the paperwork drawn up by my solicitor but for now let's just make the offer.'

'Very wise.' Ross was now itching to call John at Knight Frank. 'I could give them a call now from my mobile if you like? Their number's right here,' he said looking at the screen.

'Let's go for it.'

'Your house sounds amazing!' Katie was charmed by this artist who had only compliments to deliver to her and her family. She watched Sylvia as she hung on his every word and could not help being so very pleased for her.

'But three floors, five bedrooms and a wine cellar sounds a lot for one person.' Alice was imagining his elegant nineteenth century town house and was impressed.

'Well you see the first floor is my studio, which leaves just three bedrooms on the top floor.'

'But still room for guests,' Katie pointed out.

'Ah, funny you should say that.' Jack's big brown eyes twinkled in Sylvia's direction.

She bit her lip for a second but then said, 'yes, well I might as well tell you, Jack has asked me to go back to the Languedoc with him and stay for a while and so...'

'A while?' Birch suddenly perked up and looked inquisitive.

'Well yes, a while.'

There was an awkward pause around the table which Jack broke. 'At our time of life you have to grasp opportunities when they come your way, don't you agree?' He was looking at Katie.

She smiled at them both. 'Of course I do. I think it's wonderful that you've found each other after so long. Don't you agree Birch?'

'Absolutely,' he said but with an air of sadness.

'Right now,' Sylvia said decisively as she rose to her feet, 'who's for coffee in the lounge?'

152

'What on earth's going on?' Elaine seemed agitated when she opened her front door to Ross.

'I'm so sorry, darling, but it is good news in the end. Well, sort of.' He went to kiss her but she turned away. 'They've actually started lunch. I'm sorry but Jess and Mum were starving. I've waited though.'

'Oh thank you and I'm so sorry. You know me, I wouldn't be late if it wasn't for a very good reason.'

'Well you'd better come through.' Elaine led him through to the dining room.

Jess was tucking into her pudding. Connie looked up and said, 'Ah Ross, at last. Good to see you.'

'Thank you, yes, sorry I'm late. I'm so pleased you started without me.'

'I would have waited but Jessica's more used to a routine,' Connie explained, 'Now, may I pour you both some wine?'

Ross looked at Elaine. 'I think that would be a good idea, especially after the morning I've had!'

Elaine looked curious now. 'So, what's this sort of good news then?'

Connie passed them their glasses.

'Well..' Ross looked very pleased with himself, he turned to Connie, 'with a bit of luck you're looking at the new owners of Fegos!'

Elaine looked dreamily into his eyes. 'Oh Ross! Oh that's brilliant!'

Connie smiled to herself. 'How marvellous.'

# Chapter 16

Birch opened the front door to a very tall black man who reminded him of Morgan Freeman. He wore a branded blue overall.

'Ah! You must be the CCTV installation guy?'

'The very same. Tiny,' he said as he offered his hand.

'Tiny?' Birch hesitated before shaking it.

'Yes, Tiny's my name.'

'Oh, I'm Birch. Do come in.' He towered above Birch who was a respectable six foot one himself.

'Birch? Are you serious?' Tiny chuckled to himself.

'Totally. Now, how do we do this? I haven't told Katie about it yet but it's okay because she said she'd be out most of the day.'

'Right,' Tiny looked puzzled.

'Katie's my partner.'

Tiny still looked confused. 'You hoping to catch your wife on camera?'

'No, I mean yes. Katie's not my wife, she's my partner. I'm trying to divorce my wife, Celia.'

'Sounds complicated.'

Birch sighed. 'Listen, let's just get on with it, shall we?'

'I can't really remember. It was ages ago and Birch was driving so I wasn't taking much notice.'

Julia tapped her satnav screen and when it didn't respond she growled at it.

'I think we went through the Blackwall tunnel,' Katie said nodding her head. 'In fact I'm sure we did.'

'That makes sense if we're heading for the M20.'

'Good,' Katie sat back looking pleased with herself. She put a hand briefly on Julia's arm, 'thanks for driving me in your car. I didn't want Birch to get suspicious.'

'No, well, it's bad enough that we lied to Jonathan about who we are.'

'Yes, I do feel a bit bad about that but there's no way he'd have agreed to see us if we'd told him.'

'I even lied to Andrew about it.' Julia cringed at the thought. 'I know it sounds silly but to say you're off to Sandgate to meet up with a divorce lawyer who thinks you've just separated from your husband and needs his help, is a bit above and beyond the realms of plausibility.' They both laughed.

They were in a queue of traffic when the satnav burst into life again. 'Oh thank goodness for that,' Julia said relieved. 'It's one thing trying to drive to the back of beyond with some help and entirely another when the blind are leading the blind.'

'It's not quite the back of beyond,' Katie said apologetically. 'Look it says we'll be there by midday.'

'Not if this traffic keeps up we won't.'

Tiny was holding the camera so that it looked down on the path leading up to the front door of 12 Bisham Gardens.

'I can see how being tall is useful in this job,' Birch remarked.

Tiny had heard that comment too many times so ignored him. 'So you see at this angle you've got this area here.' He was waving his free hand around. 'Which will catch anyone approaching the front door.'

'Yes, that's good. That's what I want.' Birch scratched his head. 'But what if she barged into the house?'

'Well we can put a second camera in the hallway. Then your front entrance is covered, but not your back.'

'No, don't worry about that. I really can't see Celia scrambling over that high wall at the bottom of the garden.' He chuckled to himself at the thought of her attempting it.

'She's not into mountaineering then?' Tiny joked.

'No, just trying to ruin my life,' Birch said in a matter of fact tone.

'Women hey.' Tiny was smiling to himself.

'Tell me, do you use these cameras?' Birch asked.

'Me, I've got them everywhere. But for burglars you understand. I ain't got no women trouble.'

'Pleased to hear it.' Birch considered the rocky road ahead to what seemed like the heady goal of divorce and sighed. He considered the set up that Tiny was installing for him. 'What about sound? Will it record anything she says?'

'No, not these cameras. But you could use a recording device on your smart phone.'

'Oh really? Okay I'll look into that.'

'You can download an app for it,' Tiny added helpfully.

'Right, there seems to be an app for everything these days.'

'Yeah, even divorcing your wife.' Tiny chuckled to himself.

Julia parked up outside the address that Jonathan had given them. 'Do you think it will be okay to leave the car here?'

'Looks like it's two hours free parking,' Katie said craning her neck to read the sign.

'Well, we can't really be any longer than that, can we?'

They both felt stiff as they got out of the car. 'How long have we been in there? I can hardly walk!' Julia stumbled onto the pavement before straightening herself out.

'Too long,' Katie said. 'I feel awful you doing all the driving.'

'Oh don't worry,' Julia brushed it off.

'Right, now for the fun bit,' Katie was bracing herself. They linked arms and approached the offices of Bradley Hall & Taylor with a determination to succeed in their mission on this undercover trip.

Katie reminded Julia, 'this Jonathan seems like a bit of a wimp so we shouldn't have any trouble sorting him out.' They both knew that wimp or not they were on very dodgy ground even being there.

The entrance was like a shop and had a window inviting you in for your family law, wills and conveyancing needs. A secretary with a large forehead and spectacles manned the front desk and didn't bother to look up as they approached. Julia cleared her throat and tried to get her attention, 'excuse me?'

The woman looked up at her, her mouth open with concentration. 'Yes?' she asked as if ordinarily you would expect to wait an hour or so before anyone noticed you.

'We're here to see, I mean, I'm here to see Jonathan Taylor.' Julia smiled in a demanding sort of way.

The secretary picked up the phone on her desk. 'Name please?' she asked.

'Julia Redgrove.'

She spoke into the handset. 'Jon, two women to see you.... Yeah, okay.... Yes.' She put the phone down. 'Do you want a coffee?'

'We certainly do! We've just driven all the way from North London,' Katie said not impressed with the client service so far.

'Right.' She looked at them as if they were strange as she walked away.

'Two coffees, milk, no sugar!' Julia called after her and Katie stifled a laugh.

Just then Jonathan appeared. He was tall, slim and grey and his suit looked like it had seen better days.

'Julia Redgrove?'

'That's me,' she shook his hand and threw a sincere smile at him.

'And you've bought a friend I see?' He had the sort of voice that a Radio 4 presenter might have, calm and melodious.

'Yes, Katie Green.' She decided she was going to own up as to who she was from the start, after all it could be pure coincidence.

Jonathan looked quizzically at Katie.

'Right, are we going through to your office?' Julia asked before Jonathan twigged who they really were.

'Er, actually we have a consultation room just here.' He led the way into a small meeting room which was devoid of any character with bare walls and a simple table and chairs. This was certainly not a legal practice that exuded wealth.

Both women offloaded Macs and handbags and made themselves comfortable on one side of the desk. Jonathan looked like he was miles away but sat opposite them and brought a pen out of his pocket.

'So, how can I help you?' He looked tired and they hadn't even told him why they were here yet.

They looked at each other. This is where the charade had to end.

'Actually, we are here on a matter of divorce but not my divorce,' Julia said.

'I see.' Jonathan immediately looked worried.

'Jonathan, we don't want to cause trouble,' Katie began to explain in a pleading sort of way, 'but, in fact we're here to talk about Birch's divorce. You see, from my point of view, it is all proving rather difficult.'

'To put it mildly,' Julia added.

Jonathan put a halting hand up as he said, 'let me stop you right there. You see I simply cannot discuss this matter with you without my client's permission. I mean, does he know you're here?'

'No,' Julia said and immediately regretted it. 'I mean, he doesn't know we're not here, so to speak.'

Everyone looked confused.

'The fact is,' Katie took over, 'Celia's behaviour is beyond unreasonable! Birch is close to being bankrupt and that's making life very difficult for me, financially, I mean. He used to be my lodger and now I'm having to support him!'

'Why don't you ask him to leave and get a new lodger?' Jonathan wasn't going to get drawn into this easily.

The surly girl on reception opened the door and placed two mugs on the table.

'Thank you.' Julia was pleased for the distraction. She gathered her thoughts. 'Listen, you must know that Katie and Birch are now in a relationship. He doesn't have much choice but to live with her, as he doesn't have any money to get his own place, until his house is sold.' She took a sip of her coffee and winced at the bitter taste it left.

Jonathan took a deep breath and sat back in his chair. 'It doesn't alter the fact that I cannot discuss this with you.' He was beginning to feel ruffled.

'Okay, well how about this,' Katie said deciding she wasn't going to give up that easily. 'We will tell you what we think and you don't have to respond. This meeting isn't going to be on record, in fact Birch doesn't ever have to know about it. We just need you to understand that Celia is a dreadful, demanding, ridiculous woman who's spending HIS money like there's no tomorrow and is even refusing to put their house on the market! Last week Birch arranged for three estate agents to go round to give him some valuations and she wouldn't even let them in!'

'Yes, she's changed the locks and Birch can't even get into his own home!' Julia added. 'That can't be right, can it?'

Jonathan was feeling outnumbered and struggling to keep to his original line with these two assertive women. His face showed he had some sympathy for Katie.

'Surely you can talk to us in general about divorce law? I mean, can a woman, any woman, in Celia's position actually refuse to sell the matrimonial home?' Katie raised her eyebrows as she stared at Jonathan.

'No,' Jonathan replied quietly.

'No!' Julia said triumphantly. 'No, she can't! So, what can be done about it?'

Jonathan squirmed in his chair and looked very uncomfortable. 'Well, her husband would have to get a court order.'

'Right, so his lawyer would take the necessary steps to get one of these court orders?' Julia goaded him for more.

Jonathan paused and then chose his words carefully. 'These things take a long time to come to fruition, possibly years.'

Katie showed her frustration and changed tack. 'And what about the money side of things? Is it reasonable that the husband who is now the only breadwinner, is left with nothing?'

'Of course it's not reasonable!' His buttons were pushed now.

The two women stared at him demanding more.

'It is, of course, important that any client keeps his lawyer fully informed and instructs him as to how heavy handed he wants him to get,' Jonathan said straightening his tie.

'Do you know that this all started because Celia had an affair with some chap called Alistair?'

Jonathan did not respond. This was too specific.

Katie realised why. 'Okay, let's put it this way. If a woman, any woman, leaves her husband for another man that she's been having an affair with and later decides she wants her husband back... and is obstructive in him getting a divorce from her...'

'Can he divorce her on the grounds of adultery?' Julia completed the scenario for her friend.

Jonathan pursed his lips. This meeting was becoming more and more galling. He chose his words carefully.

'It is possible to apply for a divorce on the grounds of adultery but there needs to be sufficient proof. If there is no evidence of the affair and the affair has stopped, and the adulterer is now denying that it ever happened, it would be very difficult to find a way forward.'

Julia was itching to say something but Jonathan continued steadfastly saying, 'this route is highly inflammatory and therefore I would always advise any client to take a "no fault" approach.'

'But if the "no fault" approach is not working?' Julia's eyes drilled into his.

'Then an alternative approach may be the only answer.'

'Too right!' Katie looked very pleased with herself. 'Thank you, Jon,' she said and gave him a warm smile. 'I do understand you're in a difficult position and I appreciate you seeing us today.'

Jonathan looked only a little relieved and said with emphasis, 'Not a word of this to Birch!'

Katie emerged from the offices of Bradley, Hall and Taylor feeling like she was one small step closer to helping Birch release himself from the claws of Celia. She looked at Julia and they both looked at her parked car.

160

'Surely we can have lunch first? I'm not sure I can negotiate my limbs back into the car just yet; they haven't forgiven me for this morning!' Julia joked.

'Of course.' Katie agreed. 'As it happens I know a little place near here,' she said playfully.

'Would that be where Birch took you?'

'Yes, but first we need to move this car down to the seafront where it's free parking.'

'Even better.'

They ordered a seafood sharing platter and two glasses of Pinot Grigio and as the sun had come out, making this April day unseasonably warm, they sat outside the hotel looking straight across to the pebbled beach and glistening sea.

Julia raised her glass to her friend. 'Here's to you and Birch, you make a fine couple.'

'I could have picked someone easier, I mean without the excessive baggage.'

'I think everyone's got baggage by the time they get to our age, so unless you fancy a toy boy?'

Katie laughed. 'No, I don't think so.' She contemplated what was ahead of her. 'The big problem, as Jon implied, is proving that Celia had an affair. I mean she's now saying she wants Birch back so presumably she's dumped poor Alistair.'

'I wouldn't assume anything with that one, I mean she might still be seeing him, keeping her options open. She does seem to be pretty crazy.'

'Yes, you're right. But how do we prove it?'

Julia's face lit up. 'I've had an idea. It's brilliant! Why don't we hire a private detective?'

Katie immediately looked concerned. 'I'm not sure..'

'But don't you see? If we can get Alistair to admit his affair, and after all he's probably feeling pretty sore if she has jilted him, then we've got our proof!'

'But hiring a detective? That's the sort of thing they do on the telly.'

'No! My friend Jenny hired a PI because she suspected her husband was cheating on her. He'd started working late a lot more often and got through a whole bottle of aftershave in a month. Anyway she hired this woman to find out the truth and it turned out he was seeing someone from work. Not his PA, not quite so clichéd, but some woman in accounts.'

'How awful! Poor Jenny.'

'Yes, it's not very nice but not knowing the truth must be worse.'

'I suppose so. But wasn't it expensive?'

'I think she paid about eighteen hundred.'

Katie sighed. 'I certainly don't have that kind of money at the moment.'

'I'll lend it to you,' Julia said without hesitation. 'We've got a bit put by, which isn't earning any interest these days, so you might as well have it.'

'Oh no, I couldn't.'

'Yes you can! You can pay me back when it all comes good!'


Birch was in the attic room playing with his new toy. As Alice got home she appeared via the CCTV on his smart phone, firstly at the front door and then in the hallway. She obviously hadn't noticed the cameras. His face lit up. 'This is brilliant!' he said aloud. He'd even seen someone approach the house earlier but then change their mind and disappear. Without this new gadget he would never have known about them.

His writing was going better now. He was clear on his plot line right to the final chapter and he was pleased with how it was taking shape. The lunch with Henry had helped, if only to give him a chance to vent his anger and frustration with Celia, but it was the call from PC Blackwell which had really lifted his spirits.

He looked at his watch. It was ten past five. Katie had been out all day which was unusual but she had said she had a full day with Charlie which he could well believe. Charlie was proving quite a handful and made her other clients seem very straightforward.

Just then she appeared at the door way. Again the cameras weren't noticed. Tiny had done a good job of hiding them whilst still getting a clear picture. She looked exhausted so he decided to go down to greet her.

'Oh that's good timing,' she said putting the kettle on. 'Or did you hear me come in?'

'Well actually,' he said looking sheepish.

'What?' She was curious.

'I've got something to show you.'

# Chapter 17

Fegos was stripped back to bare walls. There were dusty marks where pictures had hung and the floor was marked with ghostly impressions where furniture had once stood. The kitchen at the back was very functional with the shiny new espresso machine standing out and looking odd amongst its sterile neighbours. Ross paced the room as he looked around him. His footsteps were loud and echoed in the empty space. Far from being disheartened by what he saw, he was excited because he could see his vision for this place in its new guise.

Harry arrived at the same time as Elaine. 'We're not late are we?' Harry asked.

'No, Ross is always early.' Elaine smiled at him.

'No bad thing,' Harry said and then looked around him. 'I see they've taken all the chairs.'

'Yes, there's not much to see,' Ross said as he swivelled around, 'except potential.'

'And it needs a good clean,' Elaine added.

'And a lick of paint,' Harry agreed.

'Oh yes!' Ross was looking forward to his new life and had given this venture a lot of thought. 'I think we need a whole new look for this place and a new name: The Friendly Bean!'

Harry and Elaine laughed gently. 'The Friendly Bean?' Harry thought about it. 'Yes, I like it.'

'I think it will work.' Elaine was nodding her head with approval. 'It means we can position the cafe as a good place to meet your friends.'

'And what about the deli?' Harry asked. 'Any thoughts?'

'Well I thought if we position it near the exit so customers will be tempted to buy on the way out,' Ross replied as he walked over to the space he had in mind.

'Makes sense.'

'I've also looked into how we could have our own branded coffee beans and ground coffee which we could sell in the deli section.' Elaine looked pleased with herself.

'That's interesting, so would it be The Friendly Bean coffee?'

'Yes, that's right.'

'That's really good. How do you do that then?' Harry was interested.

'Well there are companies that do what they call white label products which you can put your own brand on and I've been talking to one about it.'

'You two have certainly done your homework. I'm really impressed with all you've put into this so far. And all your ideas. I think I'm going to really enjoy this new venture!'

'We can't thank you enough.' Elaine felt like her dreams were coming true.

'Not at all. I have an eye for a good investment. I'm certainly happy about investing in you two. But are you still okay about leaving your job at Le Bistro? This is going to be quite different for you.'

'Oh yes! I couldn't be more pleased. This is going to be so much better.'

'Oh right.' Harry was slightly surprised but then he said, 'It's a funny place isn't it? I mean fine dining is great but the restaurant always seems to be empty so there's no atmosphere. I suppose as it's so expensive people think of it as a special occasion only place.'

'Yes, well let's just say that the owner and I don't really see eye to eye.' Elaine wondered if she'd said too much even though she had tried to hold back. The truth was that Adrien Moreau drove her crazy.

'Do you know I think I may have met him once.' Harry thought hard and then said, 'is his name Adrien?'

'Yes, that's right.'

'He's based in Paris, isn't he? Oh well, his loss is my gain.' Harry seemed sure that the three of them would make a winning team. 'Well partners,' he looked straight at Ross and Elaine, 'how about a drink at The Flask to celebrate?'

Delores de Clancy sat back on the shabby brown leather sofa in the Ginger & White cafe, tucked away on a side street in Hampstead, looking as vintage as her surroundings. She wore a pretty forties style floral dress patterned with turquoise and burnt sienna and a fox fur stole round her neck complete with head and feet. Her hair, which was unashamedly silver grey on top, was swept back from her forehead and fell in soft black waves down her neck. She sipped a cappuccino and looked like she had all the time in the world.

Katie and Julia walked into the cafe and looked around for the private investigator they had arranged to meet.

'I bet that's her,' Julia said, nodding discreetly in Delores' direction.

'You are joking,' Katie said. 'Is that a dead fox round her shoulders?'

'Oh my God! Well I did tell you she sounded quite eccentric,' Julia muttered under her breath and she smiled across to the woman who gently nodded her head.

Julia walked confidently over to her. 'Delores de Clancy?' she asked, half hoping she was right.

'The very same.' She stood up and shook Julia's hand.

'I'm Julia. This is,' she turned round to find Katie who was hovering uncertainly, 'Katie. Katie Green.'

'Lovely to meet you,' Katie said trying to keep an open mind. She had no idea what a private detective would look like but this woman was nowhere on her scale of possibilities. She wondered how on earth she was discreet in her work. They all sat down.

'Do come closer,' Delores said, 'we don't want any prying ears.' She spoke so quietly that they could only just hear her.

Katie sat on the same sofa as Delores on her right and Julia sat on the other side on an arm chair which she shuffled up as close as the table between them allowed.

'Perfect,' Delores said still with a lowered tone. 'Now, the first thing we're going to do is change all the names of the people involved. So, you are Katrina,' she nodded to Katie, 'and you are Janey,' this time to Julia.

Her listeners were somewhat taken aback but could see the sense in this. 'Okay,' Katie said uncertainly.

'Now, tell me who we need names for.'

'Celia,' Katie whispered.

'Zelda,' Delores said deliberately. Katie and Julia stifled a laugh but nodded in appreciation.

'And?'

'Birch,' Julia whispered.

'Oh! How sad to change such a beautiful name!'

A waitress appeared. Delores cleared her throat and looked pointedly at her.

'Oh, err a latte for me,' Katie said.

'Me too,' Julia added.

Delores was thoughtful. 'Benedict,' she said not inviting comment. 'Very now,' she added looking pleased with herself. 'Anyone else?'

'Alistair.'

'Andrew,' Delores said immediately.

'No, no.' Julia shook her head. 'My husband is Andrew.'

'Ah! Alan, then.'

'How are we going to remember all these?' Katie was concerned.

'I've used the same initial letter in all cases apart from Zelda. You won't forget that one.'

'How do you know she's the troublemaker?' Julia asked.

'Because she was the first name you mentioned and I could tell just by the look on your faces.'

The coffees arrived. As soon at the waiter had gone Delores started hunting around in her large silver sequined handbag. She pulled out a notepad and pen, then a pipe, 'shame I can't smoke in here,' she commented, and finally a pair of black round-rimmed glasses which she popped on the end of her nose. 'Now, tell me all about Zelda.'

The shop window had a sign which said: We speak English – do come in for a chat! Sylvia smiled and went in. As well as lots of adorable pieces for the home there were books in English, and in one corner there was a range of typically British foods including Twining teas, Branston pickle and Marmite.

'Hello,' the woman sat by the till greeted her.

'What a lovely idea!' Sylvia replied.

'Are you on holiday here in Pézenas?'

Sylvia cocked her head, 'sort of, I suppose.'

'Don't tell me, you came here on holiday and it is such a beautiful town you now want to stay.'

Sylvia laughed, 'It's certainly a lovely place and I am having the time of my life.'

'That's wonderful. Where are you staying?'

Sylvia decided to throw caution to the wind, something she seemed to be doing daily at the moment. 'I'm staying with the artist, Jack Harvey. Do you know him?'

'I do indeed. Lucky you! I hear he has a fabulous town house here. Are you a relation?'

'No.' Sylvia was coy now. 'Just a good friend.' She wanted to add lover and the man of her dreams, but she didn't need to.

'I see,' the woman said. Sylvia was wondering if she should read something into that. Did Jack have lots of female friends? Was she just one of many? That was too dreadful a thought. She knew now for certain that she was in love with Jack; probably had never fallen out of love. She distracted herself by perusing the greeting cards and quickly picked one out that showed a dramatic line of London Planes, dark against a blue sky. It was a typical sight along the roadways of the Languedoc. She looked at the back and read: blank for your own greeting. 'I'll take this,' she said to the shop owner. She would send it to Bisham Gardens.

'Thank you. And do pop back if you are missing a good cup of tea!'

'I will, but for now I am immersing myself in all things French.'
She looked at her watch, she just had time to walk back to the
square where she was meeting Jack for lunch.

As she approached Le Jardin, Jack was waving to her and as soon
as he caught her eye he blew her a kiss. Surely her doubts were
unfounded?

'Sylvie! Mon chérie! Where is your shopping? I don't see
anything.'

'I was browsing, there's so much to see here.' She sat down next
to him. 'I bought a card to send to Katie and Birch.'

'That's good but tomorrow we go shopping together and I will
buy you something special.'

Sylvia laughed. 'Okay,' she said lightly. Why not. If he wanted to
spoil her then she would let him.

'Now, the sea bass is very good here...' he said glancing at the
menu but then discarded it. 'Perhaps with some salad?'

'Sounds lovely but not too much for me.'

He looked puzzled. 'Are you feeling okay?'

'Of course, it's just that I've eaten so much lovely food since I've
been here and I don't want to put on weight.'

'Oh please don't become like a French woman, smoking
cigarettes and drinking espressos all day to stay skinny.'

'No, no, I'm not going to those extremes. But you've got to admit
I am surrounded by sylphlike women with their skin tight jeans I
could only dream of getting into.'

'Pah! You are ten times more beautiful, ma belle!'

She looked at him in wonderment. It was not in her make up to
have regrets but just at that moment she had a twinge in her heart
as she thought of all the lost years.

'Now,' he said as if he could read her mind, 'forget all these silly
thoughts and let us order some fine Chablis to go with our fish.'

'Good idea,' she said.

Delores had sat silently, almost in a trance for a couple of minutes
now and her clients were beginning to feel a little uncomfortable.
Perhaps the task they were presenting was too difficult, after all

they didn't know anything about Alistair, not even what he looked like. If Zelda, Katie was beginning to think her name as well as say it, was not in contact with him anymore, how would they track him down?

'Ah!' Delores sprang back to life. Katie jumped.

'Aha! I've got it! You say Zelda frequents The Lemon Tree where your daughter works, Katrina?'

It took Katie a moment to realise that was directed at her. 'Yes, that's right. She seems to go about once a week much to Alice's annoyance.'

'Annabel,' Delores corrected her, nodding her head slowly. 'Your daughter, Annabel.'

Katie was thinking here we go again, this was going to get very confusing.

'Would it be possible for Annabel to alert me the next time Zelda enters The Lemon Tree?'

Katie thought about the implications of getting Alice involved but decided it was worth the risk. 'Yes, I don't see why not.'

'Excellent! Annabel's mobile number, please?'

'Oh yes, I can give you that but you won't phone her until I've had chance to explain who you are and what we're up to will you?'

'Of course, it will be better coming from you.'

'So do you think you will be able to help Ka... Katrina?' Julia asked correcting the name.

'I think it's going to be tricky but not impossible.' A broad grin crept across the investigator's face. 'I think I'm going to like this one!' she added looking delighted at the prospect.

Katie and Julia both wondered if they had crossed into the twilight zone.

Delores stood tall. 'Now I must go, I have somewhere I need to be.'

Katie and Julia got up from their seats to shake her hand.

'Thank you,' Julia said not quite sure what she was thanking her for.

'Thank you, my darlings! À bientôt!' She glided across the room and out onto the street.

Katie and Julia looked at each other and burst out laughing.

'Can you believe she's real?' Julia sank back in her chair.

'I was itching to ask, but somehow daren't, how does she disguise herself when she's out doing surveillance? I mean you'd never forget her!'

'Especially if she started smoking her pipe!'

'Oh gosh yes, I couldn't quite believe that. She's certainly different. Where did you find her?' Katie asked.

'She comes highly recommended,' Julia said and looked like a naughty school girl with her fingers crossed behind her back.

'Well it will be fun finding out.' Katie looked around her. 'I rather like this place.'

'Yes, it's lovely and I'm starving, shall we get some lunch?'

Ross was writing furiously as the others called out one action point after another. The list seemed endless. He didn't allow himself to contemplate how he was going to achieve them all.

'I think that covers most of the points for the set up, branding and refurbishment phase...' he said, taking a sip of his pint and hoping they would be able to leave it there for today.

'But Ross, there's a hell of a lot there. You can't do it all,' Elaine said looking at him wide eyed and tilting her head. She had finished her glass of red wine and had refused a second glass from Harry.

'It's okay, I'll find time.' He knew he was in denial; he would have to work all hours, especially if they were going to launch in the summer which Harry had intimated. What really niggled away was the thought that his relationship with Elaine might suffer when it was going so well to date.

'I take it you've still got your local magazine business?' Harry asked him.

'Well yes, and you know I've been thinking about that, it could be a really useful vehicle for us to promote The Friendly Bean leading up to the launch. It will be part of a big marketing campaign. I was thinking we could use Facebook, too. '

'Great idea but we need to share the workload out somehow,' Harry said as he touched Ross's arm lightly.

'I'll resign from Le Bistro today,' Elaine said as if her mind was made up.

'Isn't that a bit rash?' Ross looked worried. She had protested that she needed the money when he had suggested as much.

'No, it's okay, I've talked it over with my mother and we've found a way of managing.'

'Are you sure?' Ross so wished he could support her himself. It was a huge blow to his ego that he was not in that position.

'Yes, it's fine. Listen, you know I really want to leave the restaurant, and what's more I want to be able to help you, otherwise you're going to drown under all this!'

They all looked down at his list on the pub table. Ross had managed to keep the notepad pristine despite the spillages and lack of beer mats.

Elaine smiled at him. 'I admire you, I really do, for all your plans and innovations; it's all wonderful but let me help,' she pleaded.

'I think it's a good idea,' Harry added. 'I mean I'll do all I can but with my investment business it's not going to be a lot.'

'You could invite all your clients to the launch.' Ross hoped Harry wouldn't take that the wrong way.

The others laughed together and then Harry said, 'Of course I will but listen mate, I think it's a good idea that Elaine resigns..'

'Here here!' She was jubilant.

'You may have to give notice,' Harry pointed out.

'I suspect Adrien will be glad to see the back of me!'

'Okay, I give in,' Ross finished off his pint.

'Now,' Harry said picking up his glass, 'for pity's sake, let's have another drink and relax for half an hour. Think of it as the calm before the storm.'

'I second that,' Elaine said.

'Oh, you've changed your tune,' Ross teased.

'Well, I'm feeling demob happy right now. Who needs a well paid job when you can have all this excitement ahead of you?!'

'Good! Drinks all round.' Harry made his way to the bar.

Katie paced up and down the pavement outside The Lemon Tree. She wasn't sure when Alice's shift was due to finish but was hoping it would be soon. She peered inside but couldn't see her. Suddenly Alice appeared from round the back of the restaurant.

'Mum! What are you doing here?'

'Thought I'd surprise you. Would you like a lift home?'

Alice looked puzzled. 'Yeah okay,' she said vaguely and followed her mother down the street to where her car was parked.

Back at Bisham Gardens Katie put the kettle on. 'Cup of tea?' she asked her daughter.

'You okay, Mum?'

'Fine!' she said a bit too loudly.

'Yes, I'd like some tea.'

'Good I'll make a pot.'

'Oh, is Birch joining us?' Alice asked looking thoughtful.

'No, he's out.'

Alice sat down perplexed but then shook her head and said, 'Celia came in again today.' She took the scrunchy out of her hair and let the auburn waves fall loose. 'Bloody woman!'

'Was she awful to you?' Katie looked uneasy.

'Actually Margaret's been quite good about it. She always tries to make sure I don't have to serve her.'

'That's something. So does she come in on a set day or is it just random?'

Alice considered this. 'You know I hadn't really thought about it but it does seem to be Thursdays. I always seem to work Thursdays. Maybe she does it deliberately.'

Katie put the tea pot on the table with a couple of mugs and a jug of milk.

'Is it ready to pour?' Alice asked.

'Yes, but I'll be mother.' They shared a warm smile.

'Perhaps I should ask Margaret if I can avoid working on Thursdays.'

'No, don't do that,' Katie interjected a bit too quickly.

'What?'

'I've got a favour to ask you,' Katie said looking culpable as she came clean.

'That's what all this is about,' Alice realised as she raised her eyebrows and leaned back in her chair sipping her tea. 'So what's this favour then? Not spying on Celia, surely?!'

Katie took a deep breath. 'Well, it's a long story and probably one you're going to struggle to believe but....'

Elaine was slightly tipsy when she walked into Le Bistro and had a confidence about her that her staff had not seen for a long time.

'Elaine,' Emma called as she approached her. 'I thought it was your day off?'

'It is! Don't worry I haven't come to work.'

'Right.' Emma looked puzzled now.

Elaine whispered into Emma's ear, 'I've just got an important email to send to our esteemed leader,' and then giggled.

'Do you think this is the right time to be doing that sort of thing?'

'Absolutely! Definitely the right time! Oh yes!'

'You're not leaving, are you?' Emma looked worried.

'I am! Hurrah, I'm leaving this dreadful place for good!'

Emma blushed with embarrassment. Elaine was oblivious to the attention she was attracting from a couple of diners as well as the rest of the staff.

'So have you told Adrien?' she asked keeping her voice lowered.

'Not yet, but I'm going up to the office to email him now,' Elaine shouted regardless.

Emma hurried Elaine through the restaurant and up to the office before she could cause any more damage.

'It might be better if you leave by the back door,' Emma suggested as Elaine sat down at her computer to write her letter of resignation.

'Back door? No! Why should I?'

'Well it's always best to do these things amicably isn't it? I mean you wouldn't want to go without being paid, would you?'

Elaine thought about it. 'No, you're right. Bit of a shame but I do need the money.'

'Do you need any help with the letter?'

'Probably,' Elaine said reluctantly. 'Probably best you check it over before I send it. Maybe tone it down a bit.'

'Sounds like a good idea. Do you want me to call Ross and ask him to come over?'

'No! Ross is a good man but right now I think us girls can manage without him.' She gave Emma a hug before sitting back down and switching her computer on.

# Chapter 18

'Blimey O'Riley doll!' Charlie was red in the face. He swung round in his chair and hit his knee on a metal filing cabinet. 'For goodness sake! I can't work in this bleedin' hut!'

Katie said nothing but was mildly amused. They sat in a small Portakabin in the garden of 4 Cholmeley Crescent which had a desk in it for the foreman, a few fold up chairs, a kettle and some rather dubious looking stained mugs sitting on the filing cabinet. Katie had looked at the drinks set up, smelt some milk which was past its sell by date and decided against any ideas of making coffee.

'Where is Andy, anyway? I thought he was meeting us here?' Charlie continued to rant.

'Yes, he text me to say he's running late.'

'Useless man! Sack him! Let's sack him!' He looked over at Katie who had her eyebrows raised now. It had taken her a long time to find anyone to manage this project.

'Sorry doll, I'm sounding off aren't I? But the building regs guy is doing my head in.'

'Why don't we go through his report and create a schedule of works? I don't see any other way round it.' Katie was amazed at how much she had learnt about building and refurbishment in the short time she had been working for Charlie.

'But what about using someone under the competent person scheme? Can't we find anyone who's willing to do the job? Then we can by-pass the whole regulation nightmare.'

'I've tried finding trades under the scheme in this area and I'm drawing a blank,' Katie said patiently despite the fact that they had been through this before, at least once.

'There must be someone, surely doll?'

'There are some and I've spoken to them and they said they couldn't fit the work in until November at the earliest.'

'They're a bloody law unto themselves! November! They're 'avin' a laugh!'

'They're in demand.' Katie couldn't help herself. She expected Charlie to hit back at that but he didn't. His fuse was lengthening at last.

'Right! Well! I suppose we'll have to go through this horrendous report then.' He stood up and picked up a mug from the top of the filing cabinet, sniffed it, pulled a sour face and put it back down again. 'Right!' he took his mobile phone out of his pocket, found Andy's number and called him.

'Andy! You still on this planet? Where are you?'

'Not far off boss. I'll be with you in...'

'Right, well, find the nearest Costa first, in fact there's one at the petrol station on the main road and get the three of us a half decent coffee will you?'

'Yes, boss.'

'The lady drinks a latte, okay mate, and make it quick, we've got a lot of work to do here.'

Katie smiled to herself. You certainly couldn't describe working for Charlie as dull.


Elaine checked her emails. Still no reply from Adrien. Was he just ignoring the fact that she had resigned? She looked at the clock. Five minutes since she'd last looked. Why was the time dragging so? Perhaps because they had only had six covers all lunch time. Then it dawned on her that if she rushed she would be in time to pick Jessica up from school. Why not? Suddenly with a spring in her step she went up to the office to get her jacket and handbag and met Emma on the stairs coming back down. Emma looked worried.

'Going somewhere?' she asked.

'Yes,' Elaine replied deciding to come clean, after all she trusted Emma. 'Yes, I've decided to pick Jess up from school. I'll make it if I rush.'

'Probably not a good idea.' Emma looked awkward.

'It sounds like a good idea to me.' Elaine didn't want to argue with her.

'The thing is...' Emma was fiddling with a gold chain round her neck. 'Adrien said he would be paying us a visit soon.'

'Soon? What does that mean? When did he say that?'

'He rang me yesterday.' She hung her head.

'He rang you? What's all that about?'

Emma looked sheepish, 'I don't know,' she said innocently, 'perhaps because you are leaving?'

'Mmm.' She thought better of her reaction. 'Well, what do I care?'

'I'm sure he was on a train when he rang,' Emma added. He said that thing he says in French, "À toute à l'heure!" I think it means see you later.'

Elaine sighed. 'Oh, bother,' and she turned to go back up to the office. 'Well I hope he does turn up because he hasn't even acknowledged receipt of my email yet!'

'Yes, exactly. When he comes in you can broach the subject.'

'Broach the subject! Confront him more like!'

For once Alice was pleased to see Celia walk into The Lemon Tree but her heart still skipped a beat. She knew what she had to do; Delores had given her strict instructions.

'Act natural,' she'd said. 'Whatever you do, go about your business like it was any other day.'

Alice didn't hesitate to make the necessary call. She went straight out to the yard at the back of the restaurant and found Delores' number. She answered after just two rings.

'Annabel?'

'Yes, it's me. She's here. Zelda, I mean.'

'Great, what's she wearing?'

'Oh, er, a blue dress I think.'

'Okay, well text me more info on that when you've got it. She's got dark hair, hasn't she?'

'Yes.'

'And who's she with?'

Alice had a vague recollection of a man but in the heat of the moment she'd forgotten to look at today's dining companion. 'Let me double check; I think it's a man.'

'Ooh that could be excellent,' she said and paused before she added, 'okay Annabel, check the details and text me. I'll be there in fifteen minutes. Make sure they don't leave.'

Alice was left wondering how she would act natural whilst somehow stopping them from leaving before Delores arrived, but up until now Celia had lingered for ridiculous amounts of time even if she had only ordered coffee. As she walked back into the restaurant she crossed paths with Margaret who looked slightly puzzled but thankfully she was in deep conversation with someone on her mobile.

Celia was sat at one of Alice's tables and she decided that today that would be a distinct advantage. Another table with a couple of business men were beckoning Alice over so she went to them first. The younger of the two looked Alice up and down and had a grin on his face that made him look foolish.

'Can you tell us what the specials are?' the other one asked.

'Seabass with a beure blanc sauce, crushed potatoes and seasonal vegetables,' Alice trotted out without a problem. They both looked disappointed.

'Steak for me. Medium rare.'

'Likewise,' the younger one agreed. 'And two glasses of the Chianti.'

'Thank you,' Alice said and took their menus away efficiently. From the back of the room she eyed up Celia. She was right! It was a man and he was wearing a suit. Celia had a blue top on and white trousers. She needed to amend that information for Delores. She grabbed her mobile and started thumbing out a text, praying that Margaret would not re-appear.

'What you up to?' Rick, a waiter who had started a couple of weeks ago, came up behind her and made her jump.

'Nothing,' she said as she pressed send.

Rick nodded towards Celia's table. 'Looks like you're wanted by your favourite customer.'

Celia was looking daggers at Alice. 'No problem,' she said, and went over to them.

'Oh you are serving me today then.' Celia wore a sarcastic smile.

Alice ignored her. 'What can I get you?' It was easier knowing what fate awaited this witch.

'This menu really isn't inspiring me,' Celia said rather too loudly as she wafted the menu card around before dropping it in a dismissive fashion.

'We have a special which is seabass with a ...'

'That will have to do,' she handed the menu to Alice with a sigh.

Her companion looked kind. He smiled at Alice, 'I'll have the lamb,' he said.

Celia stared at him in disapproval but didn't say anything.

Just then, what looked like a mother and son arrived and they went straight up to Alice. 'Could we have a table by the window please?'

It was Delores' voice and the only table left by the window was the one next to Celia's. 'Of course Madam.' Alice smiled and showed them to their seats. She handed them the two menus she had just collected and noticed that the man with her was about her own age and rather gorgeous. Delores had her hair in a red bob, which if her mother's description was anything to go by must be a wig. She wore a conventional navy blue suit and cut a lean tall figure. She bought out a pair of red rimmed spectacles and popped them on the end of her nose before looking at the menu.

'Any drinks while you're choosing?'

'Sparkling water for me. What would you like, Adam?' She spoke to him like a mother would speak to her son.

Alice liked the name Adam but it occurred to her that his real name might be something quite different.

'I'll have a beer, please. What would you recommend?' As he looked up to her she noticed his blue eyes. His hair was chestnut and cut short and he looked like a man who spent time in the gym.

'The Spitfire is popular,' she said as warmly as she could without making an idiot of herself.

'Excellent,' he replied simply.

Delores, who had her back to Celia, winked at Alice who returned a knowing smile and left her to her earwigging.

'Okay, you've sold it to me, new PVC windows equals double glazing equals much easier to sell on. It also means I'm going way over budget on this one as things stand..'

'Yeah, but PVC is about half the cost of wood.' Andy had already made this point but Charlie seemed to be on an impossible mission to save money.

'Point taken. But if there's anywhere else we can cut corners I'd appreciate it.' Charlie looked expectantly at Katie and Andy.

'There's some ex-display kitchens and bathrooms going cheap I could lay my hands on,' Andy said making a note as he did.

'That's the kind of thing. Let Katie know who the supplier is so she can check them out. Alright doll? And do a bit of compare and contrast as to what we can get on the internet. As long as we've got neutral colours.'

'Okay.' Katie quite enjoyed this aspect of working for Charlie, it was finding reliable tradesmen that always proved to be a nightmare.

'Now we haven't decided who we're getting in for the initial build and damp course but as we're going down the building regs route we're not restricted so who do we reckon?'

'I could check to see if Dave Harrison's available?' Katie had already sounded him out as she had got on well with him on other projects but up until now she hadn't been able to confirm with him as Charlie had had her chasing only those listed on the competent persons' register.

They both looked at Andy. 'Yeah, well I know quite a few who could do it but we're talking short notice I s'pose?'

'Short notice indeed! I need to get this place turned around quick. I've got a lot of money riding on this.' Charlie was agitated at best during this meeting.

'I'll get on to Dave straight away.' Katie made a note.

'Actually a mate of mine is just finishing a job, I might be able to call in a favour.'

'Whatever it takes.' Charlie glared at Andy willing him to get a move on.

Adrien Moreau walked stealthily through his restaurant, throwing a patronising smile at any diners, and approached Elaine who had her back to him.

'Elaine,' he said, as if they'd already greeted each other that day.

She turned and viewed him with suspicion; there was no need for pretence any more. 'Adrien,' she said frowning at him.

'Shall we convene in your office?' He didn't wait for a reply but walked through the door at the back of the restaurant and up the stairs.

Elaine took a deep breath and composed herself. She nodded to Emma who nodded back and then followed him.

He was sat in her chair, adjusting the height which was far too low for his tall and bulky frame, leaving Elaine to stand impotently on the other side of her own desk. She told herself that it was not for much longer and to hold her head high. He was opening a brief case and taking out some papers. She had had enough of his delaying tactics and spoke first.

'I take it you received my letter of resignation that I emailed to you three weeks ago?'

He looked up at her unfazed by her question. 'Yes, I did and that's what I'd like to talk to you about.'

This puzzled Elaine. Why was there a need for a face to face conversation?

'Would you sit down?' he continued calmly.

She felt a little weak at the knees and so, although she would have preferred to stand to give her petite frame some slight advantage over him, she pulled up a chair and perched on the end of it.

'I was disappointed to read your email, after all the autonomy I've given you to run this restaurant for me, after all the time I've invested.'

This was unbelievable. He lived in Paris and only turned up when it suited him and usually to criticise the way she ran the place.

Elaine was dumbstruck and didn't bother to hide it in her face but she heard Ross's voice of reason in her head telling her to keep her cool and not to let him rile her.

'I'm sorry you feel that way and I'm sure as a result you'll be happy for me to leave as soon as possible. That is what I would like.' She stared back at him unblinking.

He sighed and let his eyes drop. 'You leave me in a difficult position. How am I supposed to replace you in a mere four weeks?'

Elaine had checked her contract since she'd written her letter and to her surprise she did only have to give four weeks' notice. She also wondered why he'd wasted three weeks before even highlighting this issue.

'I'm sure you'll find a way,' she said simply unwilling to take on board this problem of his own making.

'Indeed I will take on the role myself until I find the right person even though it's terribly inconvenient with all my other business interests.'

Elaine immediately felt sorry for Emma and the rest of the staff but her concern for Ross was stronger. 'I'm sure you'll do a great job,' she said her voice ringing with insincerity.

'Well if that's your attitude you might as well leave now. I'll pay you for your full notice period.' He looked up at her and foolishly seemed to think he'd scored the winning goal in this game.

'Thank you,' she managed to say calmly despite the glee welling up inside her. She stood up and took her jacket off the coat hanger on the back of the door. When she turned round he looked puzzled.

'I assume you'll need a reference?' he said.

'Oh, no. No reference needed where I'm going.'

'So where is it you're going? I think you should tell me.' At last he was showing some emotion.

'You don't need to worry. I'm not going to any competitor of yours.' She swung her handbag over her shoulder. 'You're looking at one of the joint owners of what was Fegos and will be The Friendly Bean when it re-opens this Autumn.'

'You've bought that dreadful cafe?'

'Oh don't worry,' Elaine said proud of herself for not rising to his bait. 'It won't be dreadful any more. In fact it is going to be just what the villagers of Highgate are looking for.'

Alice was collecting plates from Delores' table when she realised that her partner in crime, Adam, was providing the necessary eyes to compliment Delores' ears.

'Can I get you anything else?' Alice put the dessert menu in front of them both.

'Let me see,' Delores paused. It was a long pause during which they overheard Celia talking to her lunch companion.

'But Alistair I must be true to myself. Angela, my therapist, she's told me time and time again that, when it comes to choosing new partners, we just keep making the same mistakes if we're not careful.' She then leaned in towards him and lowered her voice. All ears were pricked at the next table, as she added, 'I mean you could turn out to be just another Birch. Just imagine. Where would that get us both?'

Alistair looked thoroughly fed up. 'Celia, I do understand and I'm sorry that I've troubled you today. I thought that maybe...'

Celia missed the point entirely and continued, 'You mustn't be sorry. After all there's no reason why we shouldn't be friends.'

'I think there is actually,' he said flashing a derisive smile at her.

'What do you mean? We can't even have a spot of lunch together? Don't be ridiculous. I'm sure we can be grown up about this.'

Margaret appeared at Alice's side. 'Is everything alright here?'

'Wonderful,' Delores said beaming up at her. 'You have an exceptional waitress in this young girl.'

'Oh,' Margaret was taken aback.

'Yes, a coffee, I think, to round things off.' Delores handed her menu back to Alice. 'And for you Adam?'

'Yes, the same, please.'

'Coming up,' Alice said and returned to the kitchen. She half expected Margaret to follow her, but she didn't. In fact when she turned back she saw Delores had engaged her in conversation. She had to smile. This private investigator that her mother had hired was quite something. And as for her male companion, if only circumstances had been different and she hadn't been so nervous about playing out this charade, she might just have allowed herself to flirt with him.

When Alice returned Celia had left the cash on the table to pay for the meal and there was no sign of either of them. Margaret approached. 'They had a falling out and left. I managed to get the bill to them; I think they've left enough?'

'Right.' Alice picked up the cash from the table and handed it to her.

'Thanks and I'm sorry I didn't manage to switch you with another waitress today.'

'Oh that's okay.' Now that she was part of a plan to bring down Celia it was so much easier to cope with her put downs and ridiculous behaviour.

'Has something changed?'

Alice hesitated before she answered. 'Yes, I suppose it has.'

'I'm going to miss you when you go off to university.' It was a rare moment when Margaret let her guard down.

'Thanks Margaret.' Alice looked pleased with herself. 'Now I better get the bill to table nine.' She walked over to her partners in crime and placed the bill on the table.

'Thank you,' Delores said with emphasis.

'Can I get you anything else?' The question was superfluous but was an excuse to take a last look at the gorgeous one.

'I like it here, we must come again mother.' He flashed a smile at Alice.

'We'll see,' she replied.

# Chapter 19

Katie walked along an unfamiliar street, map in hand, getting increasingly frustrated. The Haberdashery cafe on Middle Lane in Crouch End was proving strangely elusive. She had hoped to travel with Julia but a meeting first thing with Charlie scuppered that idea. Delores had said very little on the phone except that a rendezvous of the three of them was advisable as soon as diaries permitted.

Alice had been more forthcoming, filling her in on the conversation she had overheard between Celia and Alistair. What a scoop, they had both agreed. Alice had been quite excited by how it had all gone and even said that she was pleased that she had been instrumental in making it happen. Katie had hugged her as she thanked her and there was a warm feeling between them that had been missing for a long time.

Finally Katie breathed a sigh of relief as the cafe's facade appeared on the other side of the road. It looked a bit drab on the outside and not the sort of place she would choose to come to but maybe that was the point. It would have been so much easier if they could meet at Bisham Gardens but as she still hadn't told Birch what they were up to, that was not a good idea. She felt a twinge of guilt every time she thought of their decision to keep him in the dark.

'It will have its advantages,' Delores had said. 'There is no one more innocent than someone who genuinely doesn't know what's going on.'

That had made Julia laugh but Katie had simply felt even more empathetic towards him. There had been no further contact with his lawyer, Jonathan. Delores had advised that it was for the best until they had got the evidence they needed. Birch had had at least two disheartening telephone conversations with Jonathan and had remarked to Katie about how he was really struggling to make this divorce happen. She had reacted by comforting him and being understanding whilst coming very close to spilling the beans.

Delores was sat in one corner of the cafe wearing a leopard print silk blouse over a denim skirt and had a black beret perched on her greying hair. Today's spectacles were tortoiseshell. Katie felt quite plain in comparison in a pair of jeans and a floral top. She noticed the tables were about half full as she went over to join her. They greeted each other like old friends and Katie felt odd acting out this role but was thankful that the dead fox hadn't made another appearance.

'So good to see you Katrina. Is Janey joining us?'

'Yes, I'm sure she'll be here soon. She was at the...' Katie suddenly remembered protocol; she shouldn't mention the charity shop where Julia worked.

'The gym?' Delores helped her out. 'You just can't keep her out of there, can you?'

'No, she loves it,' Katie joined in hoping that Julia would be looking suitably fit today even though she knew she had a strong dislike for gyms and was happy with her curves.

'Ah, there she is now.' Katie smiled across to her friend and waved her over.

Julia looked as if she was concentrating hard before she opened her mouth. 'Katrina,' she said. It was almost a question.

'Janey, darling. Did you find it okay?'

'Not really but never mind I'm here now.'

'Sorry girls, I know this is a bit out of the way but the latte is particularly good and I know you're both partial.' Delores attracted a waitress and ordered for them all.

'Now,' she said moving closer to them both, 'my recent visit to see Annabel was most beneficial. Quite revealing. You must thank her for me.' She gently placed a hand on Katie's knee.

'Do tell us more,' Julia said, all ears.

'Well, Zelda met Alan for lunch. It was his idea. He misses her. He wants her back but Zelda is not interested. She seems to think that she will return to Benedict one day.'

Katie had a pained expression; this PI certainly lacked sensitivity.

'By the way,' Delores leaned in even further as she continued, 'frightful woman. I was amazed Alan wasn't moved to slap her.'

They both stifled a laugh.

'Yes, Annabel filled me in on that,' Katie nodded to Julia, pleased she'd remembered her daughter's undercover name.

Delores continued, 'She has recruited an interior designer to refurbish the downstairs of their house. She wants to do the upstairs as well but she thinks that Benedict won't be able to afford it at the moment. She was quite frustrated at how little he earns.'

'Huh!' Feelings of anger welled up in Katie every time she heard about this woman's reckless spending.

Delores continued, 'She wants all new furniture and a brand-new state-of-the-art kitchen. She thinks this will mark a new beginning for her and Benedict.'

'But doesn't she realise that Benedict is very happily cohabiting with Katrina?' Julia interjected giving Delores a hard stare.

'I think she's in denial of that fact. The woman is deranged at best.'

'The simple fact is that Benedict is having to pay for all this!' Katie didn't hold back now.

'Yes, I know,' Delores said calmly, trying to diffuse the tension in the room. She laid her palms down flat on the table between them and smiled sweetly before resuming. 'So, we know Zelda's off her rocker and doesn't want Alan back.'

'But surely we're trying to prove she had an affair with Alan, so how does that help us?' Katie asked, exasperated by this whole charade at this point.

'Ah! Now bear with me ladies, I have a plan. The fact is we now know what Alan looks like and this is valuable information.' She picked up her mobile from the table, tapped it a few times and then passed it to Katie and then Julia. The screen showed a shot of a middle-aged man, slim, fair and looking quite disillusioned with life.

'Did you take this?' Katie asked.

'No, my dining companion did. Don't worry they were both unaware of it. Adam, my son, was pretending he wanted a photo of his dear mother.'

'Oh, yes, him.' Katie remembered Alice saying he was about her age and rather nice. 'So he's really your son?' It slipped out. Delores looked ruffled. Katie quickly added, 'Sorry, I know it's not relevant, it's just that....'

Delores puffed up her chest and moved on. 'Now, armed with what I know, I have managed to track down Alan on a dating site, called match.com.'

Katie's eyes widened. 'Really? How did you manage that?'

'I wonder if Zelda met him on there?' Julia asked. 'Could we get the evidence we need from the dating company?'

'No no no! Zelda is not on there. I checked and match.com would consider such information confidential. I've also checked their terms and conditions; we can't go down that route.'

'Okay, so I'm still not sure how all this helps.' Julia was looking perplexed.

'Well, this is where you, Janey could become extremely valuable in our mission.'

Delores continued in steadfast fashion despite the look of horror on Julia's face. 'I would put a profile on match.com, which would have your photograph and a name we would agree.'

'Another name?' Katie considered that this was getting too confusing.

'Hang on a minute!' Julia said alarmed. 'Not wishing to state the obvious, but I am a married woman.'

'Of course you are darling and this will simply be an investigation exercise to get the incriminating information we need. We can't use Katrina for obvious reasons. I'm sorry but you are the perfect person for the job.'

Katie was looking very uncomfortable, 'can't you do it, Delores?'

'Not being funny darling, but even with the best photography in the world, I just know I wouldn't be his type.'

'But what do I tell Andrew?'

'Andrew?' Delores asked.

'Yes, Andrew, my husband.' Julia gave Delores a wide eyed look to emphasise her point.

Delores took a sharp intake of breath. 'Ideally nothing. Does he need to know?'

'Well, yes! No! Oh, I don't know. What do you think Katie?' In her worked up state, Julia forgot to use Katie's undercover name. Delores closed her eyes in dismay.

'It's a tricky one, I mean if you didn't tell him and he found out...' Katie was beginning to wish they hadn't gone down this investigation route at all.

'Exactly,' Julia agreed.

'He won't find out as long as we're careful,' Delores added in a dismissive fashion.

'Well, if I agree to this, and that's if, I will decide whether or not to tell my husband.' Julia lengthened her spine and looked like she meant business.

Delores looked uneasy. 'Okay, well as long as he is sworn to secrecy.' She rolled her eyes.

'Anyway, what makes you think he'll be attracted to me?'

'We'll make sure he is. I know how to work these things, Janey. I have a brilliant photographer and makeover artist who will make you look very alluring.'

'Oh charming!' Julia responded.

'Darling, you are beautiful,' Delores said treading more carefully, 'it's just that to get the best photo we need to get in the professionals.'

Julia tutted with raised eyebrows and Katie continued to look pensive.

'But surely there will be hundreds of women on this dating site?' Katie pointed out.

'Don't worry, I've got experience in this area, we will make sure you tick all Alan's boxes; he won't be able to resist you! Once we have everything set up all we need to do is send him a friendly message. The bait will be laid. Then we wait for him to bite.' Delores was the only one looking excited at the prospect.


Alice had had a difficult shift. The warmer weather was attracting more tourists to London and The Lemon Tree was packed out even between three and five o'clock when there was usually a lull. People were coming in wanting afternoon tea and Margaret was quick to accommodate by buying some cakes in, even though they didn't normally have that sort of thing on the menu. Alice had suggested they use The Cup Cake Company which had pleased Bethan no end and Margaret had been very appreciative when she saw her customers enjoying the cakes.

As well as being busy there had been some demanding diners including an elderly couple who wanted to move tables as they felt they were in a draught at the window, normally a prized position. When Alice pointed out that all tables were taken the man had suggested that she asked a couple at the back of the cafe if they wanted to swap tables. The couple in question had just received an order of food and drinks making this too inconvenient to even contemplate.

'I'm really sorry but that won't be possible as they have their food already,' she explained.

'Well I don't think we'll stay then,' the man said crossing his arms over his beige cardigan which was buttoned up over a large paunch, but making no attempt to leave.

'As you wish,' Alice said glancing at the queue forming at the door. The table would be easily filled in an instant. The couple seemed to realise this and so changed their minds. 'I suppose we'll just have to put up with the draught and hope it doesn't kick off my arthritis in my neck again,' the woman said and they looked up at Alice as if she was somehow responsible for their ailments now.

'Okay, what can I get you?' she said as politely as she could manage under the strain.

At the end of her shift she was looking forward to going home and having a hot bath. She grabbed her raincoat, shouted out a general goodbye to the kitchen and slipped out the back. Out on the High Street she was barely looking where she was going when Adam appeared right in front of her.

'Hello Annabel,' he said cheerily, looking as handsome as she remembered. He wore a black leather jacket over a cobalt blue T-shirt which matched his eyes and a pair of casual jeans so that he wasn't trying too hard.

'Oh hi.' She hadn't meant to sound disappointed to see him but he'd caught her at a bad moment.

'I take it you've been working?'

'Yes, it's been quite a day.' She raised her eyebrows not wanting to elaborate and ran her fingers through her hair pulling it back from her forehead. If only she had washed it this morning.

'How about I buy you a drink?' He was grinning, head cocked to one side. 'You look like you deserve it.'

Alice wondered if that meant she looked as wasted as she felt. 'Oh thanks, that would be great but...'

'But I'm the son of your mum's PI and we have to be careful...'

'Do we?' Alice was too tired for games.

'Listen, just one drink at The Flask and then I'll let you go. How bad can that be?'

Having agreed to a glass of dry white wine, Alice was sat on a comfortable sofa, laden with cushions, as Adam went up to the bar. He came back with a smile on his face and put a bottle of Chablis and two glasses down on the low table in front of them. Well, he certainly had style, Alice thought to herself.

He sat down next to her, poured the wine and chinked her glass. 'Cheers Annabel.'

'Actually my name's Alice,' she now felt moved to tell him, even if it was the wrong thing to do.

'Ah, yes, my mother's always changing names. I prefer Alice, that's good,' he said.

'And you? You're really Adam?'

'I think so,' he said putting on a mock puzzled face. 'It gets confusing. I have to check my own birth certificate sometimes.'

'Ha, ha. So Adam, what do you get up to when you're not trying to remember who you are?'

'I'm a carpenter,' he replied simply. 'I make furniture, basically, high end stuff.'

'That sounds good and who do you work for?'

'Me. I set up a workshop a year ago. Mum helped me out and I now employ a couple of guys.'

'That's impressive.' Alice wasn't lively enough to hide her admiration for him even if this was some sort of date.

'It's hard work and I have to help my Mum out occasionally with her work.'

'Really? Why's that?'

'Well I sort of owe her, I mean if it wasn't for her I wouldn't have been able to set up on my own.'

'Fair enough. She seems nice, your Mum.'

'Nice? I haven't heard her called that before. Strange, eccentric, anything on those lines.'

'She seemed fairly normal to me but then I've only met her in unusual circumstances I suppose.'

'Ah well she was in detective mode. She had a blonde wig on, if I remember correctly, and was dressed conventionally so as not to draw attention. Normally she looks like something out of the 1940s.'

'Vintage! That's very trendy these days.'

'Maybe for someone your age.' He took in her delicate features and allowed his eyes to travel the full length of her long legs.

Alice could feel herself blush which she hated as it always looked awful against her red hair. She took a large glug of wine and was pleased when he said, 'have you worked at The Lemon Tree for long?'

'Since last August. I was going to go to uni but my dad died and everything just fell apart; I couldn't leave my mum.'

'Oh you poor thing, how awful. Was it sudden?'

'Yes, heart attack, in a restaurant. It was too dreadful for words.'

He looked genuinely concerned and tenderly brushed a hair away from her face as a tear appeared. She was moved to tell him more. 'He was the best dad you could ever want but he left us with no money.'

'Right,' Adam said looking concerned.

'So I decided I'd better earn some.'

'That's really noble of you.' He smiled at her and noticed her glass was nearly empty so he poured some more wine into it.

'Not really. My mum's been amazing. She's set herself up as a virtual assistant and she's earning good money now.'

'Phew, that's good.' He looked thoughtful. 'Do you still plan to go to university?'

'Yes, this September. Nottingham. That's the plan. And after the shift I've just had, I can't wait.'

# Chapter 20

Ross decided the anaglypta wallpaper had to go. Especially as it was painted lilac. He did think about covering it with a dark blue to save time and money but Elaine had turned her nose up at that idea.

'But if you're going to be living here,' she had pointed out, 'you need to make it half decent.' She always followed a remark in this vein with a coquettish smile.

He knew, with the amount of work he had to do to get The Friendly Bean up and running, that the flat above would be a place for crashing only. But as his love for Elaine grew he also knew it would be the one place they could be alone together. Much as he was fond of her mother, Connie, and little Jessica, their presence in the same house, was not conducive to romance.

It was Elaine's idea to use the flat as an office as well and they had found a second hand desk in a junk yard and revamped it with a sander and a lick of sage green paint. It actually looked pretty good now. He looked again at the lilac walls and quickly found a scrap of paper and started to make a shopping list to take to the DIY store, starting with white paint, when Elaine appeared holding a bag of groceries.

'Thought I'd get you some tea, milk, bread etc..'

'Oh thanks, that's great. I hadn't really thought about food.' He took her in his arms and held her for a moment kissing her lightly at first and then passionately until she pulled away. 'We've got so much to do!'

He laughed. 'Yes, I know.'

'When are the shop fitters going to arrive to refurbish the cafe? That's the bit I'm really excited about!'

'Yes, it will be great, won't it? But first we need to sign off on the design. Actually I can show you the latest version on my laptop.' He took the computer out of its case and opened it up on the desk.

'I'll just find the latest email from Phil.... Ah yes, this is it.'

The screen was lit up with a vision for The Friendly Bean. The colours were warm with reds and yellows and the floorboards a cherry wood. The seating was provided by long bench tables and there were pendant lights hanging down at different levels across the serving counter which was laden with cakes displayed on stands.

'I like it!' Elaine declared.

'Do you see the black board at the back, that's for us to write the list of food and drinks on offer but this section on the right is for customers to chalk messages for friends.' Ross was really pleased with himself.

'That's brilliant! Well as long as they don't write anything rude!' Elaine pointed out and they laughed together. 'And is that a magazine rack?'

'Yes, that's right, I thought we could get the local media to donate their editions each month.'

'I think it's fabulous; well done you, Ross.'

They both came down to earth with the same thought. 'Is Harry okay with the cost of all this?' Elaine asked.

'Yes, thankfully.' Ross looked concerned. 'When he saw the illustrations he thought it was worth the additional investment. He did point out that he is relying on us to make a success of it.'

'Oh we will, I'm sure we will.' Elaine took another look at the screen before her, eyes full of wonderment. 'With a cafe like this, we'll be full of customers all day!'

They looked straight at each other. Despite the bravado there was a nervousness in the air.

'It's quite a responsibility isn't it?' Ross said, taking her in his arms again.

'We can do it.' Elaine smiled at him. 'We make a good team,' she added, standing as tall and proud as she could.

'We certainly do.'

Julia was staring at Katie's computer screen. 'It makes me feel really strange. I mean, it's a great photo of me, but me on a dating site? For goodness sake. What would Andrew say?'

Katie came and stood beside her and tried to make the whole experience more palatable by saying, 'At least she hasn't used your real name.'

'Yes, now I'm Jennifer! Another new name to remember! And he's no longer got the code name, Alan, but is back to his real name, Alistair! Talk about confusing!'

Katie cringed in sympathy. 'Honestly, I know this is above and beyond the call of duty. I will owe you big time and I'm not sure how I'll repay you but I'll think of something.'

'Oh darling don't be silly. It was my crazy idea to employ Delores in the first place. I might have known it would all get really dodgy.'

Katie looked thoughtful. 'Perhaps we should tell Andrew. Just be straight with him. I'm sure he'll understand and then at least you won't have to worry about him finding out accidentally.'

'Yes, that has been on my mind a lot. Particularly when the photographer was getting me to "look alluring". He even asked me to pout at one point. "Forget it!" I said. I draw the line at pouting.'

Katie couldn't hide her amusement.

'Yes, bloody funny for you, darling,' Julia retorted but then she started laughing too.

'Would it be better if we told him together?' Katie added trying to be helpful.

'But Delores said don't. She seemed very much against the idea.'

'Never mind her, we need to do what's best for your marriage.'

Julia sighed. 'I know but I've been thinking, I mean, how would he find out unless he was searching for women on match.com. It doesn't bear thinking about. And then if he saw me on there where does that leave us?'

'Yes, I take your point. Of course he won't be on there. Your marriage is as rock solid as they come.'

'What makes you think that?'

'Isn't it?' Katie asked a little too alarmingly.

'Yes, I'm sure it is. It's just all this dating malarkey and having to meet with Alistair on some kind of pretend date, I mean I'm dreading it frankly. What if I fluff my lines? Or forget my name?'

Katie put an arm around her friend's shoulder. 'I so wish I could come with you. You know, just sit a few tables away to make sure you're alright.'

Julia's frown changed into a broad smile. 'What are we like? I should just have some fun with this and not take it so seriously. You know I've made up my mind; I am going to tell Andrew. I'll feel much better if he's in on it too.'

'Yes, I think you're right. Anyway, Alistair's not agreed to meet you yet.'

'No, but Delores is hellbent on it happening. I suggested we could perhaps just talk over the phone but she said he's more likely to open up face-to-face.'

'So how are we going to attract him so to speak?'

'Oh haven't you seen her email? She's drafted a message that she wants me to send directly to him.'

'No, I've not seen it.'

'Here,' Julia reached for her mobile from her handbag and scrolled down to find Delores' email. 'Look.' She passed her phone to Katie who read out the proposed wording.

'Hi HandsomeFromHampstead.' Katie stifled a giggle. 'I couldn't help noticing that we're both in NW3..'

'Which I'm not,' Julia interjected. 'So I've got to pretend I live in Hampstead!'

'Yes, but it's probably safer than saying you're from Highgate.' Katie was looking increasingly apologetic but continued.

'...and if I may be so bold, from your profile, you look like just the kind of guy I have been looking for all my life. I'm actually new to on-line dating and feel quite nervous about it all but you have such a kind face that I plucked up courage to send you this message. It's all a bit two dimensional on here, isn't it? I was just wondering if you'd take a risk and meet me for a coffee? You can always run away if you don't like what you see! Hope to hear from you. Jennifer.'

Katie bit her lip. 'Oh dear.' Then laughter burst from her face. 'Oh you've got to admit that's quite funny!'

'Funny! Funny for you! I've got to pretend I'm this dreadful Jennifer woman! From bloody Hampstead!'

'Just a minute.' Katie rushed off down the hallway to the kitchen and returned with a bottle of red wine. 'Here. Take this for you and Andrew this evening. Oil the wheels first.'

'Oh thanks.' She looked at the label. 'Hey this looks like a very fine Rioja. Andrew's favourite.'

'Yes, one of Birch's actually. I'll have to replace it before he notices. Anyway, best of luck, my friend.' Katie hugged her again.

Birch looked up from his laptop and rubbed his forehead with his finger tips, massaging his temples. He looked at his watch; it was later than he had imagined; the writing had flowed today. Quickly he checked his tablet to see if he'd missed anything on the CCTV at the front door. He saw that Bethan was home, but not Katie, and then remembered that she had a late meeting. He considered that Bethan was very likely to be up in her bedroom by now and so it would be safe to venture down to the kitchen.

'Ah, Bethan, hello,' he said as he walked over to the fridge feeling awkward. His mind had been set on a glass of white wine.

'Hi,' she said as she looked up briefly from her mug of tea. She had her laptop opened in front of her at the table and some papers to one side.

'Working?' Birch asked tentatively and decided he would make himself a cup of tea instead.

'Er yes. It's for Carol actually. Just preparing for a meeting we've got tomorrow with Waitrose.'

'Gosh, that sounds exciting.'

'Yeah, I can't believe it.' She looked up from her screen and straight at Birch. 'A lot rests on this. I mean if she manages to get some sort of contract with them she'll be able to take me on full time at the end of my apprenticeship.'

'So I take it Web Dreams don't know about it?'

'No, they just think I've got a meeting with Carol and luckily Matt seems to be off my case now.'

'That's good. He was out of order, I mean the way he treated you.'

'Thanks,' she said looking surprised.

His drink made, Birch hovered. He wasn't keen to go back to work.

'I'm just trying to think of lots of reasons why they should give Carol a chance,' Bethan said looking thoughtful.

'I take it they'll be sampling some of the cup cakes she makes?'

'Yes, Carol's going to bake three different kinds first thing in the morning so they're super fresh. She's doing double chocolate with blood orange, Madagascan vanilla with strawberry and apple with cinnamon.'

'All sound delicious. And very upmarket which the Waitrose customers are, I suspect.'

'Yes, I was thinking that. But there's a lot of students around Bloomsbury; that's the branch we're going to.'

'Mmm, I see what you mean. Of course U.C.L. is all around there. But Bloomsbury is a pretty nice area of London so there'll be lots of rich people too. I mean Waitrose wouldn't have a branch there otherwise.'

'Good point. I was just wondering if we should offer a cheaper alternative for students, you know, part of their essentials range?'

'Mmm,' Birch slid into the chair opposite her as he considered this carefully. 'If I were you I'd go in with one solid proposition. Don't try to be all things to all people. I think it will make you seem more sure of your own product.'

'Right, yes that sounds good.' Bethan scribbled on a notepad as she spoke.

Birch decided he was on to a good thing and continued. 'Anyway the students will probably see the cakes as a way of treating themselves occasionally.'

'Yes, yes that's right.' Bethan continued to make notes before turning her laptop round so Birch could see the screen. 'And do you think they'll like our branding?'

He was looking at The Cup Cake Company website. 'Yes, I do. It's a fine site; I've looked at it before actually. You've done a great job.'

'Oh thanks,' Bethan looked genuinely pleased.

Birch smiled back at her. This was quite a moment. For the first time there was a convivial atmosphere between them. She seemed to appreciate his point of view, even admire it possibly.

'You're welcome,' he said and relaxed back in his chair.

Katie was disappointed to find that only Andy was left at 4 Cholmeley Crescent even though it was getting late in the day. She found him at the back of the house where the damp issue was at its worst.

'I thought you'd agreed with Charlie that the trades would be here until six o'clock during these summer months?'

'Yes, I did but you see it's six o' clock now.'

'Only just!'

'Yeah well Rocket was here earlier but his missus couldn't pick the kid up from school so he had to scoot off early, but normally he could stay 'til six.'

'And the others?' Katie tried not to sound too like a school teacher ticking off her pupil but, having looked around the house, progress was clearly slow.

'Well you see until Rocket's sorted the damp proofing we can't really do much. I mean the windows haven't arrived yet and...'

'What about organising a skip for all the rubbish,' Katie reminded him as she kicked a broken chair that she was sick of the sight of.

'Yeah, I'm on to that.' He sounded unsure.

'So when is it coming?'

'Tuesday next week. Or was it Wednesday? One of those.'

Katie sighed as she shook her head. She decided to try another approach. 'Do you have time for a quick drink at the pub on the corner?'

Andy looked surprised. 'What, you buying?'

'To put together a project plan,' Katie said firmly in case he had got the wrong idea.

'Oh project plan. Yeah, well I've got one of those already actually.' He walked out of the back door into the Portakabin in the garden and Katie followed him.

'Now, where'd I put it.' He started to scan read and discard pieces of paper on his desk, opened a draw and closed it again and then went over to the filing cabinet. He searched through the top draw and scratched his head. 'I'm sure it's in here somewhere.'

'Andy,' Katie drew on every ounce of patience she could find, 'a project plan should be visible at all times. Maybe stuck on the wall. Or at least the first thing you see on your desk.'

'Yeah you're right Mrs. Sorry about this; I'm usually a bit more organised. It's just that with Charlie breathing down me neck and everything.'

'Leave Charlie to me, okay? Now bring your laptop and let's sort this out over a drink.'

Andy looked uncertain but then reading Katie's expression he decided to do as she said. 'Right you are Mrs G.'

'Please! Call me Katie.'


Alice found herself day dreaming about Adam. He had been on her mind a lot since the evening he'd taken her for a drink. 'Table nine are beckoning you over,' Sophie, one of the other waitresses, said softly in her ear.

'Right, yes.' Alice shook herself from her thoughts and hurried over to the young couple who, luckily for her, seemed to be enjoying each other's company enough not to mind her tardiness. The young man had his hands cupped over hers in the centre of the table and was transfixed on her pretty face. He looked up briefly to ask, 'Could we have some coffee and the bill please?'

'Yes, of course.' She smiled at them and felt a tinge of jealousy.

She finished her shift at seven o'clock and as she was picking up her handbag she heard a text coming through. She took a quick look to see who it was and when she saw Adam's name her face lit up.

Hi Gorgeous, how's it going? Just wondering if you're free for dinner this evening? Adam x

Her heart skipped a beat. It had been over a week since he had turned up at the restaurant unexpectedly and she'd convinced herself that even though they had exchanged mobile numbers he wasn't really interested in her. And surely that was for the best. She was going to university in September and needed to stay focused on that. It was important to her. It was what her dad would have wanted. And after the way Jacob, her last boyfriend, had responded to her going away to Nottingham, was it worth the heart ache? Looking at Adam's text now and re-reading it she decided that he was more mature than Jacob, more intelligent even. And he had his own business. And she really fancied him. And she hadn't been out with anyone for ages. What the heck, she would say yes.

Adam was waiting for her just inside the restaurant so that he didn't miss her as she walked through the door.

'Ooh!' Alice exclaimed in surprise.

'Hello!' Adam looked no less beautiful than he had the last time they met.

'Hi,' was all she managed as she looked with wonderment into his eyes.

'You okay with this? Been here before?'

'Oh yes, I like this place. Food's much better than The Lemon Tree. Oops, shouldn't have said that.'

'Don't worry I won't tell.'

A waitress showed them to a table in the corner of the room; Alice quickly realised it was probably the best table in the house.

'Did you book?' she asked.

'Yes, of course. And I asked for a nice romantic table. I told them I was bringing someone rather special.' He was beaming. Alice felt herself blush and hoped her foundation was hiding the redness of her cheeks.

'Are you always this much of a smoothie?' she asked trying to laugh it off even though she was loving the attention he was giving her.

'No,' he said simply. 'But then I've not been out much. The business has been pretty full on. Anyway, what I meant to say was,

I haven't met you before now... but I suppose that gets the smoothie supreme award!'

'Don't worry, I'm not complaining.'

'Good. Now if you can take your eyes off me long enough to look at the menu, shall we order?'

Alice giggled and looked down. Suddenly she wasn't hungry at all. She started looking round the room for something to distract her from his handsome face.

'Chosen already?'

'Oh.. No, erm..' She turned her attention back to it. Her eyes fell on the words 'fish cakes'; that sounded manageable. 'Fish cakes for me.'

Adam looked up. 'Me too. With a side of chunky chips and you can pinch a few.'

Alice smiled.

'How was your shift?' he asked as he searched her expression for clues.

'Oh usual stuff, grumpy oldies in cardigans, American tourists having orgasms over the vintage tea cups...'

He was laughing already. 'And morose mothers trying to get their children to eat salad.'

'Sounds like a bundle of fun.'

Alice waved a dismissive hand in the air. 'You get used to it. Anyway, how about you? Make anything wonderful today?'

'I'm working on a sideboard actually.' You could tell from the way he extended his spine that he was proud of his work. 'It has to be Art Deco style for this woman who's turning her house into a homage to the twenties.'

'Wow, that sounds difficult.'

'I'm working from a picture which isn't too bad but it's getting the grain of the mahogany to look right on the front which is tricky.'

'Do you love what you do?'

'Totally. It's not like work really. Well, apart from the fact that it takes up a lot of my time.'

'Do you spend all day making furniture?'

'I wish. I do most of the time but that's only because I'm avoiding the admin and marketing. That part of the business gets seriously neglected.'

'So how do you get new commissions?'

'Word of mouth, mainly. My mum's quite good at handing my business card out.'

'It sounds great. It's got to be better than working at The Lemon Tree.'

'But that's just a filler for you, until you go to uni, isn't it?'

'Oh yes. I can't wait to leave.'

He looked surprised and slightly miffed. She realised what she'd said and added quickly, 'The Lemon Tree, I mean.' Then she looked straight into his eyes as she took her time to add, 'I'm not so keen to leave Highgate.'

'Well it has its attractions I suppose.' He grinned cheekily and she didn't take her admiring gaze away from him.

A waiter appeared and said, 'Ready to order?' breaking the spell between them.

Adam reeled off their order efficiently and dispatched the waiter. Then he asked Alice, 'so why do you have to go all the way to Nottingham to study French?'

# Chapter 21

Julia waited nervously in the Hampstead coffee shop, Ginger & White. She had already had to pretend to Alistair that she was very familiar with the place, after all she was claiming to live in Hampstead. She didn't order anything deciding it would be better to wait for Alistair to appear. Instead she sat upright and rigid, her heart skipping a beat every time a man entered until she decided that there was no way it could be him. He had said that his profile picture on the website was a good likeness; she only hoped that she wouldn't be a disappointment to him after the elaborate photo shoot Delores had put her through.

She could not help feeling self-conscious about the microphone under her lapel and was convinced that everyone could see it even though Andrew had told her several times that it didn't show. It had been his idea to get there early. He was sat a few tables away from her with a newspaper and a cappuccino and was either doing a good job of acting nonchalant or she had finally put his fears to rest the other evening when she told him about this charade.

It hadn't started well.

'A dating site? Why you? Why not Delores? She's the private investigator whose getting paid handsomely for all this!'

'Yes, I did make that point but Delores felt she didn't look the part. And she does have a point.'

'Look the part! Oh, and you do! What does all that mean?'

'Darling it just means that she thinks I'm attractive. You should be flattered.'

He took a deep breath and gathered his thoughts. 'Of course I think you're beautiful. But surely all the more reason not to put yourself on mix 'n match dot com or whatever it's called.'

Julia laughed and felt relieved that her husband didn't even know the name of the website. 'It's match dot com actually,' she said gently.

'So you're actually on there already?' Andrew looked pained.

'Yes, I am and nothing terrible has happened so far. I haven't sent the message to Alistair yet, though. I wanted you to know first.'

Andrew took a large slug of his Rioja. 'Well if you do meet this Alistair chap I want to be there.'

'Good!' Julia realised that she was genuinely pleased to have an escort on this scary venture. 'Obviously you'll have to sit a few tables away.'

'Yes, of course, I realise that,' he said but even so he looked put out.

'Look, I'm pleased. I mean I wasn't looking forward to doing this on my own and it was so awful you not knowing. You do understand, don't you?'

This time it did look like Alistair. The man scanned the coffee shop obviously looking for someone and Julia raised her hand tentatively and smiled at him. He smiled back. He looked friendly. Actually quite handsome and not scary at all. Phew.

'Jennifer?' he said as he offered his hand.

'Hello Alistair,' she said remembering Delores' brief and shook his hand. Act normal she'd said, whatever it was to be normal in this contrived situation.

'Have you ordered?' he asked before sitting down.

'No, I thought I'd wait for you.'

'Oh have you been here long?'

'No, no, just got here,' she lied.

'Oh good. What can I get you?'

With two coffees on the table between them Julia felt more apprehensive than ever. Could she really go through with this? She lifted her cup to drink and managed to spill some with the first sip. The coffee dribbled down her chin. As she used a paper napkin to dab it away, she noticed Andrew laughing.

'Are you new to on-line dating?' Alistair looked sympathetic.

'Er, yes.' Julia decided that as well as being the truth that would provide a good cover for her nerves.

'Don't worry, I'm new to this too. In fact I was in a relationship until recently but,' Alistair lightly slapped the side of his cheek. 'Sorry, that's a big no no, isn't it? I mean talking about your last relationship?'

That was exactly what she needed him to do. 'Oh I think it's an inevitable subject when you first meet someone.'

He looked surprised. 'Well I'm happy to move on. Now why don't you tell me about you?'

Damn. This wasn't going well. 'What do you want to know?' she asked wondering what her husband was making of all this. His presence was making it doubly awkward now.

'Do you have children? Do you work?'

'Oh well yes, I have a daughter. She's at uni doing website development. And I sit on one of the local charity committees.'

She was sticking to her brief which was not to give too much away and this resulted in her appearing cagey. Alistair looked frustrated. 'Right,' he said but nothing more.

'Sorry I'm not very good at this. You see I've...' she managed to look longingly at him. 'Well, the thing is...'

'Yes?' He was willing her to say more through his widened eyes.

'Oh but you don't want to hear my sad, pathetic story.'

'Well actually I do. Whatever it is. Please Jennifer. I mean how are we to get to know each other if we hold so much back?'

'You're right. Okay, well you must stop me if you've heard enough but here goes.' She took a deep breath. She was in character. Her natural acting talent seemed to have kicked in. Her husband peered over his newspaper and straight at her and she deeply wished he would look away. 'You see I was married and, well, I met this man and I knew it was wrong but he swept me off my feet.'

'Really?' Alistair was already intrigued.

'Yes, and he promised me everything! I really thought that I'd finally met my soul mate. I mean, you must understand, my marriage had gone stale some years ago. We were living together like brother and sister. There was no passion. So when I met Phillip it was so exciting, I felt alive again.'

'Really?' Now he was hooked. 'So what went wrong?'

'You know he never really explained properly. He just dumped me from a great height. I had left my husband for him! Can you believe it?'

'He sounds like an absolute scoundrel. What a way to treat such a.... sensitive and... attractive woman, if I may say so?' He was obviously feeling her pain. Had she overdone it?

From a few metres away Andrew cleared his throat loudly and rustled his paper to the table as he glared at his wife.

'So you see I find myself single for the first time in many years,' Julia managed to look coy while she prayed her husband would forgive her.

'Yes...' Alistair was thoughtful.

Julia waited. Had she done enough to get him to open up? Delores seemed to think that he would. She willed him to spill his story as she fingered her lapel making sure the microphone was still in place. It was.

'It's just that...,' he started but stopped himself.

'Please, do tell me.' Julia had no trouble sounding genuine as she said that. This could be it. What they had all been working towards. His confession.

'My experience as it happens has been...' His mobile rang and he took it out of his top pocket. 'Sorry about this.' He looked at the screen and then turned the phone off. 'There, that won't disturb us again,' he said smiling at her. He noticed she'd finished her cappuccino. 'Do you want another drink?'

'No, no,' she lied hoping he would continue his story.

'Well I think I'm going to have one,' he said.

The disappointment must have shown in her face. 'But perhaps in a minute,' he added, 'now where were we?'

'You said something about your experience...'

'Oh yes! Of course. You're a good listener. It's so refreshing to meet someone who actually listens to what you say, don't you think?'

'Essential, I would say, for a good relationship.'

He looked adoringly into her eyes and Julia was very pleased at that moment that Andrew could only see her face and not Alistair's.

'So?' She could not help but prompt him.

'Yes, well, what I was going to say was that my experience was very similar to yours. It's an amazing coincidence, don't you think?'

'Amazing! Goodness, I find it hard to believe. Do tell me more.'

'Well I don't want to bore you with all the details but..'

'Oh you won't bore me. Never.'

'You're very kind. Anyway, needless to say I met a woman who I thought was the answer to my dreams. She was very unhappy in her own marriage to a well-known author, would you believe?'

'Oh, who's that?' she asked trying to sound casual.

'I shouldn't say really.'

'Does it matter? I mean after the way she's treated you.'

'Yes, you're right. His name is Birch. He refuses to use his first name.'

'Really? Do you know what it is?'

'No, she didn't tell me and I didn't want to know.'

'Of course not. So how did you meet... sorry, I didn't catch her name?'

'Oh I would rather not say.'

'Of course, I'm sorry, you must only tell me what you feel comfortable with.' She heard herself say the words; they were the words she needed to say to appear normal to him but equally she desperately needed him to say Celia's name.

'She taught my son violin actually.'

'Ah, a music teacher.'

'Yes, at first I thought she was everything I wanted from a woman and she was desperately unhappy in her marriage so...'

'One thing led to another,' Julia added trying to be helpful.

'Yes, we were together for over a year. She kept saying she would leave her husband, you know, getting my hopes up, and then one evening she came over to my place and announced she'd left him. She had a suitcase with her, would you believe it?'

'So she expected to move in with you?'

'Oh yes! She said she couldn't live with Birch a moment longer. It turned out that she hadn't actually told him about us! He rang her mobile the next morning wondering where she was and why she hadn't been home that night!'

'Really, so this woman, left her husband for you but didn't tell him? She sounds incredible.'

'Oh, let me tell you, it gets worse!'

'Really?!'

'Oh but first I'm going to get another coffee. Are you sure you don't want one?'

'Actually I would like another one, please.' It would give her a couple of minutes on her own to gather her thoughts.

'No trouble,' he said, a glint in his eye as he stood up.

As he went up to the counter to get more drinks, she was racking her brain trying to work out how she would tease her name out of him. Just one word she absolutely needed to hear. Celia.

He returned with the drinks and sat opposite her looking very pleased with himself. 'You know you have lovely eyes. That's what I first noticed about you in your photograph.'

Julia looked sheepish and tried to hide how worried she was that she was going to fail in her mission.

'It's a great photo, I mean you look lovely too in the flesh but that photo really does you justice. You must be very photogenic.'

Julia only managed an embarrassed smile. How was she going to get him back on the vital subject. She took a conservative sip of her drink before saying, 'anyway, you were telling me about this dreadful woman.' She saw his face drop. He looked genuinely hurt. 'Oh, I'm really sorry, this must be painful for you. Perhaps you're not fully over her?'

Alistair looked flustered. 'No! No, I am! I mean I want to be! And I'm sure meeting you is just the distraction...' He shook his head admonishing himself. 'Sorry, sorry, I didn't mean that to come out quite like that. Oh I'm making a mess of this now, aren't I?'

'No, not at all.' Julia tried to calm him down. 'It takes time for the wounds to heal,' she said soothingly as she remembered he had had lunch with Celia only a few weeks ago.

'Yes, it certainly does. I mean she rang me only recently wanting to see me. I fell for it again! How stupid am I? And she was spouting some rubbish about us remaining just good friends! Pah! I told her! "Listen Celia, if you think I can just forget about the last year..."'

He'd said it! Hoorah! He'd said her name.

'...and turn this into a platonic relationship!'

'Of course.' Julia tried to look sympathetic and hide her joy. She decided not to point out that he'd said her name. Perhaps he hadn't realised. It didn't matter. He had finally said her name. He'd also said Birch's name. Surely that was enough to provide the damning evidence that Katie needed.

'Oh, I've said too much haven't I?' Alistair looked down into his cup.

'Not at all. As you said earlier, how are we to get to know each other if we don't open up?'

'You're very kind, Jennifer, but I feel as though...'

'Alistair, this is our first date. It's just coffee. Don't worry.'

'So you've not been put off?'

Julia noticed the urgent expression on her husband's face. As he caught her eye he pointed to his watch in an exaggerated fashion. The cafe was beginning to fill up with lunch time trade. The one thing Delores hadn't briefed her on was how to get rid of him at the end. Julia looked at her watch and feigned astonishment. 'Gosh is that time. I'm meeting my daughter for lunch actually. She's back from university for a few days.'

'Isn't it term time?'

'Something to do with a thesis. Working on their own. Who knows? I don't argue with her!'

'No, of course not. Well maybe I'll meet her one day?' He looked hopeful.

'Yes!' she said sounding more alarmed than convincing.

'So shall we meet again soon?' He sounded desperate now. She felt sorry for him. How would she get away without saying yes?

'Well you've got my number, why don't you give me a call?' It was a fake number that Delores had told her to use. Up until this point all contact had been through the dating website.

'Oh yes, of course,' he said looking doubtful.

She stood up and he stood too looking expectant. How did they part? She noticed her husband staring at her unhelpfully. They walked out of Ginger & White together leaving Andrew behind. Julia thought on her feet. 'Which way are you going?' she asked.

'Up towards the common,' he said and thankfully and waved an arm to the left.

'Ah, well I'm going this way,' she said indicating to the right.

'Well, it's been lovely to meet you, Jennifer,' he said sincerely, his hand on her elbow. He went to kiss her and she turned her head, offering her cheek and then quickly stepped back.

'Yes, it's been good to put a face to a name.' She thought how stupid that sounded as she said it.

'I'll call soon.' He turned to go. She turned too and wandered down a narrow street, not knowing where she was going. She didn't care. It was all over. Before she knew it her husband was at her side.

'Alright?' he asked. His face showed hurt. He stopped her and turned her towards him.

'Careful!' she looked up the street to make sure Alistair had gone. She couldn't see him.

'He's gone. Don't worry I checked.' He looked at his wife. 'You look pale, are you okay?'

'A bit jittery. That was pretty hairy.'

'Yes, it took a lot longer than I thought it would.'

'Alright for you,' she said, 'you just had to sit there.'

'And watch my wife being chatted up by some bloke on a dating site. It was bloody awful.'

'Oh for goodness sake. I was the one who had to get him to say her name.'

'And did you?'

'Yes, I did. But it wasn't easy.'

'Right.' He lowered his eyes. 'Is that it then?'

'Yes, that's it. Mission accomplished. Now are you going to take your wife out for lunch or what?'

# Chapter 22

Bethan's face lit up when she read Carol's text message. It read simply:

*Hi Bethan, must see you asap. It's good news! C x*

'Heard from Harry, have you?' Matt said in a patronising tone as he stood over her desk.

'No, no it's not that.' She was pretty sure he knew she wasn't seeing Harry anymore. Certainly the rest of the agency had cottoned on. He was obviously being deliberately nasty.

'Oh, moved on already have you? Working your way through all the unsuspecting males in Highgate, I suppose?'

'I'm not seeing anyone if you must know. Not that it's any of your business. Did you want something work-related or did you just come over to be spiteful?' She gave him a hard stare.

'You two are still getting on, I take it?' Paul appeared from nowhere.

'Of course,' Matt smiled unconvincingly.

'Good. I don't want to hear otherwise.'

Bethan kept a serious frown. Matt had left her alone of late and she had thought that she would be able to make it to the end of her apprenticeship year. Paul looked at her questioningly and then turned to Matt. 'You must have a lot of work to be getting on with,' he said pointedly.

'Yes, of course,' Matt replied and scurried back to his desk.

Bethan gazed at her computer screen, willing Paul to leave her alone.

'I hear you've been into Waitrose with Mrs Cup Cake. How did it go?'

'It went well, thank you,' she said not wishing to go into any detail.

'Good, well perhaps you could keep me posted on any outcomes?'

'Of course,' Bethan said. She desperately wanted the outcome to be that Carol offered her a job and she could leave Web Dreams.

'Good,' he said and he hesitated before he moved away.

Left alone Bethan went straight to her mobile to reply to Carol's text. The sooner she saw Carol, the better.

Katie put her mobile down on the desk and ran her fingers through her hair. It was the fifth call she'd made in a row, chasing the various trades working on 4 Cholmeley Crescent. Each time she had been disappointed with pathetic excuses ranging from 'the wrong kind of rain' to 'Rocket's knee's givin' him gyp.' Her notepad was covered in ink but looking at it now the general conclusion was that progress was slow. That's all Charlie would be interested in. He would not suffer all the endless drivel she had just put herself through. As if he could read her mind a call came up from the man himself.

'Hello Charlie.' She didn't try to hide the deflated feeling she had.

'Alright Doll? he asked sounding concerned.

'Not really. I've just been chasing updates on Cholmeley and it's been like pulling teeth.'

'They're little buggers those trades. So go on then give me the low down, what progress have we actually made? There must be some, it's been weeks?'

'To be honest Charlie, without actually going there and seeing for yourself you can't be sure. Last time I went I asked Andy for the umpteenth time why he hadn't organised a skip to get rid of the rubbish and he came up with something on the lines of a general shortage in the area.'

'God give me strength! Do you think it's him? Is it Andy that's the problem? I mean should we just sack him and find someone better?'

'It's not easy.' Katie didn't relish the thought of finding someone new. 'Most local foremen are tied up in the summer months. But you know I am beginning to wonder what he does all day.'

'Probably working a couple more developments and ours is bottom of the pile. You know what I think?'

'What's that?' Katie braced herself. That sort of question from him usually spelt trouble.

'I think we should sack Andy and you should project manage the whole kit and caboodle.'

Katie's eyes widened in disbelief. She imagined herself stuck in the Portakabin in the back garden of number four, arguing with Rocket all day. Despite her stunned silence Charlie continued, 'With what I save from Andy's wages I could afford to up your hours quite a bit. Do you have the capacity for that?'

At least he'd asked the question. 'I could do some more hours but I need to be based in my office, Charlie. I can't be on site all the time.'

'No, no, I don't expect that. You could just pop round each day to make sure they're all doing their bit. Only I've heard they're all a bit scared of you,' he added carefully.

'I find that hard to believe, having just spoken to most of them. They're just full of excuses.'

'Right, I tell you what, send them all an email asking them to meet us both at number four tomorrow, say about two-ish? Don't bother inviting Andy. Tell 'em it's a progress meeting and we want updates from all of them.'

'Okay, that might help as long as you are there.'

'Yes, of course. And also tell them that if they want their invoices paying they'll be there.'

'That will work.'

'Yeah, so is two o'clock okay with you?'

Katie checked her paper diary on her desk. 'Yes, that's fine.'

'Excellent.'

After putting her phone down she tore off the sheet of notes from all the phone calls she'd made earlier, screwed it up and threw in the bin.

Birch popped his head around the door. 'Busy day?' he asked.

She turned to face him. 'Challenging,' she said before breaking into a smile.

'Yes, you look like you need a break. How does tea on the patio sound? I'll put the umbrella up, that sun's really strong today.'

'It sounds lovely.'

Bethan felt like she was breaking free as she walked out of the offices of Web Dreams in the direction of Carol's home. She had told the colleagues that happened to be around at that moment, that she was taking a lunch break and they had hardly reacted. Kelvin had looked up from his screen, still deep in thought and said vaguely, 'right...'

It took just twenty minutes, in flat pumps and with a spring in her step, to reach Carol's house and she grew more excited as she contemplated what the good news might be. She arrived slightly out of breath, with flushed pink cheeks and went round to the back door as previously instructed.

'Come in,' Carol shouted from inside. The door of the garden room was already open and Bethan could see her bringing a tray of fresh cakes out of the oven. The air was filled with a delicious fragrance of chocolate and orange. Carol's home was always so inviting.

'You look well. Did you walk?' Carol released one hand from its oven glove and lifted each cake carefully, placing it on a cooling rack.

'Yes and I've got flat shoes on today,' she said lifting one foot high, 'so I could be quick.'

'I take it you haven't got long then?'

'Well, I didn't tell them I was coming here. Just said I was taking a lunch break.'

'Which you're entitled to, surely?'

'I suppose so but most don't seem to.'

'Have you eaten?'

'No, but don't worry, I'll be fine.'

'How about a cup of tea and a cup cake?'

'Oh go on then. You've twisted my arm,' Bethan smiled and settled herself down at the kitchen table.

'Good!'

'But first you must tell me. What's the news from Waitrose?'

'Oh God, yes, of course! Well, they said they were very impressed with both of us and the product and..'

'Really?'

'Yes, and they want us to start supplying the Bloomsbury store from next week!'

'That's fantastic! How many do they want?'

'They've asked for a hundred a day to be delivered fresh each morning, four in each box, for the first week and they will see how it goes and amend the order accordingly.'

'That sounds like a lot of baking. And have you sourced the packaging yet?'

'No! I've really got my work cut out to get this out on time.'

'I could help you, after work and weekends.'

'Oh Bethan that would be fantastic but I don't want you run ragged.'

'I don't care! I'm so happy! This is the best news!'

'Oh look at you!' Carol went over to her and hugged her. She eased back. 'Not very professional, I know, but hey we're entitled to celebrate, aren't we?'

'Definitely!' Bethan started laughing as Carol went to put the kettle on and find some mugs.

'This really means a lot to you, doesn't it?' Carol said as she turned back to Bethan.

'Well yes, but I was just thinking.... stuff.... Harry!'

'Who's he?'

'Oh just some bloke.'

'Obviously not worth worrying about,' Carol said winking at Bethan.

'Exactly.'

With the tea made they sat devouring the delicious cup cakes that had just come out of the oven. 'They should cool a bit more really but...'

'They smell too good,' Bethan said eyes wide on the chocolate orange delights.

'Anyway, let me tell you what else Hans from Waitrose said.'

'Yes, tell me everything.'

'He was really impressed with your promotional ideas for point of sale and on their website.'

'Oh good.' Bethan was really chuffed.

'And he said he'd like you to work with their e-commerce team to promote the new line in their weekly email newsletter.'

'Wow, that sounds fantastic.'

'Yes, but how are we going to play this? I mean you're tied to Web Dreams until November aren't you?'

Bethan sighed, 'Oh you know I'm so fed up with the way Matt treats me, I really feel like walking out.'

'Ooh, no! Don't do that. You'll get me into trouble.'

'But the thing is, Matt is so horrible to me, if I told Paul then he'd probably say that one of us has to go. He's as good as said that already. And you know it will definitely be me. I mean, Matt might be a twat but Paul really rates him and I'm just the lowly apprentice girl.'

Carol frowned with concern. Eventually she said, 'Well okay, let's see how the trial goes and if Waitrose want to roll out I could definitely take you on.'

'That would be so good!'

'More fool Paul for not appreciating your talents!'

'Exactly!'

Carol chinked Bethan's mug of tea. 'We should be drinking Champagne really, not Twinings!'

'I'm happy with tea for now but when Waitrose roll out..' Bethan was beaming.

'When! I like your positivity.'

They laughed together and Carol said, 'I think we make an excellent team, you and me.'

Bethan suddenly thought of her father, he would have been so proud of her, and a tear appeared in the corner of her eye.

Carol stopped laughing and reached over to Bethan. 'Are you okay?'

'I was just thinking about my dad. It's silly...' She tried to wipe the tears away but they kept coming. 'Really I'm all right. It's just in moments when I feel happy I remember he's dead and I'm never going to laugh with him again.'

Carol squeezed her hand. 'He'd be pleased for you. I'm sure of that.'

Julia poured out two glasses of wine and handed one to Katie. 'Shall we sit here?' she asked nodding at her kitchen table. 'Andrew's in the living room and even though he's in on all this now he can be so childish about it at times.'

'Poor Andrew having to sit through your "date" with Zelda's jilted one.'

'Poor me actually!'

'Yes, of course. Was it too dreadful? I'm so sorry you had to do it.'

'Actually when I look back on it now I can laugh about it. I mean he was so easy to wind up!'

'Really? I thought he looked quite nice on his profile.'

'Yes, he is! I must admit when he walked into the cafe I was actually quite pleased that he looked okay, you know quite friendly. I mean from what we know of Zelda he could have been a weirdo!'

'I wonder what Andrew made of him?'

'We didn't go there. After it was all over he took me out for lunch, a nice little gastro-pub in Muswell Hill.'

'How lovely! Was he trying to woo you back?!'

They were both laughing as Andrew popped his head round the door. 'Joke at my expense by any chance?'

Katie got up and went over to hug him. 'What's that for?' he said looking puzzled.

'That's a big thank you for letting Julia go on a pretend date to gather the vital evidence we need.'

'Mm,' Andrew flicked his eyebrows heavenwards. 'I see you're tucking into a good bottle of Rioja?'

'Would you like a glass?' Katie offered.

'Yes, actually, I would.'

'Oh all right.' His wife begrudgingly reached for another glass. 'But you're not staying. I told you this is a girly evening.'

Andrew rolled his eyes. 'Yes dear, you made that very clear earlier. I shall go and watch the blokey football on the telly,' he said disappearing with his wine.

'See what I mean!' Julia turned to her friend.

'Oh he's being pretty stoic really. You can't expect any more than that.'

'I know, I should be more understanding. If the shoe was on the other foot...'

'Exactly. Anyway getting back to the dirty deed, is the recording all right? And more to the point did he spill the beans?'

'Yes and yes! He mentioned Birch by name and eventually, even after he said he didn't want to.... it was in a moment of being flustered, wound up by yours truly of course, he said Celia! I thought alleluia!'

'Oh well done!'

'Anyway, I've sent the recording to Delores. She rang me to congratulate me on a sterling job!'

'Did you listen to it first?'

'Yes, I did and it made me cringe! I hate hearing my recorded voice at the best of times but this was excruciating!'

'Oh how funny,' Katie chuckled to herself. 'I'd love to hear it.'

'Too bad, it's gone.'

'So what's happened about your profile on match dot com?'

'Well, Andrew wanted me to take it down straight away when we got home but I emailed Delores and she said I should keep it there just a little bit longer until the evidence has been presented to Zelda.'

'Oh, so are you getting many messages from admirers?'

'I daren't look! Andrew has forbidden me.'

'Spoil sport! After all you went through for that photographer, you might at least have a bit of fun seeing how many David Beckham look-a-likes you get!'

'Now you're just being silly!' Julia giggled. 'Would be fun though. Naughty but fun. More wine?'

Birch found himself looking for distractions. With Katie out for the evening there was no excuse not to work on into the night. The deadline for his next book was looming, something Henry had reminded him of earlier today. He heard the house phone ringing and decided he'd answer it in case it was important even though it was most likely to be Charlie or an Indian call centre. Rushing down the stairs he reached the hallway just before the answer machine kicked in. The caller display said international and he rolled his eyes expecting a nuisance call, so was more than pleased to hear his mother's voice.

'Mum! It's so good to hear from you!'

'It's good to hear from you too. I'm getting quite homesick out here.'

'So you're still at Jack's?'

'Yes, yes, as I said in my email, it's a wonderful townhouse he's got in Pezenas which is just the most delightful place.'

'And how's it going between you two?'

'It's amazing. I still have to pinch myself when I wake up in the morning. But I am missing good old Blighty.'

'You must be. It's been a while. Are there many ex pats out there?'

'Yes, lots actually. In fact, I've made a few friends which, of course, helps. But when they ask me how long I'm staying I don't know what to say.'

'What does Jack say?'

'Oh Jack is very zen, live in the moment and don't even think about tomorrow.'

'Probably a good way to be.'

'Yes, well I've hinted that I want to go home soon. He just smiles and says nothing.'

'Perhaps you could persuade him to come with you? We're having a good summer here. It was about twenty-five degrees today.'

'That sounds wonderful. It's more like thirty-five here! You just can't do anything after midday except sit in a dark room, shutters all closed up!'

'Yes, that sounds too hot.'

'That's a good idea of yours, I'll ask him. He'll be encouraged by your weather report. Anyway, how's Katie?'

'She's good. She's getting lots of work from Charlie which is good news even if he is a bit of a handful at times.'

'He sounds like good fun, Charlie. Far better to be working for him than some boring type. And what about Alice and Bethan?'

'How would I know? Except to say I think Bethan is finally beginning to accept me. I would go as far as saying she doesn't totally hate me these days.'

Sylvia laughed, 'Does that mean she might actually like you a bit?'

'Steady on mother. No, I was helping her prepare for a meeting at Waitrose she had with the cup cake woman.'

'Oh yes, I remember Bethan mentioning that. Do you know how it went?'

'She said it went well but they're waiting to hear from them.'

'Will you give her my email address? Ask her to give me an update on her cup cake making.'

'Yes, I'm sure she'll like that. She was really taken with you.'

There was a thoughtful pause before Sylvia said, 'and dare I ask how the divorce is going?'

Birch sighed loud enough for his mother to hear.

'That good, hey?' Sylvia said gently.

'Well actually Jonathan's talking about a more confrontational approach; he seems to think it's going to be the only way now.'

'Good,' Sylvia said simply.

'I do have CCTV set up at the front door and in the hallway.'

'Really? What's that for?'

'In case Celia comes round again. I mean if she did I'd have everything she said on record. I've got this app on my phone which will record what she says.'

'That sounds really good. So how are you going to entice her round?'

'You know I hadn't thought of it that way. I was just waiting for her to appear of her own volition.'

'Oh darling, that could be forever. Why don't you send her an email suggesting she pops round?'

Birch's mind was whirring. 'Yes! Bloody good idea mother! I could just say I think we need to talk.'

'Exactly. Don't give anything away. Just invite her round.'

'I won't be able to let her go beyond the hallway.'

'That's okay. Just say Katie's in and you need to talk there.'

'Yes, you're right Mother. Fantastic idea. And Mum?'

'Yes?'

'Come home soon. We all miss you.'

# Chapter 23

Ross stood in the middle of a hive of activity. He rubbed his chin and remembered he hadn't shaved for a couple of days now. He'd caught himself in the mirror that morning and liked what he saw. The beard coming through was a salt and pepper mix and he decided then and there to leave it and see what Elaine thought of it when she saw him. There were shop fitters all around him now seemingly calm and focused on their work, unperturbed by the intermittent screeching of tile cutters which was still making him cringe.

Harry came through the door with a bounce in his step. He was early but Ross had prepared for their meeting in good time.

'Morning Ross.' They shook hands amiably. Harry looked around him as he said, 'This all looks very industrious.'

'Yes, progress is good.' Ross leaned in to add quietly, 'helps when you're project managing from your home upstairs.'

'Of course.' Harry looked up to the ceiling. 'You okay up there?'

'Yes, it's fine for me. Elaine's talking about adding cushions and vases and things!' He raised his eyebrows. 'But why don't you come on up, we can talk more easily there,' he shouted over the sound of the electrician's drill.

'Good idea,' Harry replied raising his voice too.

The flat was devoid of personality with beige carpets throughout and cream walls thanks to its new owner and a paint brush. There were piles of boxes still unopened and very little furniture but the kitchen looked fully functioning if cosy. Ross put the kettle on and made them both a drink while Harry found the room designated as the office.

'This is all right, isn't it?' Harry said as he found a chair to sit on. 'You still running My Mag from here?'

'Yes, yes, but it pretty much runs itself now. A lot of my advertisers repeat their ads each month and I'm getting it distributed with the local paper now instead of doing it myself.'

'What? You used to hand deliver it to all of Highgate village?'

'Yes, well it was good exercise and I had more time then but now what with The Friendly Bean and, of course, Elaine, life's got a bit busier.'

'It certainly has old chap. Quite the entrepreneur these days and Elaine's a lovely woman. Good for you.'

Ross was beaming from ear to ear.

'And I like the beard,' Harry continued nodding towards it, 'Very distinguished. Is that keeping up with the trend or no time to shave?'

'Definitely the latter but I actually quite like it. I'm just hoping Elaine does too.'

'Good luck with that.' Harry looked doubtful.

Ross was shuffling papers. 'Anyway, I've got a full update for you. What we've spent on the refit so far and where we are on the schedule.' He handed Harry some pristine papers in a plastic wallet.

'Oh thanks, very efficient.' He started scanning the content. 'And when do you think we'll be able to launch?'

That was the burning question that had been on Ross's mind. A casual remark that Harry had made early on when he agreed the funding which was on the lines of 'the sooner we get this cafe open the better,' had played on his mind. He had stared at his carefully drawn up project plan on more than one occasion and tried to work out how he could get to D day more quickly but it only served to overwhelm him and add to his stress levels. He decided to be straight now for his own sanity. 'I'm hoping September, I mean being realistic I think it's going to be then. A summer opening would have been nice but if we push it too far...'

'September is good,' Harry interrupted his stream of consciousness. 'After all coffee is more of a cold weather drink so I think it would be best to establish ourselves in the Autumn and Winter.'

'Good thinking.' The relief was clear in Ross's face. 'There is still plenty to do. The plastering's done and the tiles on the back wall are going on today. Rick says he should be finished by the end of the week.'

'What about the flooring?'

'Ah! I wanted to ask you about that especially as it's the next thing to go in after we've painted the walls. The wooden boards that are already down are a bit of a mess but we could hire a sander and then paint them. I'm sure they would look fine.'

'Sounds good to me.'

'Yes, you see the other options are very pricey and so...'

'I like the idea of keeping the original boards. Recycling is a good thing and painted up... what colour were you thinking?'

Ross reached for a paint swatch. 'This one here, castle gray, is quite neutral but dark enough not to show the dirt.'

'I like that. Castle gray did you say? Yes, I think that will work well.'

'We'll keep the walls light so that the overall space isn't too dark.' As Ross said that he remembered all the black in Harry's apartment and bit his lip.

'Yes, well we've got the big windows at the front; they always let a lot of light in.' Harry was going with the flow.

'And we've got spot lighting in the ceiling which gives a natural light and they're very low energy bulbs. Elaine found them on the internet.'

'Great and what about the tables and chairs?'

'Ah well, you mentioned recycling and that's what we were thinking of. You can pick up decent second hand stuff and do it up. It will mean we have different sized tables, some big, some small but I think that fits into our theme of being a friendly cafe.'

'Could work,' Harry sounded uncertain. 'Must be a lot of work for you, I mean sourcing it all and then having to sand and paint.'

'Well actually Elaine has been working on that side of things. I was just waiting for your approval to go down this route before we start buying.'

'Oh okay. So Elaine's much more involved now is she?'

'Yes, she's brilliant. Great at finding the things we need and choosing colours etc.. Much better eye for that kind of thing than me; in fact she reckons I'm colour blind!'

'Good to know Elaine's involved then! I don't want a lurid pink cafe.' Harry looked thoughtful. 'Can I see what it will look like when it's all finished?'

'Yes, you can,' Ross opened up his laptop, 'we've got this clever app which shows the finished room and you can change things on it as the project develops.'

'Oh yes, that looks good.' Harry looked carefully at the screen. 'So are these the blackboards on the side wall where people can leave messages?'

'Yes, they will be near the exit door so people see them on their way out.'

'And the deli! Oh I like that. It blends in well. Are we still going to be able to sell the branded coffee?'

'Yes, Elaine's progressed that. We should be getting some sample packs soon with the new Friendly Bean logo.'

Harry sat back and looked straight at Ross. 'You're doing a splendid job.'

'Thank you Harry, I mean it's all down to you really.'

'Well I stumped up the cash but you and Elaine are doing all the hard work.' There was a thoughtful pause which worried Ross for a moment and then Harry said, 'I'm just wondering if we should fix a date for the launch so we can start advertising. A guy I know in the retail trade said it's vitally important to have a first class launch; gets the business off to a good start. What do you think?'

'I couldn't agree more. How about Saturday 10th September? Summer holidays over, back to school...'

'Mmm..' Harry considered this. 'I was rather thinking we might go for a weekday, just from the point of view of attracting the working population. And all the people I have earmarked to invite would prefer a weekday.'

'Yes, I take your point. How about we make it the Friday and then continue it on into Saturday for those who can't make the Friday.'

'Yes, that would work. Are we going to be running some sort of promotion during the launch?'

'I was thinking of something on the lines of a free prize draw to win, say, a free coffee every day for the first month.'

'Yes, that would be doable. Okay so let's say definitely the ninth and tenth. Elaine will be okay with that, will she?'

'I'll double check but I'm sure she will be.' Ross suddenly felt nervous; there was so much riding on this.

'Great. How exciting! Let's get some invites printed and I'll start telling people.'

'Ah yes, invites,' Ross said making a note to add this item to his never ending 'to do' list.

Sylvia was enjoying the last piece of shade on the balcony before the Languedoc morning sun gripped it with a stifling heat. Despite the white floaty cotton dress she was wearing, she could only bear to consume ice cold sparkling water, and had said 'no' yet again earlier that day to an espresso which Jack enjoyed regardless. He spent the mornings in his studio, which adjoined the balcony where she sat, claiming that the light was at its best at that time of day for painting. When she'd asked him what he was working on he'd grinned and said, 'you'll have to wait and see.'

She had broached the subject of a trip back to England the evening before after an excellent meal in the nearby restaurant, La Mamita, and a few glasses of a delicious cold Chablis. It felt like a good moment.

'I spoke to Birch a few days ago.'

'Yes, you said.'

'Oh did I? Sorry.' This hadn't started well. 'I was just going to say that I quite miss him. And Katie and the girls actually, even though I've only known them a short while.'

'Well from what you tell me, Katie is a remarkable woman.'

'Yes.' She was going to have to get straight to the point. 'Anyway I was thinking about a trip home.' She left it at that carefully looking for a response in his face. He looked as calm and unruffled as he always did and didn't say anything at first so he must have considered his response before he said, 'good for you.'

Where did that leave her? 'Would you like to come with me?' There, she'd posed the question. She felt nervous waiting for the response.

'Perhaps later. I'm in the middle of a painting I want to finish. And I'm not sure I want to leave the beautiful heat again so soon. It's so cold in your country.' She noted the way he referred to England as her country even though it had once been his.

'Birch said they're having a lovely summer. In the high twenties; it would suit me down to the ground.'

He put his wine glass down and leaned towards her and gently stroked her face, his eyes full of affection. 'You're finding this heat too much, mon amour?'

'Well yes.' She was flustered now. 'No! No, not really. I mean it's a bit too hot for me right now but I was just saying it's a really nice temperature back home and I just thought you might want to...' she trailed off feeling discouraged.

He continued to watch her face. 'You must do what's right for you,' he said which only served to exasperate her even more.

'Right.' She tried very hard to take any drama out of her voice as she said, 'yes, well I think I will go back for a while.' For a while was Jack language, casually vague.

The ice had melted in her drink now and she turned to look in to Jack's studio and was surprised to see him staring at her, paintbrush in hand. He smiled and almost looked embarrassed as he went back to his canvas. She decided to go inside and get another cold drink and found herself drawn to the cool of the bedroom at the back of the house, where she noticed her ipad on the bed. There was no harm in looking. It didn't take her long to find a suitable flight from Montpellier to London Gatwick. She had entered 'one person travelling' and 'one way' with a heavy heart. There were plenty of options even if they were with a budget airline. She decided to ring Birch and tell him of her plan and rang the land line at Bisham Gardens.

'Katie?'

'Hello Sylvia, how lovely to hear from you.'

'Oh Katie! What a joy. How are you?'

'I'm good, yes.' She sounded uncertain.

'How's it going with Charlie?'

'Gosh his reputation precedes him, doesn't it?'

'Just something Birch said.'

'Yes, well he's certainly keeping me busy. You know that house we bought at auction?'

'How could I forget.'

'Well, he's sacked the foreman and given me the role of project manager now. He reckons the tradesmen are frightened of me!'

'Oh how wonderful. I hope you're giving them all hell.'

'Not exactly. Pleading with them would be more like it! The only real clout I have is that I pay their invoices.'

'Yes, that's usually the only route to compliance.'

'But enough about me! How's it all going out there?'

'Good! Yes, it's all good. Well, apart from the heat which is exhausting!'

'Oh dear. And how's Jack?'

'He's,' Sylvia surprised herself as she thought about what she would say next, 'he's preoccupied on some painting at the moment. I suggested we both take a trip back to Blighty and he said something vague about "maybe later".'

'Oh. Well we'd love to see you. Bethan's always asking about you.'

'Bless you. You know that gladdens my heart.'

'Oh Sylvia. Why don't you come. Come on your own and straight to us from the airport. We'll meet you off your flight, if you like. Jack can manage without you for a while; it will do him good.'

'You know I think you're right. He might appreciate me a bit more if he misses me.'

'That's decided then. And you and I shall go out and have some fun while you're here.'

A tear appeared in Sylvia's eye. 'Oh thank you. Thank you darling, you've been just the tonic I need.'

Birch was pacing the kitchen at Bisham Gardens. He looked at his watch. She should be here at any minute but he just knew that his wife would be deliberately late to spite him. Maybe even half an hour late, it would not be the first time. And then there would be a chance that Katie would get home in the middle of it all. That would be a disaster. He decided to have another espresso even though he had already had two. Far from calming his nerves it was firing him up but that was how he wanted to be. Fired up, able to think quickly and confident enough to railroad his wife into a confession. This was a golden opportunity to finally progress his divorce despite the laissez faire attitude of his lawyer. He checked his mobile again to make sure the recording equipment was working okay and the cameras were on. That was the fifth time he had checked. Yet again, as far as he could tell, it was all okay but still no sign of Celia.

With the unwanted coffee made he sat at the kitchen table and opened up his laptop. He went to his emails and found her reply to his simple invitation to come round to talk. It was deliberately vague and had prompted questions from her. Talk about what? But the essence was that she agreed to come round at two o'clock that afternoon and so it had achieved its objective. Birch was mid-sip of his coffee when the doorbell rang loud and shrill causing him to splutter and spill coffee over his keyboard.

'Shit!' he grabbed a damp cloth and wiped the laptop down. Then a tea towel to make sure it was dry and no damage done. He could not afford a new one. Then he practically ran to the door worried she might not wait even thirty seconds. He flung the door open.

'Celia, hello.' His voice was curt and he didn't step aside to invite her in. It was important that she stayed in camera shot which meant no further than the hall. He knew she would worm her way in to the house if she could. She was wearing a pretty summer dress and had obviously done her hair and makeup. She was here on a very different mission to the one he had in mind.

Celia looked bemused. 'What's going on Birch? Aren't you going to ask me in? After all this was your idea.'

'I said we need to talk.' He held his ground.

'On the door step? You don't honestly think...'

'No, not on the doorstep, but in the hallway.'

She still looked baffled and stared at him as he moved to one side and she stepped in. He shielded the living room door which was closed as were all the other doors off the hallway. She looked around her as if trying to find an escape route.

'Can't we go somewhere more comfortable?'

'No. This is Katie's house. You must remember that,' he said cringing inside; that did not sound plausible.

'Is she here?' Celia asked looking bemused.

'Yes, she's upstairs,' he lied.

'Perhaps we should go out? I don't want to cause any awkwardness,' she said as she appealed to him with her eyes and just fell short of fluttering them at him.

'No! No I think it's best we talk here. I mean.. what we have to say is private, isn't it?'

She eyed him suspiciously. 'So what are we talking about, then?' she demanded.

'Celia,' this speech was prepared, 'so much has gone wrong between us. We find ourselves in this ridiculous situation..'

'But it doesn't have to be like this.' She moved towards him. He moved back even though there was little room between him and the doorway and raised a palm to indicate he wanted her to keep her distance. She wasn't supposed to interrupt him.

He continued, 'I just want to understand what happened, at the start I mean, when you started seeing Alistair behind my back. What was I doing so wrong?'

'Oh Birch I forgive you now. I'm so sorry about all that. I know now that I..' She hesitated for some time before adding, 'I was misguided. I didn't understand what was happening between us. You could say it was my cry for help.' She was trying to affect a damsel in distress demeanour which was only serving to annoy Birch. He needed her to admit to the affair.

'So what actually happened when you first met Alistair? How did you meet? I need to know.'

233

'Oh but Birch, it can only be upsetting for you raking all that up again.'

'No,' he said firmly. 'No, I need to know for my own peace of mind. Otherwise, how do I know it won't happen again?' he said throwing her a life line to reel her in.

'Oh Birch does this mean that you might come back to me?' She'd fallen for it.

'I need to know,' he said resolutely. He gave her a very serious look to ensure she knew he meant it.

She sighed deeply and gulped. 'Right.' The wind was out of her sails. 'Well, if you really must know..' She looked around her once more. 'Can't we go into the kitchen? I'm feeling quite weak. I could do with a chair.'

'Tell me,' he said trying to take the anger out of his voice, 'just tell me.'

'Okay, well I was feeling neglected. I realise now through my work with Angela, my therapist..' She broke off and Birch thought he might explode. He said nothing. She continued, 'By the way Angela is more than happy to do some joint sessions with us and you know she's really good.'

'Right,' he managed in response. 'But we digress.' His expression urged her to continue.

'Yes, okay.' She sounded irritated. 'Well as I was feeling low, probably depressed, that's what Angela said anyway, when I met Alistair and he was so kind to me, he's a very generous man actually...' She broke off and leaned back against the wall behind her. Birch wondered if she was still in camera shot but forced himself not to check by looking up. His face did give something away, though.

'Is Katie listening in to all this? Is she at the top of the stairs?'

'No! No, she's in the attic room. I made her promise to stay up there.'

'She must think it's all rather strange.'

'She's an understanding woman,' he said and wondered how that sounded. 'Anyway you were saying that Alistair is a generous man. So how did you meet him?'

'Through a girlfriend actually. She knew how unhappy I was and Alistair was single at the time and so...'

'So you started an affair?' Birch interjected.

'Yes, I'm sorry to say we did. But I have explained and it won't happen again. I mean it really won't because I know now that it was just a stupid attempt to make things better, just a sticking plaster over our marriage.'

'And when did all this happen?' Birch needed to keep her on track.

'Oh do we really have to go through all this.' She looked pained as she said, 'You know! It was about a year before I told you.'

'Before you left me to go and live with Alistair?'

'Yes! Before then. Look I've said I'm sorry, I don't know how many times now. I really am sorry. I don't know what else to say.'

Birch found his eyes smarting. They may have been tears of relief or tears of joy but Celia misinterpreted them. And so he got away with saying, 'I think you should go now,' with quiet determination.

She started weeping. 'Oh Birch! Come back to me soon! Please! I miss you so much!'

He blinked his eyes, encouraging the warm wetness. 'I think you should go.' He opened the front door and left the way clear for her before turning away and dipping his head to the ground, one arm across his waist, the other hand holding his face. He waited.

'Tell Katie we're going to try again; tell her I've changed; tell her you're coming home to me.' She walked slowly out onto the street. Birch waited a moment before turning to close the door. To his astonishment he really was crying now.

# Chapter 24

Birch called his lawyer the very next day. 'I have the evidence we need to go down the adultery route!' he had almost announced, pleased as punch.

Jonathan sounded puzzled. 'Yes, indeed,' he replied simply.

'I'm going to deliver it in person,' Birch told him.

'Is that really necessary?'

'Oh yes. I'm not having anything go wrong with this. We're talking blood sweat and tears to get this far. I will drive down and hand it to you myself.'

Sitting in the reception area of Bradley Hall & Taylor, Birch was clutching the damning evidence to his chest. The receptionist's expression was somewhere between doubtful and bored. Jonathan appeared, his suit slightly crumpled and lines deep across his brow. 'Birch,' he said as if it had been a long day already despite being before noon.

'Jonathan.' They shook hands and Birch followed him into his office. A woman appeared and handed Jonathan a file.

'Oh thanks Sandy. Do sit down,' he said to Birch.

He opened up the file before looking up at his client. 'How can I help you?'

It seemed like an odd question to Birch. He carefully peeled away the envelope from his person and presented it to Jonathan. 'A confession of adultery from Celia on film and with a voice recording.'

'Interesting.' Jonathan opened the envelope carefully and took out the DVD and what looked like a mobile phone. He held up the handset. 'Is this your phone?'

'Yes,' Birch said nodding. 'The voice recording is on there. It's fully charged. You can play it now if you'd like to.'

'I take it you'll be wanting the mobile back?'

'Well yes. I mean I'm sure it's possible to transfer the file thingamajig, but beyond me.'

Jonathan picked up the phone on his desk and dialled an internal number. 'Siobhan, could you pop down to my office. Little technical task for you.'

Siobhan appeared. She must have been about nineteen and wore black shorts over opaque tights. Jonathan handed the phone to her and explained what they needed.

'No problem,' she said and turned to leave.

'Er, you will be careful with that won't you?' Birch almost pleaded.

'Of course,' she gave him a warm smile. 'Don't worry, I won't lose your data.' She was gone.

'Don't fret,' Jonathan added. 'She's young enough to know what she's doing.'

Birch rolled his eyes. Jonathan sat back in his chair looking thoughtful. There was an uncertain pause between them during which Birch became increasingly anxious. He broke the silence.

'You're not going to tell me that this evidence I'm giving you on a plate isn't enough for us to file for divorce on the grounds of adultery? Please God! No!'

Jonathan quickly collected himself and sat upright. 'No. No, I'm not. I was just wondering if Katie has told you yet that she too has pretty conclusive evidence to the same end.'

'What? What are you talking about? How can she? She was out when I got Celia to come round.'

'Have you told her about what you've done?'

'Well... not really. I mean she knows about the CCTV I had installed. And I said what it was for and... well...'

Jonathan was unable to repress a smile.

'What's so funny?'

'It just seems that you and Katie have both been a bit secretive recently.'

'I've not been secretive!' he protested. 'Just rather busy with one thing and... Anyway! She's been tied up working on this project with this developer, Charlie boy. He's quite a handful at the best of times.'

'I see.'

'Well I'm not sure I do. What's this about her having the evidence too?'

'I'm not sure I should be the one telling you this.' Jonathan looked worried.

'Oh for goodness sake, Jon, spill the beans.'

'Okay, but don't blame me if you don't like it.'

'Now you've got me really worried.'

'Look, calm down old chap. What Katie's done was purely an attempt to help you get the divorce you want.'

'So cut to the chase. What has she done?'

'She and her friend, Julia, hired a private investigator.'

'They what?'

'One Delores de Clancy,' he said reading from the file in front of him.

'Is this some sort of joke?'

'No. No, I received a recording from her of a conversation between Julia and Alistair.'

'Julia and Alistair? What the f..?' Birch was incredulous.

Jonathan sighed. 'Listen, I think it would be best if you went back to Bisham Gardens and spoke to Katie about all this.'

'Don't worry. I will. But first do tell me, what was Julia doing with Alistair?'

'He was set up basically, through this dating site.'

'Dating site! This gets worse!'

'It was purely a device to get Alistair to talk about his affair with Celia.'

Birch's eyes were so wide they might have popped out his head. He blinked as he took in this last piece of the tale. 'And did he?'

'Yes, he did.' Jonathan left it at that.

'My God. Well would you Adam and Eve it.' Birch's mind was whirring. 'But.., but where do we go from here? What do we do next?'

There was a knock at the door and Siobhan appeared with an MP3 player attached to a speaker. 'It's all on there,' she said placing it on top of a pile of papers on the desk.

'Thank you,' Jonathan replied. Birch was staring at the speaker.

Siobhan looked at the two men. 'Well, I'll leave you to it,' she said as she sidled out of the room.

Birch still looked like he was in shock. 'So are you going to play it?'

'Listen, I have an idea. My next client is not until two, why don't we go for a pie and a pint at the pub?'

It took a few moments for Birch to realise what he'd suggested. 'Yes, good idea, I think I need a drink.'

Katie watched as the passengers alighted the Gatwick Express at Victoria station. Although she had sent Sylvia a text message explaining it would be her, and not Birch, meeting her she had not had a reply. Katie spotted her from the barrier being helped off the train by a smartly dressed man. Her face was lightly tanned and she was wearing a lime green mac and a tangerine silk scarf. He was putting her suitcase on the platform for her and extending the handle so that she could wheel it along. Katie stood on tip toe and waved. Sylvia spotted her and waved back enthusiastically. She hurried up to where Katie stood and threw her arms around her.

'Katie! So lovely to see you!'

'Oh Sylvia, it's good to see you too. Did you get my text?'

'No, I've had my phone switched off. Anything the matter?'

'No, no, it's just that Birch couldn't make it today. He's off on some secret mission.'

'Planning to assassinate Celia, with a bit of luck,' she joked.

Katie laughed. 'Hopefully he won't need to; there have been some interesting developments on that front.'

'Oh marvellous. Let's get a cab and you can tell me all.'

239

Birch was halfway through his pint. Jonathan was outlining his proposal for how they should proceed. It was straight forward and seemed like the best way to go. He had suggested that they simply present the evidence directly to Celia in the hope that it would persuade her to go ahead with the divorce without further obstruction. This would hopefully avoid going to court.

'So would her adultery still be cited as the reason for the divorce?'

'Yes, it would have to be as there has to be grounds.'

'What's her solicitor going to think of that? Shouldn't we be going through them?'

'We could do and we will if necessary but I think presenting the evidence we have in a discreet way, to begin with, would be less inflammatory.'

Birch took another sip of his beer. 'It doesn't take much to inflame Celia.' He was thoughtful. 'Okay, so how exactly do we let her know?'

'I think initially a letter from me outlining the evidence we have and making it clear what we want her to do.'

'Do you think she'll believe you?'

'If she doesn't we'll have to invite her to hear the evidence for herself.'

Birch looked worried. 'I'm just concerned how she might react. I mean she might come after me?'

Jonathan stifled a laugh. 'Good job you're bigger that her then.'

'Ha ha. Doesn't stop her being vicious.'

'She's certainly a formidable woman.'

There was an amiable pause before Jonathan said, 'now all you have to do is talk to Katie. The last thing we need is you two falling out after all this!'

'It's so lovely to be able to sit outside and not swelter!' Sylvia laughed at herself. 'And drink tea! I've been reduced to iced water for the past couple of months.'

'How hot is it there?' Katie asked.

'Oh about ten degrees hotter than here. Up in the high thirties during the day.'

Katie hesitated before she asked, 'how's it going with Jack, you two still okay?'

'I think so.' Sylvia looked thoughtful. 'He's very much used to living on his own so I sometimes feel like a spare part.'

'But he's good to you, isn't he?'

'Oh yes. I can't fault him for generosity when it comes to shopping, dining out, anything I want really. But of course he has his art and he gets very wrapped up in all that.'

'I see.' Katie lifted the teapot. 'More tea?'

'Don't mind if I do,' Sylvia held out her cup.

'Have you made any friends in Pezenas?'

'Oh yes, there's quite a big expat community. Jack's not so bothered with them. He's become very French since he's been there. It's almost as though he's a native now.'

'You must miss Sandgate.' Katie suggested.

'I do a bit but you know there wasn't really a lot keeping me there.'

'What about your adorable apartment?'

Sylvia smoothed her shift dress over her thighs and avoided Katie's gaze. 'I haven't done anything about it apart from getting my friend, Joyce, to pop in every now and then to make sure it's all okay. Joyce said she wouldn't mind renting it out for me..'

'That sounds like a good idea.'

'Yes, it's just that, well, what if it all goes horribly wrong with Jack and I come back for good?'

'Do you really think that might happen?' Katie asked carefully.

'It's crazy really. I mean it's all based on a kooky affair many years ago when we were both too young, too reckless... to get back together at this stage in life, well...'

'I think it's wonderful,' Katie interrupted.

'Yes, it is, I suppose.' Sylvia sounded like she was trying to convince herself.

'So enjoy it,' Katie squeezed her hand.

'While you can...' Sylvia had a cynical smile on her face. 'That's what they say, isn't it?'

# Chapter 25

The Waitrose promotion was going really well. Hans had cautioned that most new products outperformed their nearest competitor in the first few weeks, as they put so much promotion behind them, but nothing he said had dampened Bethan's spirits. She had spent as much time as she could helping Carol, going straight round to her house after work and sometimes not leaving until she was too tired to think straight.

'Darling! You must go home to bed now!' Carol had caught her momentarily asleep standing up propped against the counter.

Bethan stirred herself. 'But we've just put a fresh batch in. And don't we need to do another one?' She looked anxious. 'How many have we got now?' She started counting the rows of cup cakes neatly lined up on the cooling racks but lost count. 'Oh bother.' She had to start again.

'I'll do the rest,' Carol insisted, 'you go now.' She put her hands on Bethan's shoulders and stared at her with concern.

Bethan rubbed her face and decided she did need her bed. She thought about walking home in the dark and remembered the tramp who'd accosted her last winter. 'I think I might ring my Mum for a lift.'

'It's too late for that!' It was quarter past eleven. 'I'll drive you. Oh damn, my car's in the garage and Jeremy is away.'

Bethan's eyes flicked upwards as she had an idea. 'Do you have a spare bedroom?' she asked hopefully, too tired to worry that she may be being impertinent.

'Yes! Yes, of course. Charlotte's at uni; you can have her room. But hadn't you better let your Mum know?'

'Okay, I'll call her.'

Sylvia had answered the phone and said she'd leave a note for her mum who had gone to bed. She had added that she thought what Bethan was doing was brilliant. 'Go girl,' she said.

'Thanks Sylvia. I think right now the only place I'm going is to bed.'

On Saturday the buyer from Waitrose telephoned mid-afternoon and said they wanted to double the order for Sunday. Was that okay? Apparently they had run out already that day and they were expecting higher sales due to the bank holiday on Monday. Carol sat down feeling exhausted at the mere thought of the additional work it entailed. Her body was already aching in protest. Up until now she'd been telling herself she could do this, after all it was only a hundred cup cakes a day. It was so important to maintain a high quality. Every batch was taste tested at each stage from batter through to final bake. By succumbing to using external premises she would lose total control which seemed to be essential right now. But that last phone call had deflated her. What was she going to do? She toyed with the idea of ringing Bethan. It was ridiculous as she had strongly protested against Bethan doing any more that weekend. She had insisted that she should have the time off to recuperate. After all, she had a full time job to do as well. But the more Carol thought about it the more she thought it was too bad, she was desperate. She called Bethan's mobile and it went to voice mail so she left a message. As if on autopilot on some desperate mission, and forgetting to take her apron off, she decided to drive round to Bisham Gardens.

Sylvia answered the door to her. 'Hello? Are you Carol, the cup cake lady?'

'Yes.' Carol smiled at the tag line she used. 'You must be Sylvia. So sorry to bother you today.'

'Come in,' Sylvia said warmly inviting her into the kitchen which Carol noticed was a lot calmer and tidier than her own. 'Coffee? You look like you need one.'

'Oh that's very kind but is Bethan here?'

'She's out with a friend.'

Carol sighed and raised her palm to her forehead. She felt like crying.

'Are you all right?' Sylvia looked concerned now. 'Is there anything I can help with?'

She turned to go. 'Thanks, but I'd better get back to the kitchen. I've got so much to do. Could you ask Bethan to call me when she gets home?' She spoke so quickly her words fell over each other.

Sylvia put a gentle hand on her shoulder. 'Darling, please let me help. Surely a quick coffee wouldn't hurt?'

Carol felt defeated; the kindness shown by this woman was too tempting. How could a coffee with a friendly face make much difference to the ludicrousness of her day? Once sat down, and with the first sip of silky cappuccino inside her, Carol offloaded all the dramas and worries that had come about since she had committed to the Waitrose trial. Sylvia listened making sympathetic noises and when she'd finished she was quick to make a suggestion.

'Well, I can make cup cakes. Just give me the recipe and I'll get going.'

'Oh that's really sweet of you but you see what with health and safety and Waitrose's exacting standards...'

'You mean I couldn't make them here? You don't need to worry about exacting whatsits, I can make cup cakes. I'm sure Bethan's told you.'

'Yes, she has, but it doesn't get it us over the safety hurdle. Your kitchen would need to be inspected...' Carol looked at her watch. 'I'd better be going.'

'Mmm.' Sylvia ignored her and tapped the side of her cup as the problem ticked over in her mind. 'Well, I'll come over to you then,' she said pleased with herself.

'That's very kind but I'd have to pay you.'

'Don't be ridiculous; I need something to do. My man, Jack, is still in France behaving in the most infuriating manner and this is just the sort of thing I need to take my mind off him. Anyway, I enjoy baking.'

Carol blinked her eyes in surprise as if a fairy God mother had just appeared.

Sylvia took that as her offer accepted. 'Now drink up, we've got work to do.'

Katie had worked out that the element of surprise worked best when you were dealing with tradesmen. So she varied the time each day for her visits to 4 Cholmeley Crescent and ignored their protests that they'd had no warning.

'Well I would've had it done, if I'd known you were coming this morning?' Ryan had argued a few days ago.

'You're not doing this for me,' Katie explained for the umpteenth time and yet again it provoked a puzzled look. 'Charlie needs to get this development finished and sold so he can move on to the next one.' This, she realised later, was no incentive to these guys.

The sun was shining as she approached the house today and the first thing she noticed was that the skip, which had been full to overflowing for several days, had gone. Someone had even swept up so that the facade was looking much more pleasing. Was this a good omen? Katie braced herself for disappointment which was the usual order of the day. She let herself in through the front door and moved slowly from room to room, through, what was now, the ground floor flat. The plasterer had been in and it really was taking shape. Katie felt relieved, almost to the point of tearful. Was this finally coming together? She went upstairs and upstairs again. More of the same. The plasterer had completed the whole building; she would be able to get the painters in. On the second floor she came across Ryan up a step ladder, adjusting a light fitting in the ceiling of what was now a living room.

'Afternoon,' he said cheerily.

'Hello.' Katie was still amazed by the sight before her. 'Are you the only one here?' she asked and almost wished she hadn't as it sounded as if she was displeased when she wasn't.

'No ma'am, Rocket's out the back. He's finishing the outside painting of the back door.'

Katie blinked in disbelief. 'Good,' she managed. She was about to head back down the stairs but then she turned to ask him, 'so I could get the decorators in on Monday?'

'Don't see why not.'

'Okay. Will you have finished the electrics?'

'Yep, just this floor to finish. I'll be done by the end of today.'

'Great. Oh and thank you Ryan.'

'Just doin' me job ma'am.'

'Yes, but thanks anyway. Charlie is going to be really pleased.'

Ryan was coming down from his step ladder as he asked, 'Will you be managing the next job he does?'

Katie was taken aback. 'Well I'm Charlie's assistant as you know but I don't usually project manage.'

'You should fink about it.'

She was suspicious now. 'Well, I have other clients too so...'

'But you're good at this.'

Katie smiled deciding to accept the compliment. 'Right, well, I'll bear that in mind.'

Ross could feel Elaine's eyes on him. 'What?' he asked slightly affronted and unaware he was stroking his beard.

'Nothing,' she said affecting innocence.

'It's my beard, isn't it? You don't really like it. You were just being polite the other day.'

'Well, I do quite like it actually.' She looked mischievous. It's just a bit scratchy.'

'What, even though it's grown a bit now. They're supposed to get softer.'

'Mmm.' She wasn't going to elaborate.

'So does that mean I have to shave it off?'

'No,' she said, as if she meant yes.

Ross sighed and raised his eyebrows. He was about to commit to going back to a smooth chin when he decided that the launch of The Friendly Bean was too important to worry about such trivial things. He surprised himself as his normal modus operandi was to please the woman in his life at all costs but he had a strong feeling that Elaine was going to stick by him regardless.

'Anyway, where were we? Cakes. Local suppliers of cakes. Have you found any?' he asked changing the subject.

'I've found one but her cakes look a bit formidable. They're gluten free and dairy free and frankly, taste free. They have a sort of saw-dust texture.'

'They sound dreadful. Forget that.'

'Well I think we'll have to look wider afield then.' Elaine yawned and propped her head up with her hand.

'You tired?'

'Yes,' she said with naked honesty.

'Lack of sleep or tired of The Friendly Bean?'

'Never, but can't we have a bit of a break; maybe take the evening off? It is Saturday.' She let her bottom lip protrude outwards.

'Yes, you're right. We deserve some time out.' Ross sat back in his chair. 'Cup cakes,' he came out with randomly.

'All the rage.'

He looked pensive as he said, 'There's someone around here that makes cup cakes; I'm sure there is.'

Adam was varnishing a small bookshelf which had ornate carvings down each side. His face held a serious expression as he concentrated on perfecting the piece with a light stain in order that the natural beauty of the oak shone through. Alice watched him silently in awe as she stood at the door of his workshop. He looked even more attractive in his scruffy khaki T-shirt and torn jeans. She couldn't quite believe that she was in love with this man and he was in love with her.

He caught sight of her out of the corner of his eye and looked up. 'Hey, you! How long have you been there?' He put down his brush and they rushed together to embrace and kiss. He pulled back. 'Hang on, I'm covered in...'

'I don't mind,' she said. Nothing mattered anymore.

'But that's a lovely top you've got on.' He checked her over, turning her with his hands on her waist. 'No damage,' he said as he broke into a broad smile and they kissed again.

'Finished work for the day?' he asked.

'Yes!' she cried triumphantly. 'No more work until Monday.'

'That's good.'

'So what about you?' She gave him a seductive smile.

'I might just have to take some time out.' He glanced at his watch. 'From round about now this second until the moment you have to go back to The Lemon Tree.'

'Ooh, that's lucky.'

'Well, we have to make the most of every day now before you head off to uni,' he said cheerfully but didn't let go of her.

Alice bit her lip. 'We do,' she said but was thinking something very different.


'That's it! Two hundred!' Sylvia said gleefully. 'I mean I've counted them twice but I think I'm going a bit gah gah, so perhaps you'd better double check,' she added as she collapsed on a chair.

'Another tea?' Carol asked. 'Or how about a glass of wine?'

'Now you're talking. After all, it is well past the six o'clock alcohol watershed.'

'Is that a French thing?' Carol asked as she pulled a bottle of wine out of the fridge.

'No, they start at lunch time there!' Sylvia's eyes were full of amusement.

'Alkies,' Carol said writing off an entire population. 'White okay?'

'Perfect.'

Carol poured them both a glass and handed one to her kitchen mate. She raised hers to make a toast. 'To Sylvia, my saviour!'

Sylvia laughed feebly. 'Just a bit of cake making. Although I must admit it's been jolly hard work. I certainly deserve this.' She took a large gulp.

'It's four in a box, so when I've boxed them up I'll know if we've got enough.' Carol waved an arm in the direction of the cooling cup cakes.

'You what?' Sylvia was too tired to think straight.

'I mean the cup cakes. To make sure we've got enough.'

'Oh, I see.'

Carol's mobile phone made a buzzing noise. She picked it up from the table and saw that there was a message from Bethan. She read it out. 'Sorry I wasn't around earlier. Is there anything I can do to help? Bethan!' She was grinning as she spoke.

Sylvia laughed. 'I think that's what you call perfect timing.'

Adam rose naked from his bed and looked for his boxer shorts which were tangled in a bed sheet. He put them on and said, 'Chinese or Indian?'

Alice was lying on her back looking serene. 'I don't mind.'

'Chinese it is then; I know you secretly don't care for Indian food that much.'

Alice giggled.

'Do you trust me to order?' he asked.

'I trust you totally.'

He looked wistfully down at her and then with a mischievous smile he whipped the sheet away revealing her naked body. 'You getting up then?'

She felt strangely calm and it occurred to her that if Jacob had done anything like that it would have annoyed her. She sat up slowly and swung her legs round, in no rush to go anywhere and looked vaguely round for something to wear. Adam threw a denim shirt her way.

'Thanks,' she said and slipped it on. It smelt of him and did nothing to wipe the innocuous smile from her face.

By the time the takeaway arrived they were lounging entwined on the sofa in front of a French film.

'With or without subtitles?' Adam had joked when he put the DVD in.

'Without is good for me.'

'Show off.'

They started watching without the English translation but it wasn't long before Adam objected.

'This isn't happening. I'm not sitting through two hours of this.'

Alice smiled and picked up the remote control to add the subtitles without saying a word.

Adam had warmed a couple of bowls in the oven and when the take-away arrived he lay the silver foil tubs out on the coffee table. 'Dig in.' He piled his bowl high while Alice picked.

Later they made love again with Adele singing one of her lovelorn ballads in the background. They were sipping wine in bed when Alice said as she stared into the distance, 'I don't want to go.'

'You don't have to, you can stay over, surely? Your mum won't mind, will she?'

Alice was smiling as she sighed gently. 'I meant Nottingham. I don't want to go up to Nottingham and be so far away from you.'

'Oh babe, I don't want you to go either but I know it's important to you, I mean for your Dad and all that. We'll manage. It won't be easy but what with Skype and the odd weekend, we'll get through it.'

Alice looked despondent. 'But will we? I mean I know I want to, I mean be faithful to you and...'

'But you don't trust me?'

'It's not that,' she said with certainty. 'Let's face it, it would be testing for any couple. Three years. And some of that time spent in France.'

Adam suddenly jumped up and went in search of his tablet. Returning to the bed he was already tapping something into Google. The results were there on the screen. Universities in London that do French degrees. He looked hopeful as he passed it to Alice.

'What do you think? Kings College, I've even heard of that one.'

'Great idea but I don't have a place on the course. I've got a place at Nottingham. Bloody Nottingham!'

# Chapter 26

Birch's stomach churned when he saw Celia's angry face appear on his mobile via the camera over the front door step. She pressed the doorbell for an unreasonably long time. Fearing that Katie might answer the door, he flew down the stairs to the hallway. He was just in time. Katie was peering through the peephole looking worried. He beckoned her into the kitchen at the back of the house.

'I suspect she's got the letter from Jonathan judging by that scowl on her face. Maybe you should stay in here with the door shut.' Birch spoke softly. The doorbell rang again. They both looked alarmed.

'Perhaps we should just pretend we're out?' Katie suggested.

'We could do but I have a feeling she won't go away and even if she does she'll be back. I may as well face the music now.'

'Okay, I'll stay in my study.'

'Isn't that dangerously close?'

'Keep her on the doorstep,' Katie suggested thinking that this was intrusion enough without her having to hide away in her own home.

'Okay,' Birch said looking uncertain. With Katie behind her study door, he opened the front door slowly and just enough to see Celia whilst still blocking her entry.

'What took you so bloody long?' Celia was at fever pitch from the off.

Birch ignored her question. 'What do you want?' his voice was shaking.

'What do I want? I want my husband back but that's not going to happen, is it?' She stood right up against him looking as threatening as a woman of five foot two can. Realising he was obstructing her way she added, 'for God's sake will you let me in?'

'No, I won't. Katie's here and I don't want you to upset her.'

'Oh she's the bloody woman of the moment isn't she! I bet she can't do anything wrong! Ms grieving widow who's snatched my husband!'

'Have you just come round to insult me?'

'I'm not insulting you. Just for the record on your stupid bloody camera which I suppose is switched on now and taking bloody notes.' She waved a fist in the direction of where the camera was partially hidden.

Birch was almost relieved; she'd obviously got his solicitor's letter. In an attempt to speed up this exchange he asked, 'What do you propose to do now that I can divorce you on the grounds of adultery?'

'Oh you think you're so bloody clever, don't you?'

'I just want a divorce!' He raised his voice but wished he hadn't.

'All I ask is that you wait five years, keep up the maintenance payments and let me stay in our home. After that, you can do what you bloody well want; I can't stop you. But maybe, just maybe you might come to your senses in that time. Maybe you'll tire of Ms goody goody! Where is she? Can she hear me? I do hope so. Ah! But silly me, she'll be able to watch me on film later!' Celia shouted and then laughed mockingly.

'I'm not willing to wait five years. I want to put the house on the market now.'

'Well tough! You'll have to fight me all the way through the courts and I hope it bloody bankrupts you on the way!'

'That way only the lawyers win.' Birch surprised himself at how clear thinking and calm that response was. 'Is that what you really want?'

'Why oh why have you turned into Mr reasonable after all your plotting and spying and underhand tactics? I hate you!' She started beating his chest with her fists and he tried to stop her by grabbing her wrists. But then, remembering the hellish time he'd had following her ridiculous assault charge, he just stood there and took the blows.

'Stop it,' he managed to blurt out and the blows weakened as she burst into tears. She wrapped her arms around him and Birch felt awkward but his instinct was to reciprocate and comfort her. He actually felt sorry for her at that precise moment. After a few seconds he gently manoeuvred her away from him and said, 'Look, let's not make this any harder than it has to be.'

'No. No! I'm not going to let you walk all over me,' she cried, exasperated by his steadfast stance.

'Look, we've written to you direct. If you don't agree to our demands we will start going through your solicitor; I'm sure you don't want that.'

'Don't tell me what I want!' She staggered away down the street crying uncontrollably and Birch watched her without a grain of satisfaction.

The sun was beating through the large window at the front of The Friendly Bean cafe. Elaine was sweating as she guided the heavy sander carefully over the floorboards keeping it in a straight line to follow the direction of the boards. At the end of the room she turned it off and found a tissue to blot her reddening face.

'Let me take over,' Ross said as he appeared from upstairs.

'I can do it. It's just so airless in here even with the door open.'

'Yes, it would be better if you could open a window.'

'Bi-fold doors across the front here,' Elaine signalled where she envisaged they would go as she said it, 'would be perfect for the summer months.'

'Yes, and very expensive right now.'

Elaine smiled as she sighed and lined herself up for another row of floorboards.

'Please let me take over; you look ever so hot.'

'I am hot! But... well you're tracking down the cup cake company aren't you?'

'Yes, I've found them and I've spoken to the owner, Carol. They're very local. One of the town houses on North Grove. I said you'd pop round.'

'Me? Oh good. When?'

'About now,' he said putting his hand on the sander and looking masterful. 'But first,' he put his arms around her, 'I haven't had a kiss for ages.'

'You really want to kiss perspiring woman?' she giggled as she leaned away from him.

'I really want to...' They kissed and she pulled away again.

'It's far too hot for canoodling,' she said with a broad smile. 'Now, I need a shower before I can face polite company.'

Matt came out of Paul's office looking pleased with himself and headed straight for Bethan's desk. She shivered with disgust as he approached.

'Bethan,' he started, his voice booming unnecessarily, 'I need a full update on The Cup Cake Company account; shall we say we'll meet in the small meeting room in ten minutes?'

Bethan scowled at him. This was open warfare. 'What's going on? You don't work on that account.'

'I do now.' He flashed a sarcastic grin at her.

'Since when?'

'Don't argue with me. Ask Paul if you're stupid enough to.' He turned and walked away as he repeated, 'ten minutes.'

Bethan tried to think of what she could show him that wouldn't reveal how much extra, out of hours work, she had done with Carol. In recent weeks the agency had given her full autonomy on the account which had made it easy to hide what was really going on. She thought on her feet; he knew about Waitrose so she would print off the media schedule she'd agreed with them; that would look good. By the time she'd done that Matt was striding over to the meeting room and so she followed him clutching some papers.

Matt sat down and she sat opposite him, rapidly scanning the schedule to remind herself what was coming up.

'What's that?' he asked. 'Do I get a copy?'

'I could photocopy it for you.'

Matt tutted and looked annoyed. 'Give it here,' he said.

Bethan handed it to him. 'We have slots in Waitrose's email newsletter, the edition that goes to customers in the Bloomsbury area, once a week where we feature a particular cup cake, so this week it's lemon and blueberries because they're refreshing in this hot weather.'

'Do people even want to eat cake in the summer?'

'Yes, of course they do. They're ideal for picnics and outdoors. We're led by Waitrose anyway. They know their customers. So I've been working with this guy called Hans there and he gives me feedback on how each line goes and then we decide what to promote next.'

'And what about Carol? Where does she come into all this important decision making?'

'She's very involved, of course she is. I talk to her about what flavours we, I mean she, can produce and send options to Waitrose.'

Matt looked confused. 'This sounds very operational. What about the online marketing? Driving traffic to the website. I thought that was your focus.'

'It is but it's all linked, I mean there's no point promoting cup cakes that Carol can't make.'

'I want to meet this Hans,' Matt said throwing the schedule back at her.

Bethan looked doubtful. 'Waitrose are happy dealing with me. So is Carol.'

'And Paul wants me involved, okay?' he fired at her in a condescending manner. 'Now, what about the website development and local promotions? Surely it's not all about one Waitrose store?'

Elaine found Carol's house easily. She was pleased that Ross had taken over the manual work back at the cafe and felt much fresher after her shower. She went round the back as instructed, where she found a wonderful orangery filled with light and adjoining an enormous kitchen. The door was open and Elaine stepped in tentatively shouting 'hello there!' The delicious smell of baked cakes was mouth-watering and Elaine's eyes widened at the sight of rows of beautifully formed cup cakes. Carol appeared from a door at the back, removing her apron and hanging it on a hook along with two other freshly laundered chef's whites.

'Elaine, isn't it?' She swept over to her to shake her hand. 'Good to meet you.'

'Well it's very good to meet you, especially in such a wonderful place!'

'Thank you. I do get some lovely comments from visitors.' Carol gestured to Elaine to sit at the kitchen table and quickly cleared some space.

'Oh don't worry.'

'Well at least let me make room for your tea and cake; I take it you would like to try one?'

'Ooh yes please! They look amazing.'

'Right, well,' Carol moved over to where the cakes were, 'we have chocolate orange, raspberry double and apple caramel.'

'They all sound wonderful.'

'How about a taste of all three? You can always take with you any you don't eat here.'

'Good idea. I'm sure Ross would like to try too.'

Carol put the kettle on and arranged the cup cakes on a pretty plate covered in pink spots and placed it in front of Elaine. 'Here you are, might as well get tasting.'

Elaine tried the raspberry one first. 'Ooh to die for,' she said with a mouthful.

Carol smiled knowingly as she poured steaming water into a teapot.

'Oh wow! That chocolate orange one is sinful! Love it!'

The tea made, Carol joined her at the table. 'So, they're up to scratch then?' she asked as if she didn't need to.

'They are fabulous. I do hope we can make this work. These could be the making of The Friendly Bean!'

'Gosh that's praise indeed.'

'Yes, now we've got to do the boring bit and talk about numbers.'

'Dates will have to be the first thing, as I said to your partner, Ross. You see I'm snowed under at the moment with this Waitrose trial and they're keen to roll out so I think I'm going to have to find premises before I commit to any more orders.'

'Oh I see.' Elaine struggled to hide her disappointment. 'We're not opening until the 9th of September,' she added desperately; the launch was coming up fast.

Carol sat back in her chair and looked thoughtful as she took a sip from her mug of tea.

'We're doing a huge promotion for the launch and expecting lots of people to turn out,' Elaine continued full of enthusiasm. 'It's running over two days, Friday for the working population and Saturday for, well, anyone really.' She was trying to read Carol's face. 'We could promote The Cup Cake Company as part of it all.'

Now Carol grinned at her eagerness but still said nothing.

'Ooh!' Elaine looked like she might burst as she had another idea, 'and we could sell your cup cakes in the deli!'

'Well this all sounds great but I need to work out how I'm going to fulfil this order. I suppose what I could do would be to take someone on full time, maybe a couple of people, and step up production that way until I can get premises.'

'Sounds like a good plan,' Elaine said and felt guilty for finishing the raspberry cup cake before she realised. 'I mean you've got a lovely big kitchen here, haven't you?'

'Yes, but only two ovens you see. I'd really need to get another one to step up production, otherwise we're going to get held up at the bake stage.'

'I see.' Elaine got up and started walking around the kitchen looking determined. 'How about here?' she asked hopefully where there was currently just about a space on the wall. 'One of those built in ovens at arm level?'

'I like you,' Carol said laughing. 'You won't accept "no" for an answer come what may.'

'Sorry,' Elaine said scurrying back to her chair, 'I do get a bit much sometimes, I know. It's just that your cakes are so delicious! I tried some others a few days ago, organic, gluten-free things. Awful!'

Carol looked awkward. 'I'm never going to have a new production unit up and running by the 9th. You'll just have to leave it with me. I'll try and find a way.'

'Your garden looks lovely; much better than mine; I don't have the time. Those agapanthus are magnificent!' Katie sat on one of the garden chairs.

'Thank you.' Julia passed her a glass of chilled white wine.

'I thought you said tea.'

'It's gone six o'clock.' Julia chinked her friend's glass and sat next to her. 'Anyway, you look like you need it.'

'Yes, it's been quite a trying day. Oh well, cheers.'

'So what exactly was Celia saying?'

'Basically she's going to fight him through the courts. She seems to think that if she makes him wait five years he'll change his mind about me and go back to her.'

'Oh how ridiculous.'

Katie was pensive. 'It's odd but Birch seemed really shaken up after she left. I mean rather than angry, more sort of knocked for six. Probably partly because she tried to beat him up.'

'What? Is this on the CCTV?'

'Yes! Can you believe it. And of course she knows about that now.'

'Which makes it a particularly stupid thing to do,' Julia added.

'Exactly. But you know it took me a while to get the full story from Birch. He didn't mention that she'd hit him at first, it was almost as if he was trying to protect her.'

'After all she's put him through.'

'Yes, I think he feels a bit sorry for her; I mean it's all rather desperate, isn't it?'

'She's brought it all on herself,' Julia reminded her.

'Yes, you're right.'

'You're not worried are you?'

'No,' Katie said unconvincingly.

Julia turned to her. 'You know what you and Birch need, a romantic night out, just the two of you. An overnight stay even, in a luxury hotel. It can't be easy with your daughters around all the time.'

'That's a lovely idea but we can't afford it.'

259

'Oh come on, I'm sure Birch can find the money. And you're earning quite a bit now, aren't you?'

'Well, yes, I must admit Charlie's invoice is big this month with all the project managing I've done. I was thinking of giving some of it to the girls. I've given them so little since their father died.'

'Forget that. They are both earning. Book a nice hotel outside London where you can spend some quality time.'

'I must admit that does sound lovely. I'm very tempted.'

'Do it! If you don't I will!'

Bethan appeared at the door of the orangery. Carol looked up from her piping and beckoned her in. 'It's open,' she shouted.

'Sorry to just turn up like this, I know I wasn't due round here this evening.' She checked Carol's expression to make sure she was welcome.

Carol's mouth was wide open as she looked back at Bethan. She dropped her icing bag and went over to her. 'Bethan, you've been crying.' She put her hands on Bethan's shoulders and then drew her to her and hugged her. The display of affection was too much for Bethan and she burst into tears.

'Oh darling, what's happening? This isn't right. Have I been working you too hard?'

'No, no,' Bethan managed between gulps, her complexion red now. 'It's Matt, I mean Web Dreams, I just can't take anymore.'

'Right, let's sit you down and get you a drink. Coffee or wine?'

Bethan took a tissue out of her handbag and blew her nose.

'Wine it is,' Carol said taking a bottle of chilled white out of her fridge and grabbing a couple of glasses.

She sat close to the injured one and wiped some wet hair strands from her face. Bethan drank eagerly.

'So,' Carol said gently, 'tell me all. Whatever has happened, I think you're wonderful.'

'You're so nice,' Bethan looked up at last.

Carol waited.

'I walked out of my job today. I've told them I've had enough of Matt's bullying.'

260

Katie entered stealthily into her own home and hiccupped. She giggled at her tipsy state and, hearing loud jazz music coming from the kitchen, she knew this would be where she would find Birch. He was sat head in hands, at the kitchen table.

'Sorry,' she said immediately feeling the need to apologise as she had been out much longer than she had estimated earlier and it was nearly nine o'clock.

Birch looked up. His face was tired; that of a defeated man. 'Don't be silly. You're allowed to have a drink with your friend.' He turned the music down.

Katie half smiled, tight-lipped. 'Are you all right?' she asked and reached her hand across the table between them but didn't find his.

Birch sighed heavily, wrapped up in his own predicament.

'Is that a no?' she asked.

'I spoke to Jonathan...' he trailed off, shaking his head, as if he didn't know what to say next.

Katie waited patiently and then asked, 'And?'

Another sigh. 'It's going to get nasty. We're going to have to take her to court.'

Katie suddenly felt sober. She had plenty of opinion on the matter; there was much she could add to his thoughts. But the lacklustre fight left in the man opposite her left her not knowing what to say. Then she decided she needed to know.

'And are you going to? Fight her, I mean?' It was a perfectly reasonable question for her to ask so why did she feel awkward?

'Yes, yes of course,' he replied feebly. 'I just wish there was another way.'

# Chapter 27

Ross had set his alarm for five thirty that morning but was awake before it went off. His mind was whirring through everything that could possibly go wrong on this momentous day. Elaine had dithered the evening before but in the end decided to sleep at her own home. She arranged for her mother to take Jessica to school, so that she could be at the cafe by eight o'clock. He motored efficiently through his ablutions, having trimmed his beard the previous day in readiness. He donned an ironed pair of beige chinos and a smart blue shirt, open at the neck to affect a look befitting the manager of a rather good coffee shop. Elaine had had smart navy blue aprons printed up with The Friendly Bean logo and he decided he would put his on later.

Downstairs he was grinning to himself as he made a coffee using the cafe's impressive shiny machine. Whilst there had been plenty of practice runs to get used to its workings, he considered this to be the first official cappuccino to be served by The Friendly Bean. He worked efficiently, wiping away any traces of spillage and told himself it wouldn't always be like this, but for the grand opening he would make sure everything sparkled. As he sipped his drink he wondered how many customers would turn up. Harry seemed to have invited a long list of clients, friends and associates. Ross, himself, didn't know that many people but he had invited everyone he could and they had all responded warmly saying that they would pop in at some point during the day.

He looked round the cafe and felt immensely proud of what he and Elaine had achieved. The painted floorboards looked very smart in grey and set off the yellow and red painted tables, all different shapes and sizes giving the cafe a quirky feel. The blackboard by the door had today's menu on one side and invited customers to add their own personal messages on the other. And the metal shelving for the deli was shiny and set off the packets of The Friendly Bean coffee beans splendidly. Just as Ross was wondering why he had got up so early and what he would do with himself before Elaine arrived, he saw Carol and a rather sleepy looking Bethan laden with covered trays, trying to get in at the cafe door.

Katie had reminded Sylvia about the opening of The Friendly Bean today.

'I'd like to support Ross; he's been good to me, giving me free advertising in the local magazine.'

Sylvia was happy to tag along. She was all for keeping busy. She sat at the makeshift dressing table, that Birch had put together for her in the attic bedroom, and decided to wear her coral necklace. It would look nice with her moss green shift dress and add some brightness to her day. She was wondering what Jack was up today when her mobile rang.

'Joyce? Is everything all right?'

'Oh Sylvia, I'm glad I caught you. I tried the land line number that you gave me but it's engaged.'

'Probably Katie.'

'Yes, anyway, I don't want to alarm you..'

'Oh my God! What's happened?'

'Well it's not too bad really, but..'

'But what?' Sylvia was beside herself.

'You've had a break-in at your flat.'

'Oh no! Oh how dreadful!' Sylvia racked her brain to think of anything there that was valuable. She had all her jewellery with her or in France. It was just the fine furniture pieces she'd carefully chosen for her home and maybe a few ornaments.

'Yes, well, anyway,' Joyce continued wavering, 'the thing is, I don't think they've taken much. I mean they seem to have overlooked your antique furniture, probably don't realise its value, but I'm pretty sure they've taken the carriage clock that was on the mantelpiece.'

263

'That's a shame,' Sylvia said remembering her mother had left it to her and she had displayed it more out of duty than love.

'Yes, I suspect it was worth something,' Joyce added.

'Anything else?'

'Well, I can't be sure. You know I do pop round regularly but you don't tend to notice things when it's not your place, do you?'

'Of course,' Sylvia said more sympathetically.

'I called the police.'

'You did. Thank you. That was kind.'

'Well, I thought it best, the insurance, you know.'

'Absolutely.' Sylvia sighed. 'I suppose I should come down. Get the next train even.' She had little appetite for returning to Sandgate. It felt like going back to her old life which seemed quite dreary compared to the one she had experienced with Jack in Pezenas.

'Well, it's up to you. They broke in the back, came up from the beach, through the French windows.'

'Oh God, so it's not secure now.'

'It's okay, the police have made sure it's all boarded up.'

'Oh Joyce, thank you. It sounds like you've done a great job.'

Sylvia felt torn and then she said reluctantly, 'Listen, I will come down later today, it's just that we're all going to this coffee shop opening in the village this morning and I don't suppose it would hurt if I'm down there a few hours later, would it?'

Alice checked her mobile phone for the umpteenth time that morning.

'Everything okay?' Katie asked casually noticing her daughter's agitated state.

'Yes, yes, fine,' she said dismissively.

Katie looked puzzled. 'You are still coming to The Friendly Bean launch, aren't you?'

'Yes, of course Mum, I'm meeting Adam there.' Her frown deepened.

Katie nodded but every time Adam's name was mentioned she worried about the distance that her university course would put between them. 'Are you going like that?' It was the sort of question she wished she didn't ask.

Alice looked down at her T-shirt and jeans. 'I might put a different top on.'

'Okay, well we're going in five minutes.'

Alice's phone bleeped. She looked at the screen, opened up the email and was wide eyed as she frantically took in the message. Katie was curious. Perhaps Adam wasn't going to turn up? Perhaps he was letting her down gently?

'Brilliant!' Alice sprung from her chair and almost exploded. 'Bloody brilliant!'

'What is?' Katie knew Alice wouldn't swear in front of her without good reason.

'I've got a place at Kings. Kings College have accepted me!'

'But you're going to Nottingham?'

'No! I've changed my mind; I want to stay in London and Kings have just accepted me on their French degree course.' She looked like the happiest girl alive.

Sylvia appeared at the door. 'Good news is it? You got in? I told you you would,' she said hugging Alice and Katie wondered why she was the only one not in on this scheme. Now she was worried that Adam would break her heart.

'Oh come here.' She held her daughter tight. 'I'm pleased for you, of course I am. If it's what you want.'

Alice moved back to face her mother. 'It is, Mum,' she said as if she couldn't have been more sure about anything in her life. 'Adam, well... he's special and...'

'But you're so young.' Katie immediately regretted saying that. 'Oh to hell with it. Good for you!'

Bethan pulled another tray of cup cakes out of the oven and set them on cooling racks. She worked as fast as she could, in what was becoming a very hot kitchen at the back of The Friendly Bean, but remembering what Carol had said about working safely rather than hastily. The noise of the crowd gathering in the cafe was getting louder by the minute. It must be packed by now. What if they all wanted cup cakes? She used a light touch of her middle finger to feel the apple and cinnamon cakes and was relieved that they were now cool enough to decorate. It was quite a responsibility Carol had given her today and Bethan couldn't quite believe that she had not felt the need to stay and oversee her work. She loved the fact that Carol had faith in her, believed in her; it was the sort of belief her father had had.

Harry popped his head round the kitchen door and Bethan braced herself.

'Everything okay in here?' he asked.

'Fine,' Bethan said, avoiding his gaze, and wished she hadn't sounded so sulky. She was determined to get over this guy.

'Great, well I'm going to make a speech in a minute; it would be good if you could come through to the front.'

'Okay,' Bethan replied obediently but wondering why it was necessary. She'd go. She didn't want to be awkward. She focused on the task at hand which was filling an icing bag with a vanilla flavoured cream.

'Oh and Bethan,' he added and she couldn't stop herself from looking up and taking in his full gorgeousness, as he said her name. She even noticed his aftershave cutting through the baking smells and it reminded her with far too much clarity of how she'd totally fallen for this man.

'Thank you. You're doing a fabulous job; you really are.'

Bethan managed a curt smile before eyes down and accurately swirling the creamy mixture onto another perfectly formed cup cake. A tear formed in one eye and she gulped forbidding any more to surface. Whenever she felt sad she thought of her father; he was worth crying about. She still missed him terribly. The next time she looked up Harry had gone.

Ross and Elaine looked very pleased with themselves, if pale with tiredness, as they stood next to Harry. There must have been at least fifty people there by now. Harry raised a hand and asked, 'may I have your attention, please? Just a few words.'

266

The general melange of voices subsided and Harry started on his prepared speech.

'Would you believe, none of this wonderful new establishment would have been possible if it wasn't for my dear uncle Jim.' He had their attention. 'Poor chap, man after my own heart, died earlier this year, leaving me a few quid to invest in this place.' Some of the audience laughed quietly at the understatement.

'It's alright, Harry, the tax man's not here!' one of the crowd heckled in a friendly fashion.

Harry responded with a broad smile and continued, 'but money alone would not have achieved so much and I have to thank Ross and Elaine who have worked their magic and turned what I'm sure you'll agree was a pretty ordinary coffee shop into this amazing cafe, The Friendly Bean.' Ross nodded to his audience and Elaine looked very proud. Someone from the back started applauding with a loud and deliberate hand clap and everyone else felt moved to join in.

Sylvia looked round to see who it was and couldn't believe her eyes. Jack stood at the door dressed in his cream linen suit and wide brimmed hat, his eyes full of amusement. He was holding what looked like a painting wrapped in brown paper. As their eyes met he grinned from ear to ear and she rushed over to him.

'What are you doing here?' Sylvia whispered as loudly as she dared. 'Why didn't you tell me you were coming?'

He shrugged his shoulders. 'I wanted to surprise my Sylvie,' he said not caring who heard him. 'And I wanted to bring you this.' He handed the painting to her and Sylvia couldn't believe how blissful this moment felt.

'And finally,' Harry searched the room for one individual. His eyes found her and rested there. 'I would like to thank Bethan from The Cup Cake Company, for doing such an excellent job today. I think we all agree these cakes are delicious.'

'Here here!' was the general cry from those who had partaken. Bethan knew it wouldn't matter that she was blushing as she was red-faced from the heat of the oven anyway. She saw the funny side of it and realised she had, in fact, done a marvellous job and without Carol's help. She loved working for The Cup Cake Company. It was so great to be away from Matt and all the politics at Web Dreams. It felt safe now that this was her focus. Her career. Men would just be an unnecessary distraction from now on.

Adam had had a busy morning at the workshop finishing a dining table for a demanding client. So he had turned up just as Harry had started his speech. He found Alice with his eyes and weaved through the coffee drinkers to be by her side.

'Where have you been?' she mouthed, mocking annoyance.

'Sorry.' His face said please forgive me. 'Have I missed much?'

'You have actually, but you'll have to wait.' She raised her nose in the air as she turned away. A man in front of them turned round and said, 'Shush,' and they both tuned into the speech although Alice wasn't really listening.

As soon as Harry had finished and the clapping had died down Adam turned Alice towards him.

'So?' he looked mischievous.

'So I've only got a place at Kings,' Alice shrieked.

'Kings College in London?'

'Yes!'

He threw his arms around her and lifted her in the air. 'Wahoo! Brilliant news! Oh Alice! Well done!'

As he put her down he started kissing her until someone shouted out, 'get a room!' and so they pulled apart just enough for him to ask, 'Shall we live together? Do you want to move in with me?'

Katie was chatting with Ross when it happened. Celia walked in to The Friendly Bean looking smartly dressed and composed. What on earth did she want now? Harry was greeting her, clearly not knowing who she was and they were obviously making polite conversation.

'Sorry Ross, I need to find Birch,' she said placing a hand on his arm as she interrupted him.

'Something the matter?' he asked.

'Celia's just walked in. Birch's ex to be.'

'Oh dear. Look he's over there with Sylvia.'

'Ah yes.' She headed straight for him, keeping her eye on the enemy to make sure she didn't move.

'Birch,' she smiled at Jack, 'sorry about this, I need Birch for a minute.'

He looked puzzled.

'Celia's just turned up.'

'What? Oh no!' He looked over to where she was and Celia caught his eye. 'Oh God, she's seen me. Listen, I'm going to talk to her. See if I can get her outside. The last thing Ross and Elaine need today is a scene.' He was talking to her but his eyes were on Celia.

'Okay,' Katie said but felt reluctant to let him go.

'Right.' Birch had a serious face on and Katie felt neglected at that moment. Why was it all about Celia? Why didn't he worry about how she felt?

'Celia, what on earth are you doing here?' Birch got straight to the point and Harry looked puzzled.

'This is my ex-wife,' Birch said filling him in.

'Oh.' Harry's jaw dropped. 'I'll leave you to it,' he said slinking away.

'Shall we talk outside? We don't want a scene.' Birch's tone was formal and abrupt.

'I haven't come to make trouble,' Celia responded eagerly. At least she was sober. She actually looked very attractive in a soft pink blouse and jeans. He couldn't remember her ever wearing jeans before.

'So why are you here?' he asked impatiently.

'Birch, whatever happens, we were married for twenty years and they were good years for me on the whole. I realise I messed up in the end.' She was a picture of reasonableness.

'Haven't we been through all this?'

'Yes, probably, I'm sorry. But I thought you might like to know that I've decided to let you have your divorce on the grounds of my adultery.'

Birch couldn't believe his ears. 'You mean you will...?' There had to be a catch.

'Yes. And I've had three estate agents round to value the house.' She took a folder out of her handbag and handed it to him. 'They're all in there. See what you think and which one you want to go with and I'll instruct them.'

Birch was amazed and delighted. 'Thank you,' he said and then he thought better of it, but still asked, 'Why the change of heart?'

'Well, your heart's obviously not going to change,' she nodded towards Katie across the room, 'and I'm done with fighting.'

He wished he didn't, but he did feel sorry for her. 'What will you do? Where will you go?'

'Oh I don't know. Well I haven't decided. There's an orchestra in Milan looking for a violinist, I thought I might...'

'Go abroad?'

'Maybe.' Her eyes were downcast, no sign of the feisty woman he had been wrangling with these past months. He felt moved to touch her, to comfort her but with a large handbag still over her shoulder and Celia making no attempt to respond, it resulted in an awkward exchange with him patting her on her arm.

Back in eye contact he said, 'Thank you,' and she turned and left the cafe calmly and without another word.

Birch stood still trying to take in the enormity of what had just happened. It wasn't long before Harry appeared.

'You all right, old chap?'

Birch pursed his lips in thought but then smiled. 'Yes, yes, I think I am.'

'All sorted with Celia? She seemed okay, today anyway.'

'She was more than okay; she's finally seen sense and is going to let me divorce her. And we're selling the house!'

'That's fantastic news!' He then looked puzzled. 'Are you going to share this with Katie?'

'Of course, yes. I was just thinking about that.' They both looked over to her. She was laughing with Elaine.

'I know I'm a fine one to talk,' Harry said, 'but if I were you, I wouldn't hang around. Katie's quite a catch.'

# Chapter 28

Katie was peeling Maris Piper potatoes with vigour and wishing she had not invited so many people to lunch on a whim.

'Blast!' She had scraped the skin of her thumb and it started bleeding. She grabbed a piece of kitchen towel, blotted the red away from the chopping board and rinsed the potato under the cold tap. Still she bled and, considering that she didn't have time to go up to the bathroom cabinet where she'd find a plaster, she made a makeshift bandage with a tissue which was bound to fail.

'Need some help?' Birch came up behind her and placed his hands gently on her waist.

'I'm okay,' she said brushing him off. She noted the hurt look on his face and added, 'It's just that there's so much to do and they'll all be here in a couple of hours.'

'Hey, you've cut yourself.' He took the peeler from her. She was frowning as he said, 'You're not okay, are you?'

'I could just do without this right now.'

'My fault,' he declared raising his hands as if surrendering. 'I invited Jack and my Mum and it sort of escalated from there.'

'It's fine, really, I invited people too but these potatoes won't peel themselves,' she said failing to hide her agitation.

'No, but I will do them,' he said masterfully. 'You go get a plaster for your wound.'

She sighed as she gave into him. 'That would be nice actually.'

'Just leave the cooking to me.'

'That would be lovely but...'

'No buts. Listen I..,' he started but the doorbell went.

'I better get that.'

'Probably Jehovah's witnesses!' Birch called after her sounding frustrated.

Katie went to the front door and was really pleased to find Julia on the other side.

'Thought you might need some help,' she said, not waiting to be asked in.

'Goodness, I'm going to be able to put my feet up at this rate! Birch has just taken over the prep.'

'Too right.'

Mellow tones of jazz were now coming from the kitchen.

'Men! Why can't they get stressed like normal people?' Katie said unable to wipe a smile off her face.

Alice was very quick to get to the front door before anyone else when Adam arrived. They couldn't keep their hands off each other. Katie accidentally walked in on them and Alice blurted out, 'Mum, we've got something to tell you.' Her skin glowed, her hair it's natural lustrous red and even her freckles, normally covered, showed. She looked so pretty but so young without make-up. Katie braced herself for whatever was coming next. Surely they weren't going to rush into something they might regret? She had only had one night to get used to the idea that Alice wasn't going away, but would be here in London, but she'd decided she liked it. She selfishly wanted her precious daughters near her.

'Mum?' Alice was trying to get her attention.

'Yes, sorry, you have something to say.'

'I've asked Alice to move in with me,' Adam said taking responsibility for the deed.

A deflated, 'oh,' was all Katie could manage.

'Mum, are you pleased for me?' Alice demanded.

'Yes of course,' she said but she wasn't. At that moment she just felt sad. Her husband was dead and her daughter was leaving home.

Sylvia let herself and Jack in with the key Katie had given her. They were laughing as they came in and Katie pursed her lips in defiance of her thoughts. She must be happy for them, not jealous.

'Katie.' Jack gave her a hug and kissed her on both cheeks before Sylvia presented her with a bouquet of tall elegant delphiniums in blues and white. 'For you, the most wonderful host.'

'They are beautiful. Thank you. And we've loved having you to stay. I suppose you'll be going back to France now. Is everyone deserting me?'

Sylvia looked blank and there was an awkward pause before she said, 'I know someone who has no plans to go anywhere; not without you anyway.' She had a mischievous glint in her eye.

Katie struggled to respond but suggested they moved out of the hallway into the lounge but then Birch appeared to announce that lunch was ready to be served.

They started to move into the dining room because with Julia's family and the two loved up couples there was not enough room round the kitchen table. Bethan was missing. On cue she waltzed in and found her mother in the general hubbub of happy people.

'Mum, I've got some great news!' Bethan's face was lit up with delight.

'Really?' Katie wondered what was going to be thrown at her next.

'Yes, Carol says I can move in with her.'

Katie blinked in disbelief. 'You want to move in with your employer?'

'Well, weekdays mainly. She says I can have her daughter's room as she's left home. I mean I'll still have my room here, won't I?'

'Of course. Look, I know you get on well with Carol but won't it be a bit much?'

'No! She's great. This is what I want. I thought you'd be pleased.'

Katie considered that a few months ago she would have been. 'Well, if it's what you want then good for you; of course I'm pleased.' She felt close to tears but gulped them back and moved away to be next to Jack. He seemed to have a calming effect on people; perhaps it would rub off on her.

After the main course, a chicken roast which Katie had played little part in as things turned out, Jack excused himself and squeezed past the back row diners to retrieve his painting from the hallway. It was still wrapped in brown paper and on returning he courteously asked for everyone's attention.

'Just a moment of your time, my good friends,' he started.

'Haven't you seen it yet, Mum?' Birch asked.

'No, he asked me to wait. All I know is that it's a painting for me.'

Jack's eyes twinkled, 'shall I do the honours?'

'Yes! Come on!' was the general consensus.

It was a stunning portrait of Sylvia, stood on the balcony of Jack's house in Pezenas. The likeness was remarkable and she looked serene and very beautiful. A tear appeared in Sylvia's eye as she took in this remarkable painting.

'Oh Jack, oh darling.' She went to him and embraced him. 'It's perfect. I love it!'

He held a broad grin and said, 'there's just one condition.'

'Oh?' Sylvia searched his face for an answer.

'I want you to hang it in my home in Pezenas and so you will have to come and live with me and then you will see it every day.'

'Now let me see,' Sylvia said with a wry smile, 'oh all right then. I will.'

Everyone cheered and Bethan shouted, 'we all expect to come for holidays!'

'Of course, you are all welcome! Maybe not all at once!' he added and there was hearty laughter round the table except for Katie who could only manage a smile.

Birch got straight up from his seat beckoning Katie to join him. She was confused and didn't move.

'Katie, I need some help in the kitchen,' he said staring at her.

'Oh and I thought it was my day off,' she said getting up begrudgingly.

As they entered the kitchen she asked, 'are we serving the dessert?'

'No.' He was back to being masterful and took her in his arms. 'What?'

'No, we're not serving anything, well, not yet. I have something I want to ask you.'

275

Katie didn't have time to think before he said, 'Katie, I love you and I know I've been pretty crap recently with the whole divorce thing but I promise that's going to change.'

Her expression softened. 'It's been pretty awful for me too, you know?'

'Yes, of course it has, and I'm sure I've been a bit too wrapped up in it to give you the attention I should have. Do you forgive me?'

She looked at him properly for the first time in days. He looked thin, the effects of months of stress, but his face was bright today. The huge relief brought about by Celia's decision had left him with a joyful smile. 'Yes, of course I do,' she answered finally, pleased that the tension between them was resolved.

'Good, in that case, will you marry me? And by the way what I want to serve next is Champagne. I've got two bottles on ice.'

Katie was stunned. Her mind was whirring. Did she want to marry this man? 'Yes,' she said quietly, and then, 'yes,' more emphatically. 'Yes!'

Birch held her tight for a long slow kiss before taking her hand, rushing her into the dining room to announce, 'She said yes! We're getting married!'

Everyone clapped and cheered and rose up to congratulate them. 'Now that is good news,' Sylvia said looking delighted. Alice and Bethan were both at their mother's side.

'Really pleased for you, Mum,' Alice said and hugged her.

'Yeah, me too,' Bethan said and joined in the embrace and then she released herself and said to Birch, 'Shall I help you pour the Champagne?'

# *Thank you*

Hello Reader,

Gill Buchanan here. I just wanted to say thank you for reading Birch & Beyond, the sequel to Forever Lucky. I do hope you enjoyed it.

It would be great if you left a review on Amazon.

If you would like to email me direct, I'd love to hear from you. Alternatively, I have an author website where you can find out more and sign up for newsletters so you are the first to hear when a new novel comes out.
**Email:** words@gillbuchanan.co.uk
**Author website:** www.gillbuchanan.co.uk

Thanks again and happy reading!

# About the Author

Gill Buchanan is a business graduate who worked in marketing before writing her first novel.

Having lived a little, herself, and experienced the ups and downs of being a woman in the 21st century, Gill decided to create female characters who blossom in the face of adversity. She uses modern day dilemmas which resonate with her readers and humour to add a lightness to the story.

She has written four novels to date and her latest work, The Disenchanted Hero, is inspired by the true story of Molly and Guy who met during World War 2 with enormous hurdles to overcome before true love could run its course.

Gill lives in rural Suffolk with Tony, her husband, and Gracie, her cat. She loves to hear from her readers.

Find Gill on Facebook:
https://www.facebook.com/literallyforwomen

Printed in Great Britain
by Amazon

24514574R00162